REBECCA'S
BOUQUET

Also by Lisa Jones Baker

The Amish Christmas Kitchen
(with Kelly Long and Jennifer Beckstrand)

Published by Kensington Publishing Corporation

REBECCA'S BOUQUET

Lisa Jones Baker

ZEBRA BOOKS
KENSINGTON PUBLISHING CORP.
http://www.kensingtonbooks.com

ZEBRA BOOKS are published by

Kensington Publishing Corp.
119 West 40th Street
New York, NY 10018

All Kensington titles, imprints and distributed lines are available at special quantity discounts for bulk purchases for sales promotion, premiums, fund-raising, educational or institutional use.

Special book excerpts or customized printings can also be created to fit specific needs. For details, write or phone the office of the Kensington Sales Manager. Attn.: Sales Department. Kensington Publishing Corp., 119 West 40th Street, New York, NY 10018. Phone: 1-800-221-2647.

First Printing: October 2016
ISBN-13: 978-1-4201-4158-0
ISBN-10: 1-4201-4158-9

eISBN-13: 978-1-4201-4159-7
eISBN-10: 1-4201-4159-7

10 9 8 7 6 5 4 3 2 1

Printed in the United States of America

To the two people I love most,
John and Marcia Baker

ACKNOWLEDGMENTS

First of all, I thank my Lord and Savior for blessing me with publication after twenty-four years of prayers to see my work in print. Numerous individuals contributed to this story. Very special thanks to my mother, Marcia Baker, the most patient person in the world, for listening to me read REBECCA'S BOUQUET and other novels out loud for the past two decades, and to the world's best sister, Beth Zehr, for creating my website and spending countless hours taking on my computer challenges. Huge thanks to the Welcome Center, the Cheese Festival folks, the wonderful family who allowed me to join them in their home for a *fabulous* Amish dinner, and the friendly people of Arthur, Illinois, who've answered my questions. I've tremendously enjoyed the horse-and-buggy rides. My gratitude to the talented woodworkers who offered me an inside view of furniture making over eight years ago when I commenced this novel. This particular experience sparked the idea for Daniel's cabinet shop. I wish to extend my appreciation to the following authors: *New York Times* Bestseller Joan W. Anderson for her review and great support; Lisa Norato, true friend, writing confidante, and critique partner for over twenty years; Gina Welborn, who, through a contest entry, introduced me to my fabulous agent, Tamela Hancock Murray. Many thanks to Evansville postal employee, Rob Carpenter, for taking time to answer my questions; Steve Biever, AIFD, of It Can Be Arranged floral shop in Evansville; and also to Becky for so graciously providing me with tremendous insight about the floral business. Thanks to my computer experts: Gary Kerr, Doug Zehr, nieces Brooke and Brittany, and the Geek Squad team in Bloomington, Illinois. Thanks to Amber Kauffman, former executive director, Illinois Amish Interpretive Center. A special, heartfelt thank-you to my Amish go-to girl, who prefers to remain anonymous while loyally reading early drafts of my books, cover to cover. Last, but certainly not least, a huge thank-you to my fabulous editor, Selena James, and everyone at Kensington who has helped with the production of this book.

Chapter One

His announcement took her by surprise. Rebecca Sommer met William's serious gaze and swallowed. The shadow from his hat made his expression impossible to read.

"You're really leaving?"

He fingered the black felt on the brim. "I know what a shock this is. Believe me, I never expected to hear that Dad had a heart attack."

"Do they expect a full recovery?"

William nodded. "But the docs say it will be a while before he works again. Right now, they can't even guess at a time line. In the meantime, Beth's struggling to take care of him."

While Rebecca considered the news, the warm June breeze rustled the large, ear-shaped leaves on the catalpa tree. The sun peeked from behind a large marshmallow cloud, as if deciding whether or not to appear. In the distance, a sleek black gelding clomped its hooves against the earth.

Pools of dust stirred, swirling and quickly disappearing. Lambs frolicked across the parcel of pasture separating the Sommer home from Old Sam Beachy's bright red barn. From where they stood, Rebecca could barely glimpse the orange YIELD sign on the back of the empty buggy parked next to the house.

"I'm the only person Dad trusts with his business." William paused and lowered his voice. "Beth wants me to come to Indiana and run his cabinet shop, Rebecca."

The news caused a wave of anxiety to roll through Rebecca's chest. She wrung her hands together in a nervous gesture. A long silence ensued as she thought of William leaving, and her shoulders grew tense. Not even the light, sweet fragrance floating from her mother's rose garden could take away Rebecca's anxiety.

When she finally started to respond, William held up a defensive hand. "It's just until he's back on his feet. This may not be such a bad thing. The experience might actually benefit us."

Rebecca raised a curious brow. The breeze blew a chestnut-brown hair out of place, and she quickly tucked it back under her *kapp*. Her gaze drifted from his face to his rolled-up sleeves.

Tiny freckles decorated his nose, giving him a youthful appearance. But there was nothing boyish about his square jaw or broad shoulders that tried to push their way out of his shirt. Her heart skipped a beat. She lifted her chin, and their eyes locked in understanding.

William smiled a little. "One of these days, we'll run our own company." He winked. "Don't worry."

She swallowed the lump in her throat. For one blissful, hopeful moment, she trusted everything would be okay. It wasn't those simple two words that reassured her, but the tender, persuasive way William said them. The low, steady tone in which he spoke could convince Rebecca of almost anything.

The warm pink glow on his cheeks made Rebecca's pulse pick up speed. As he looked at her for a reaction, her lips lifted into a wide smile. At the same time, it was impossible to stop the nervous rising and falling of her chest.

She'd never dreamed of being without William. Even temporarily. At the young age of eighteen, she hadn't confronted such a difficult issue.

But her church teachers and parents had raised her to deal with obstacles. Fortunately, they had prepared her to be strong and to pray for guidance. As she stared at her beloved flower garden, her thoughts became more chaotic.

The clothes on the line rose and fell with the warm summer breeze. Their fresh, soapy scent floated through the air. She surely had greater control over her destiny than the wet garments, whose fate was dependent on the wind. She and William could get through this. They loved each other. God would take care of them, wouldn't He?

She glanced up at William. The way the sun hit him at an angle made him look even taller than his six feet and two inches. He'd always been bigger and stronger than other kids his age.

The gray flecks in his deep blue eyes danced to a mysterious tune as he darted her a grin. When she looked into those dark pools, she could drown in happiness. But today, even the warmth emanating from his smile couldn't stop the concern that edged her voice. "Don't worry? But I do, William. What about . . ."

"Us?"

She nodded.

He leveled his gaze so that she looked directly at him. "Nothing has changed. We'll still get married in November after the harvest."

Rebecca hesitated. She couldn't believe William would really leave Arthur, Illinois. But his reason was legitimate. His father needed him. She wasn't selfish, and asking him to stay would be.

Circumstances were beyond her control. What could she do? The question nagged at her until frustration set in. Within a matter of minutes, her world had changed, and she fought to adjust. She nervously tapped the toe of her black shoe against the ground.

As she crossed her arms over her chest, she wished they could protect her from the dilemma she faced. Her brows narrowed into a frown, and a long silence ensued. She looked at him, hoping for an answer. Seeking even a hint of a solution.

To her surprise, William teased, "Rebecca, stop studying me like I'm a map of the world."

His statement broke the tension, and she burst into laughter because a map of the world was such a far stretch from what she'd been thinking.

"Of course, you've got to help your folks, William. I know how much Daniel's business means to him. You certainly can't let him lose it. I can imagine the number of cabinets on order."

Surprised and relieved that her voice sounded steady, Rebecca's shoulders trembled as the thought of William leaving sank in. They'd grown up together and hadn't spent a day without seeing one another.

She stopped a moment and considered Daniel and Beth Conrad. Nearly a decade ago, William's mamma had died, and Daniel had married Beth.

He was a skilled cabinetmaker. It was no surprise that people from all over the United States ordered his custom-made pieces. Rebecca had seen samples of his elegant, beautiful woodworking.

A thought popped into Rebecca's mind, and she frowned. "William, you seem to be forgetting something very important. Daniel and Beth . . . They're English."

He nodded. "Don't think I haven't given that consideration."

"I don't want to sound pessimistic, but how will you stay Amish in their world?"

He shrugged. "They're the same as us, really."

She rolled her eyes. "Of course they are. But the difference between our lifestyle and theirs is night and day. How can you expect to move in with them and be compatible?"

William hooked his fingers over his trouser pockets, looked down at the ground and furrowed a brow. Rebecca smiled. She knew him so well. Whenever something bothered him, he did this. Rebecca loved the intense look on his face when he worried. The small indentation in his chin intensified.

What fascinated her most, though, were the mysterious gray flecks that danced in his eyes. When he lifted his chin, those flecks took on a

metallic appearance. Mesmerized, Rebecca couldn't
stop looking at them.

Moments later, as if having made an important
decision, he stood still, moved his hands to his hips,
and met her gaze with a nod.

In a more confident tone, he spoke. "It will be
okay, Rebecca. Don't forget that Dad was Amish
before he married Beth. He was raised with the same
principles as us. Just because he's English now
doesn't mean he's forgotten everything he learned.
No need to worry. He won't want me to change."

"No?"

William gave a firm shake of his head. "Of course
not. In fact, I'm sure he'll insist that I stick to how I
was brought up. Remember, he left me with Aenti
Sarah and Uncle John when he remarried. Dad told
me that raising me Amish was what my mother
would have expected. The *Ordnung* was important to
her. And keeping the faith must have also been at
the top of Dad's list to have left me here. Nothing
will change, Rebecca."

Rebecca realized that she was making too much
out of William's going away. After all, it was only Indiana. Not the North Pole! Suddenly embarrassed at
her lack of strength, she looked down at the hem
of her dress before gazing straight into his eyes. He
moved so close, his warm breath caressed her
bottom lip, and it quivered. Time seemed to stand
still while she savored the silent mutual understanding between them. That unique, unexplainable
connection that she and William had.

"I've always read that things happen for a reason,"
William mentioned.

"Me too." Rebecca also knew the importance of the Ordnung. And she knew William's mamma, Miriam, would have wanted him to stay in the faith that had meant everything to her.

As if sensing her distress, he interlaced his fingers together in front of him. His hands were large. She'd watched those very hands lift heavy bales of hay.

"Who knows? Maybe this is God's way of testing me."

Rebecca gave an uncertain roll of her eyes. "Talk to your aunt and uncle. They'll know what's best. After all, they've raised you since your father re-married."

The frustration in William's voice lifted a notch. "I already did. It's hard to convince them that what I'm doing is right." He lowered his voice. "You know how they feel. When Dad left the faith, he deserted me. But even so, I can't turn my back on him."

"Of course not."

"Aenti Sarah's concerned that people will treat me differently when I come back. She wants to talk to the bishop and get his permission. If that makes her feel better, then I'm all for it."

"If he'll give his blessing."

William nodded in agreement.

"But we're old enough to think for ourselves, William. When we get married and raise our family, we can't let everyone make up our minds for us."

He raised a brow. "You're so independent, Miss Rebecca."

She smiled a little.

A mischievous twinkle lightened his eyes.

"Your decision shouldn't be based on what people

think," Rebecca said. "If we made choices to please others, we'd never win. Deep down inside, we have to be happy with ourselves. So you've got to do what's in your heart. And no one can decide that but you."

The expression that crossed his face suddenly became unreadable. She tilted her head and studied him with immense curiosity. "What are you thinking?"

His gray flecks repeated that metallic appearance. "Rebecca, you're something else."

A surge of warmth rushed through her.

"I can't believe your insight." He blinked in amazement. "You're an angel." His voice was low and soft. She thought he was going to kiss her. But he didn't. William followed the church rules. But Rebecca wouldn't have minded breaking that one.

In a breathless voice, she responded, "Thank you for that."

As if suddenly remembering the crux of their conversation, William returned to the original topic. "I've assured Aenti Sarah and Uncle John that I won't leave the Amish community. That I'll come back, and we'll get married. They finally justified letting me leave by looking at this as an opportunity to explore *Rumspringa*."

Rebecca grinned. "I guess that's one way to look at it." Rumspringa was the transition time between adolescence and adulthood when an Amish youth could try things before deciding whether to join the faith for him—or herself. She even had a friend who had gone as far as to get a driver's license.

He paused. "Rebecca, I know we didn't plan on this." His voice grew more confident as he continued.

"You've got to understand that I love you more than anything in the world. Please tell me you'll wait for me. I give you my word that this move is only temporary. As soon as Dad's on his feet again, I'll come home. Promise."

As William committed, Rebecca took in his dark brown hair. The sun's brightness lightened it to the color of sand. For a moment, his features were both rugged and endearing. Rebecca's heart melted.

Her voice softened. "How long do you think you'll stay?"

William pressed his lips together thoughtfully. "Good question. Hopefully, he'll be back to work in no time. His customers depend on him, and according to Beth, he has a long list of orders for cabinets to produce and deliver. He's a strong man, Rebecca. He'll be okay."

"I believe that. I'll never forget when he came into town last year to see you." She giggled. "Remember his fancy car?"

William chuckled. "He sure enjoys the luxuries of the English. I wish our community wouldn't be so harsh on him. He's really Amish at heart."

William hesitated. "I used to resent that he left me."

Long moments passed in silence. He stepped closer and lowered his voice to a whisper. "Rebecca, you've become unusually quiet. And you didn't answer my question."

She raised an inquisitive brow.

"Will you wait for me?"

Her thoughts were chaotic. For something to do, she looked down and flattened her hands against her long, brown dress. She realized how brave William was and recalled the scandal Daniel Conrad had made when he married outside of the faith and had moved to the country outside of Evansville, Indiana. She raised her chin to look at William's face. Mamma always told her that a person's eyes gave away his feelings.

The tongue could lie. But not the eyes. William's intriguing flecks had become a shade lighter, dancing with hope and sincerity. His cheeks were flushed.

"William, you've got to do this." She let out a small, thoughtful sigh. "I remember a particular church sermon from a long time ago. The message was that our success in life isn't determined by making easy choices. It's measured by how we deal with difficult issues. And leaving Arthur is definitely a tough decision."

He hugged his hands to his hips. "What are you getting at?"

She quietly sought an answer to his question. What did she mean? She'd sounded like she knew what she was talking about. Moments later, the answer came. She recognized it with complete clarity.

She squared her shoulders. "I promised you I'd stick by you forever, William. And right now, you need me."

He gazed down at her in confusion.

Clearing her throat, she looked up at him and drew a long breath. "I'm going with you."

Inside Old Sam Beachy's barn, Rebecca poured out her dilemma to her dear friend. Afterwards, Buddy whimpered sympathetically at her feet.

Rebecca reached down from her rocking chair opposite Old Sam's workbench and obediently stroked the Irish setter behind his ears. The canine closed his eyes in contentment.

Old Sam was famous for his hope chests. He certainly wasn't the only person to put together the pieces, but he was a brilliant artist who etched beautiful, personalized designs into the lids.

Rebecca had looked at his beloved Esther as a second mother. Since she'd succumbed to pneumonia a couple of years ago, Rebecca had tried to return her kindness to the old widower. So did her friends, Rachel and Annie. The trio took care of him. Rachel listened to Sam's horse-and-buggy stories. Annie baked him delicious sponge cakes while Rebecca picked him fresh flowers.

Drawing a long breath, Rebecca wondered what advice he'd give. Whatever it was would be good. Because no one was wiser than Old Sam. She crossed her legs at the ankles. Sawdust floated in the air. Rebecca breathed in the woodsy smell of oak.

When he started to speak, she sat up a little straighter. "The real secret to happiness is not what we give or receive; it's what we share. I would consider your help to William and his parents a gift from the heart. At the same time, a clear conscience is a soft pillow. You want to have the blessing of our bishop and your parents. The last thing you want is a scandal about you and William living under the same roof."

Rebecca let out a deep, thoughtful sigh as she considered his wisdom. In the background, she could hear Ginger enter her stall from the pasture.

Old Sam's horse snorted. And that meant she wanted an apple.

Sam's voice prompted Rebecca to meet his gaze. "Rebecca, I can give you plenty of advice. But the most important thing I can tell you is to pray."

Rebecca nodded and crossed her arms over her chest.

"But remember: Do not ask the Lord to guide your footsteps if you're not willing to move your feet."

Rebecca was fully aware that William was ready to leave. In her front yard, she hugged her baby sister, Emily, shoving a rebellious strand of blond hair out of her face. Rebecca planted an affectionate kiss on brother Peter's cheek. "Be good."

Pete's attention was on Rebecca just long enough to say good-bye. As she turned to her father, the two kids started screaming and chasing each other in a game of tag. Emily nearly tripped over a chicken in the process. Rebecca was quick to notice the uncertain expression on Old Sam's face.

The sweet, creamy smell of homemade butter competed with the aroma of freshly baked bread. Both enticing scents floated out of the open kitchen windows. Tonight, Rebecca would miss Mamma's dinner. It would be the first time Rebecca hadn't eaten with her family.

Her heart pumped to an uncertain beat. But she'd never let her fear show. Ever since the death of her other little sister, Rebecca had learned to put on a brave façade. Her family depended on her for strength.

Rebecca's father grasped her hands and gave them a tight squeeze. She immediately noted that his arms shook. It stunned her to realize that his embrace was more of a nervous gesture than an offer of support. And the expression on his face was anything but encouraging. Rebecca understood his opposition to what she was about to do. Her father's approval was important to her, and it bothered her to seem disrespectful.

All of her life, she'd tried hard to please him. They'd never even argued. In fact, this was the first time she'd gone against his wishes. But William was her future. She wanted to be by his side whenever he needed her.

In a gruff, firm voice, her father spoke. "Be careful, Becca. You know how I feel. I'm disappointed that William hasn't convinced you to stay. You belong here. In Arthur."

He pushed out a frustrated breath. "But you're of age to make your own decision. We've made arrangements with Beth so that living under the same roof with William will be proper. We trust she'll be a responsible chaperone while you're with the Conrads. Just come home soon. We need your help with chores."

He pointed an authoritative finger. "And never let the English ways influence you. They will tempt you to be like them, Becca. Remember your faith."

Rebecca responded with a teary nod. When she finally faced Mamma, she forced a brave smile. But the tightness in her throat made it difficult to say good-bye.

Mamma's deep blue eyes clouded with moisture. With one swift motion, Rebecca hugged her. For long moments, she was all too aware of how much she would miss that security. The protection only a parent could offer.

Much too soon, Mamma released her and held her at arm's length. When Rebecca finally turned to Old Sam, he stepped forward and handed her a cardboard container with handles.

She met his gaze and lifted a curious brow. "This is for me?"

He nodded. "I hope you like it." He pointed. "Go ahead. Take it out."

Everyone was quiet while she removed the gift. As she lifted the hope chest, she caught her breath. There was a unanimous sound of awe from the group. "Old Sam . . ." She focused on the design etched into the lid. "It's absolutely beautiful! I will treasure it the rest of my life."

"You always bring me fresh flowers, so I thought you'd like the bouquet."

She glanced at William before turning her attention back to Sam. "I'm taking the miniature hope chest with me."

Sam's voice was low and edged with emotion. "I will pray for your safety. And remember that freedom is not to do as you please, but the liberty to do as you ought. And the person who sows seeds of kindness will have a perpetual harvest. That's you, Rebecca."

Rebecca blinked as salty tears filled her eyes. With great care, she returned the hope chest to its box on the bright green blades of grass.

Old Sam's voice cracked. "You come back soon. And if you want good advice, consult an old man." A grin tugged at Rebecca's lips. Sam knew every proverb in the book. She'd miss hearing him recount them.

"Thank you again. I can't wait to start putting away special trinkets for the children I will have some day."

When she looked up at him, he merely nodded approval.

William's voice startled her from her thoughts. "Rebecca, it's time to head out. It's gonna be a long drive."

Her gaze remained locked with Mamma's. Mary Sommer's soft voice shook with emotion. "This is the first time you've left us. But you're strong."

Rebecca squeezed her eyes closed for several heartbeats.

As if to reassure herself, her mother went on. "We hope Daniel recovers quickly. William needs you. In the meantime, God will keep both of you in His hands. Don't forget that. Always pray. And remember what we've taught you. Everything you've learned in church."

"*Jah.*"

"It's never been a secret that God gave you a special gift for accepting challenges. I'll never forget the time you jumped into that creek to save your brother. You pulled him to shore."

Rebecca grinned. "I remember."

"Rumspringa might be the most important time in your life. But be very careful. There will be temptations in the English world. In fact, the bishop is concerned that you will decide against joining the Amish church."

"I know who I am."

A tear rolled down Mamma's cheek while she slipped something small and soft between Rebecca's palms. Rebecca glanced down at the crocheted cover.

"I put together this scripture book to help you while you're away, Rebecca. When you have doubts or fears, read it. The good words will comfort and give you strength. You can even share them with Beth. She's going through a difficult time. Your *daed* and I will pray for you every day." She paused. "Lend Daniel your support. The bishop wants you to set three additional goals and accomplish them while you're gone. Give them careful consideration. They must be unselfish and important. Doing this will make your mission even more significant."

After a lengthy silence, William addressed the Sommers in a reassuring voice. "I'll take good care of her. You can be sure of that."

Rebecca's dad raised his chin and directed his attention to William. "We expect nothing less."

Long, tense moments passed while her father and William locked gazes. Several heartbeats later, Eli Sommer stepped forward. "I don't approve of my Becca going so far away. I'm holding you responsible for her, William. If anything happens . . ."

William darted an unsure glance at Rebecca

before responding. "I understand your concern. That's why I didn't encourage her to come."

Rebecca raised her chin and regarded both of them. "I've given this a lot of thought. I'll go. And I'll come back, safe and sound."

Rebecca listened with dread as her father continued making his case. She knew William wouldn't talk back. And she wasn't about to change her mind about going.

"Daed, it's my decision. Please don't worry."

Before he could argue, she threw her arms around him and gave him a tight, reassuring hug. After she stepped away, William motioned toward the black Cadillac. As Rebecca drew a deep breath, her knees trembled, and her heart pounded like a jackhammer. Finally, she forced her jellylike legs to move. She didn't turn around as William opened her door.

Before stepping inside, Rebecca put Mamma's scripture book inside the hope chest. William took the box from her and placed it in the middle of the backseat. Rebecca brought very little with her. Just one small suitcase that her father placed in the trunk.

With great hesitation, she waved good-bye. She forced a confident smile, but her entire body shook. She sat very still as Daniel's second cousin, Ethan, backed the car out of the drive. Gravel crunched under the tires. This wasn't Rebecca's first ride in an automobile. Car rides were not uncommon in the Amish community.

Trying to convince herself she was doing the right thing, she gently pushed the down arrow by her door handle, and the window opened. Rebecca turned in her seat and waved until the sad faces of her family, their plain-looking wooden-framed house built by her great-grandfather, and Old Sam, disappeared.

William turned to her. A worry crease crept across his forehead. The cleft in his chin became more pronounced. "Rebecca, your dad's right. I should have made you stay. The last thing I want to do is create tension between you two."

"It wasn't your choice. As far as my father's concerned . . ." She gave a frustrated shake of her head. "I don't like displeasing him either. On the other hand, it's not right for me to stay here and send you off to save Daniel's shop all by yourself." She shrugged.

In silence, she thought about what she'd just said. She nervously ran her hand over the smooth black leather seat.

"You can adjust the air vents," Ethan announced, turning briefly to make eye contact with her.

She was thankful she didn't have to travel to the Indiana countryside by horse and buggy. She rather enjoyed the soft, barely audible purring of the engine.

Next to her, she eyed the cardboard and pulled out the mini hope chest, setting the box on the floor. She smiled a little.

"Old Sam is something else." William's voice was barely more than a whisper.

"Jah. I can't wait to tell him about our trip." Rebecca giggled. "I'll miss listening to him grumble while he works in the barn. I enjoy watching him make those elaborate chests that he sells to the stores in town."

William gave a small nod. "He loves you three girls."

"Thank goodness that Annie and Rachel will be around to keep him company."

The three friends had loved Esther. Now they took care of Old Sam. He was like an uncle to them. But Rebecca was leaving the world she knew. Would she fit in with the English?

Chapter Two

The week had passed quickly. In the cabinet shop, Rebecca worked with William. She was no stranger to this trade. The large assembly building behind the Conrad home was ten times larger than Rebecca's parents' small woodworking shop. Fans whirled from the high ceilings, creating a whistling sound.

Sawdust floated in the air. Electric saws made sharp, piercing noises. Half a dozen workers completed different tasks at their own stations. Rebecca enjoyed the airy feel created by the large skylights in the roof. She loved sunlight.

From an early age, her father had taught her well. She'd done every job from running the cash register to measuring drawers. Rebecca had even known Daniel's father.

When the Conrads lived in Arthur, their shop was only two blocks from her parents'. They hadn't really been competitors, though. There had always been plenty of work to go around since each of the businesses focused on a different product.

Rebecca glanced at the beautiful, expensive furniture and smiled a little. Her father had never rushed orders. Instead, he had invested pride into his work and had aimed for perfection. Detail was the key to success. Custom furniture was a sharp contrast to assembly-line products.

Obviously, the two men operated alike. The showy pieces ready for delivery spoke for themselves. She and William had accomplished quite a bit and had come up with a plan to get Daniel's backlog of orders processed.

She wore tennis shoes. They didn't exactly flatter her in her long dress, but she was here to work, and Daniel had an order list several pages long.

Stations were spaced throughout the large room. At the staining area, Rebecca ran a cloth over an oak board. A few feet away, William put together delivery orders.

Rebecca's large cabinet glistened with cherry-colored stain. With pride, she smiled and stepped over to William to display her finished piece.

He put down what he was doing and whistled. "It's gorgeous, Miss Rebecca. You've always had a special knack for making cabinets. Only you can apply the stain to make the wood take on that unique rich appearance."

"Thank you." Rebecca dipped her head slightly and carefully placed her cabinet on a bench.

William motioned in front of him. "This must be a year's worth of work." He paused. "It's funny."

"What?"

"I've been thinking a lot. Too much, maybe. I don't care what the circumstances were. Dad should have taken me with him. How could he have left me behind, Rebecca?"

The serious expression on William's face and the tone of his voice told her he wanted to talk. She glanced at the wooden bench next to a nearby wall and motioned. "Come on."

William followed her. They sat next to each other and Rebecca turned to him. "I'm sure that leaving wasn't an easy decision. Carrying out Miriam's wishes must have been terribly important to Daniel."

"I don't care. If he couldn't take me with him, he shouldn't have gone."

"But there's nothing we can do to change what already happened."

As William looked down at the floor, Rebecca nudged him. When their eyes met, she darted him a wry smile. "Living in Arthur wasn't all bad, was it?"

He looked at her to continue.

"If you'd moved, you wouldn't be with me. And I don't know what I would have done without you to carry my schoolbooks."

He grinned. In a soft voice, he responded, "I know. You can never have everything, can you? And you're the most important person in my life. But I feel cheated that I had no father or mother. Am I wrong to think that way?"

Rebecca paused to consider the question. "William, it's not a perfect world. God has presented an opportunity to get to know Daniel. Make the most of it. At least you're playing a role in his life."

"Jah. 'Cause he needs me."

She frowned.

He pushed out a regretful sigh. "You always see the glass half-full."

"That's what Old Sam tells me to do, William."

"You're right. Ya know?"

She raised a brow.

"I feel good about helping him, Rebecca."

"And your parents appreciate it. By the way, I really like them. Daniel's a bit gruff sometimes, but he isn't well. His intentions are good. And Beth has gone out of her way to make me feel at home."

The clicking of the door handle made them turn. "William Conrad?"

"Jah." William stood and walked toward the entrance where a middle-aged man waved a hand. Rebecca followed.

In a friendly voice, the man introduced himself. "Henry Kreggs. And this here's my daughter, Natalie." He closed the door, and they stepped inside. "I hope you don't mind us coming in. Beth gave us permission."

When they met, William extended his hand and introduced Rebecca. She had never met Henry Kreggs, but knew exactly who he was from the customer list. He was Daniel's biggest client. And his order of fifty cabinets was for the family mansion he was building.

Henry shoved his hands deep into his pockets. "I was in the neighborhood and thought I'd drop by to see how things were coming along. Word has it that Daniel's under the weather. How's he doing?"

William gave a slight nod. "He'll be fine. Thanks for asking."

As William gave a time line for the cabinets, Rebecca

observed the young girl dressed in fashionable clothes. Natalie sported loads of makeup, and her long, blond hair gave her an angelic appearance.

When their gazes locked, Rebecca was quick to note curiosity in Natalie's eyes. Recognizing that her Amish dress was out of place, Rebecca guessed that Natalie was probably unsure of what to think about her. Trying to break the ice, Rebecca forced a friendly smile.

"Would you like a glass of water?"

Natalie shook her head. "No, thanks."

When it became clear that Natalie didn't intend to pursue their conversation, Rebecca returned to her workstation and opened another can of stain.

As she carefully pulled off the lid, her attention lingered on the threesome. The men talked and gestured with their hands, but Natalie's focus was on William. In fact, she looked at him with interest.

Natalie batted her eyelashes and said something that made William smile. Rebecca arched a curious brow. An unsettling feeling landed in her chest.

She knew she was naïve, but Rebecca was astute enough to see that Natalie flirted with William. And William had responded.

The moment Henry and his daughter waved good-bye, Rebecca sighed in relief. Natalie made her feel a bit odd and uncomfortable. When William rejoined Rebecca, she erased the girl from her mind. "Everything okay?"

He nodded. "I assured him we'd do our best." William paused and cupped his chin with his hand.

Rebecca furrowed her brow and motioned to the wooden bench. "Want to finish our talk?"

"Sure."

Sitting down, she turned slightly and laid a hand on her thigh. "What's wrong?"

Extending a set of long legs, William cleared his throat. "Henry asked about Dad. As soon as I said he'd be okay, I realized I wasn't sure." He moved his shoulders in a casual shrug. "I'm worried, Rebecca. The doctor said he should be doing light activities by now. But I'm sure you've noticed that he can barely get around. And he doesn't look good. The bags under his eyes, his pale cheeks . . . He's so . . . frail."

William lowered his voice. "Rebecca, what if he doesn't recover?"

She considered the potent question and pursed her lips in deep deliberation. Daniel had made little or no progress since she and William had moved into the Conrad home over a week ago.

She recalled Old Sam's optimistic approach to life and raised her chin in confidence. "Keep praying. He suffered a heart attack. Of course getting back on his feet will take time."

A grin tugged at her lips as she recalled one of Old Sam's favorite proverbs. "A handful of patience is worth a bushel of brains."

The old saying prompted a sigh from William. "Thank you, Rebecca."

"For what?"

He leaned toward her. The hopeful look in his eyes made her heart melt. She loved him so much.

"Everything. I can't believe how hard you've worked." He motioned to the cabinets in front of them. "I couldn't have finished this order without you."

She sat up straighter. "That's why I'm here."

"Most of all, thanks for being my best friend. Having you with me has boosted my confidence."

She raised a curious brow. "Confidence?"

He nodded. "I hate to admit this, but I was afraid to leave home."

"Really?"

"It's the truth. I wasn't sure I could carry this out."

She crossed her arms over her chest and lightly tapped her shoe against the floor. "I don't understand. We've done this our entire lives. Besides, we're not alone." She motioned to two women placing dividers inside of drawers.

"Not by ourselves. Aenti Sarah, Uncle John, and your folks made the big decisions."

"I'd never really thought of it like that."

"We've got a lot on our plate." He paused. "You know what I've learned here?"

"What?"

"That the world's much larger than Arthur, Illinois."

Rebecca laughed. "But we knew that."

"Of course, but what I didn't realize was how protected we were. For the first time in my life, I feel I can do anything." He hesitated. "Under one condition."

"What?"

"That you're with me."

* * *

That night, Rebecca thought of William as she sat in bed and pulled the bedcovers over her legs. The lamp on the stand next to her illuminated the area.

She had to let Mamma know how amazing the Conrad home was. On a piece of paper, she wrote as neatly as she could.

Dear Mamma, I miss you so much. The Conrads are wonderful. You wouldn't believe my room. A beautiful white fan looms from the high ceiling. Cream-colored wall paint offsets a dark oak boudoir. A large picture of a flower garden decorates the wall in front of me. You'd love the deep, rich colors. And the gold detailed frame looks like an expensive antique.

My walk-in closet is lined with sachet hangers in pastel colors. And a small television rests on a shelf in one of the corners. My purple bed comforter smells of lavender.

When she ended the letter, she put down the paper and pen, pushed an oversized decorative pillow to the side, and rested her head on a smaller cushion. Her gaze drifted to the hope chest given to her by Old Sam. She grinned, and hopped up to open it and retrieve Mamma's scripture book.

As she thought of her family and Old Sam, her heart ached for home. She would give anything to talk with Mamma while they made homemade butter. She grabbed a nearby notepad and pen, jotted the date in the upper right-hand corner, and began writing her innermost thoughts.

At home, life was carefree. There was no pressure.

Here, there's stress.

Rebecca frowned as a small yawn escaped her. As she considered the events of the day, she wrote, *Meeting Natalie was uncomfortable. She stared at me and made me feel strange. What really made me uneasy was watching her look at William. She likes him.*

Rebecca returned her new diary to the chest, and the tense muscles in her shoulders began to slowly relax. She put her written thoughts next to her scripture book and stood. She closed the hope chest and strummed her fingers over the lid. As she traced the bouquet carved into the wood, she thought of Old Sam. Salty tears stung her eyes as she turned to flip off her lamp.

In bed, she closed her eyes and prayed. As she rolled onto her side, she considered how different her life was now. She thought of her parents and struggled to keep in mind why she'd come.

As she drifted off to sleep, she dreamed of the woods behind the Conrad home. In her long, brown dress and kapp, she and William proceeded side by side through the thick brush.

Without warning, his pace quickened to a jog. She tried to keep up, but couldn't. Where was he?

Before she knew it, he had vanished. She was lost. She hollered. No answer.

The sky turned dark. A chilly wind caused shivers up and down her spine. Worse, she couldn't find William. Why had he left her? She cried out.

"Rebecca, wake up! It's okay."

When she opened her eyes, Beth was shaking her. Rebecca's breaths were rapid and shallow. Her heart beat at a sprinter's pace.

"I had a nightmare."

"Honey, I know you miss your family."

Beth's gentle smile was understanding. "It's the first time you've been away from them. But I have a nice surprise. A new friend named Katie. She's Amish and sells eggs. Tomorrow, she'll be by in her buggy to deliver them. And you'll love her."

Beth planted an affectionate kiss on Rebecca's forehead and stood. "Go back to sleep. Tomorrow will be a good day."

As Rebecca's gaze followed Beth out of the room, she considered William's kind and loving step-mother. But what Beth didn't realize was that meeting Katie wouldn't solve Rebecca's worries. Being homesick wasn't really her main problem.

It was Natalie. Rebecca feared losing William.

What had Rebecca dreamed? The following morning, William pondered the question as she placed a newly stained cabinet partition on a board to dry. In her long dress and tennis shoes, she worked hard. Miss Rebecca was definitely the practical sort. Her clothing was far from glamorous, yet there was still an incredible beauty that emanated from her.

A loveliness that even the ugliest of garments couldn't conceal. Rebecca's eyes sparkled. Her creamy skin glowed. He liked the proud, determined lift of her chin. What he loved most about her was her ability to reason. Rebecca was the most logical person he knew.

He glanced around the sawdust-filled room and

considered their future. He dreamed of giving her a wonderful life. A beautiful home. He wished he could provide her with a kitchen like Beth's.

When he rested a gentle hand on her shoulder, she turned.

"Beth told me about your nightmare. Want to talk about it?"

To his surprise and disappointment, Rebecca shook her head. "I'd rather not." She changed the subject. "William, if you could have anything, what would you ask for?"

Together, they lifted a large cherry cabinet and carried it to the delivery station. As they set it down, their eyes locked. William smiled a little.

"That's easy. You. And a house full of children." He lowered his voice. "You mean the world to me, Rebecca. I couldn't imagine being here without you."

"Do you still dream of building a house together?"

"Of course. And I want a pond so our boys can fish."

"What about our girls?"

He grinned. "You can teach them to make quilts. And to grow vegetables. You're a wonderful gardener. I can already see our little ones picking flowers. They'll be just like you." He paused. "What do you dream of, Rebecca?"

"You."

He beamed. "What else?" He took in the thoughtful expression on her face.

"Children." The excited look in her eyes turned serious. "I also pray for my parents to live to be very old." She quickly added with a newfound excitement, "And I'd like a zillion flower plants, to make arrangements." Old Sam had given her a spot in his barn to dry them.

William chuckled. "You and your plants."

"I love watching things grow. It's amazing what blessings God has given us. And the best things cost nothing at all."

They returned to the main work area. She gently touched his shoulder. "William, I've noticed your folks don't have a garden."

He shrugged. "They buy fresh produce at a farmer's market."

"Jah, but don't you suppose Daniel would enjoy a small garden?" Before William could answer, she added, "You know, just to look at while he recovers? Flowers are good for the soul."

William considered the question. "He might."

"I'd like to do that for him."

William smiled widely. "You're so thoughtful, Rebecca. That's one of the reasons I love you."

As his gaze penetrated hers, there was more he yearned to tell her. Like his longing to own a car. Of living like the English. But he didn't. Because wanting these things was selfish.

He had been raised to not place such emphasis on material possessions. And he was ashamed of himself. What would Rebecca say if she could read his mind?

Katie's friendly smile and warm green eyes immediately made Rebecca feel at home. Katie was tall and willowy with porcelain skin and a beauty that seemed to come from a centered, thoughtful personality.

At the same time, she wore a long, brown dress and black shoes. Like Rebecca, her hair was pulled tightly back on her head and covered with a kapp.

After Beth paid Katie for the eggs, she glanced at the girls and waved a hand in dismissal. "Why don't the two of you sit on the patio and enjoy a cup of tea?"

Katie grinned at Rebecca. "I have a better idea. How 'bout a ride in my buggy? I have some errands in town."

A wide smile lifted Rebecca's lips. "I'd love it."

They made their way to the "black box." An orange-and-yellow YIELD sign decorated the back. They lifted the skirts of their long dresses to step up to the bench seat.

After Katie yanked the door closed, she straightened in her seat and grabbed the reins. With a light jolt, the horse trotted. As it whinnied, Rebecca let out a contented sigh.

A soft, folded quilt of beautiful hues covered the bench seat. Rebecca felt at ease. After all, this was what she knew. Shiny autos didn't tempt her at all.

A sleek, smooth leather car seat couldn't compete with the buggy's homespun goodness. Above, the sun brightened the sky. The warm breeze loosened tendrils of hair from her bun.

"Do you like it here?"

Rebecca offered a slight nod. "I adore William's parents. Beth is so kind. And Daniel teases her about ordering him around. Their home is lovely." She hesitated. "But I feel a bit out of place."

"Of course. You're used to a simple life. Is this your first encounter with the English?"

"No. The town I'm from has them. But this is a first for being away from my family."

"Do your parents have a phone?"

"They share one with neighbors. It's in a booth between two houses. Oh, Katie, I miss little things. Chatting with my little brother and sister over breakfast. Going to church with my family. Helping Mamma in the garden."

As they proceeded down the country road, everything was familiar to Rebecca. The distinct smell of horses. The gentle rocking of the carriage.

"The English lifestyle must be tempting."

Rebecca shrugged. "At times, I think about wearing my hair down." She giggled. "And I wonder how I'd look in blue jeans."

Katie laughed. "I'm proud of you for practicing your customs. We Amish girls are a tough breed. We never take the easy way out. That would be too simple. But sticking to our beliefs when we're in the minority?" She gave a firm shake of her head. "That takes courage."

"I never thought of it that way."

"You must really love William to move so far away for him."

"Oh, didn't Beth tell you?"

"What?"

"This is temporary. William and I are only here until Daniel's back on his feet."

Katie raised a curious brow. "Are you sure?"

Rebecca frowned. An uncomfortable sensation tightened her chest. "Of course. Why do you ask?"

With a roll of her eyes, Katie cleared her throat.

"Because Beth mentioned how nice it would be for William and Daniel to become business partners."

William waved good-bye to Rebecca and Katie from the front yard. He blinked as the late June sun appeared from under a cloud. Already, he sensed Katie was good company for Rebecca. He lifted a concerned brow. Rebecca's nightmare was still on his mind. And . . . that she hadn't shared it with him. They had never kept secrets from each other. What had she dreamed about that had caused her to scream? Whatever it was must have been awful.

As he fingered the tip of his hat, he took in the Conrad estate. He'd never imagined so many luxuries. They'd been here less than a couple of weeks, but already, he knew he liked the amenities that came with the English lifestyle.

Beth's sleek BMW boasted a sunroof. The large-screen television Daniel watched from his bed was like something from the future. Cell phones. Electric garage-door openers.

Of course, Aenti Sarah and Uncle John were fully aware that all of these accessories existed. They shopped at Walmart and Sears.

While the sun appeared from behind a white fluffy cloud, William compared his new life to his old. He pressed his lips together in deep deliberation and shoved his hands into his pockets as he studied the ground.

He respected Amish ways, yet it seemed unfair that Aenti Sarah used an air compressor to power her washing machine, while Beth merely tossed her laundry into an electric Maytag and did other things while the machine worked.

Things were too easy here. But were Daniel and Beth bad people? William shook his head. To his surprise, he enjoyed their luxuries. Especially the ESPN channel.

Would God disapprove? Long, thoughtful moments passed while he wondered who he would have been had he driven a car instead of a horse and buggy. Nervous, guilty steps took him to the edge of the yard and back. Would he have become the same William his Rebecca loved? His gaze landed on Beth's silver car and he imagined cruising the country roads with the windows down.

For one blissful moment, he smiled. His imagination wandered to a land where he sat in the driver's seat. He stepped hard on the accelerator as the warm summer wind lifted his hair. He'd never felt so much power as he clutched the leather-covered steering wheel that tilted up. On the front dash were all sorts of buttons and arrows. He was in control as he swept past fields. Towns. From the open window, he waved at people he knew.

They reciprocated. In the rearview mirror he watched their gazes follow him. He chuckled. Life couldn't get better than what he saw here. A large house. A color television with tons of cable channels and a remote control.

As the engine hummed, William could do anything. Because he drove the smoothest, sleekest car around.

A squirrel dashed in front of him, interrupting his thoughts. With a frustrated sigh, he frowned and forced his mind to reality. A few moments later, he shrugged and struggled to accept what he had. He reasoned that there were definitely advantages to driving a buggy.

No gas tank to fill. Or tune-ups. And no monthly insurance payments he'd heard Daniel talk about. Still, William would love having a car.

A strong pang of guilt swept down his arms and landed in his fingertips, making them tingle. He flexed them to rid himself of the uncomfortable sensation. Temptation. It filled his heart and his soul. Was it wrong? Was it possible to be around these luxuries and not want them?

As he swatted away a fly that buzzed near his nose, William considered those challenging questions. He raised a thoughtful brow and tapped the heel of his foot to a nervous beat. What he felt was actually stronger than temptation. It was envy. His heart sank. God was surely disappointed in him.

Perhaps it would have been better to have stayed in Arthur. He wouldn't have been exposed to so much. In Illinois, he wouldn't have been tested.

Yet there were plenty of English at home. They shopped in the same stores. Dined in Yoder's Kitchen, the popular local restaurant. All the same, he had never lived in their houses.

Being isolated from evils was taking the easy way out, wasn't it? He supposed he could view this experience as an education. He smiled a little. His guilt began to slip away as he considered the word "education."

While the sun slipped behind a cloud, the temperature dropped a notch. Surely he couldn't be blamed for enjoying his father's way of life. And certainly

God wouldn't have approved of him neglecting his own flesh and blood.

William's thoughts drifted to Rebecca, and he squeezed his eyes closed in acute pain. A guilty shiver crept up his spine and landed at the base of his neck. He gave a quick shrug of his shoulders to rid himself of the uncomfortable sensation, but it lingered. So did his wants. What would Rebecca say if she knew what he was thinking?

Rebecca watched Henry Kreggs write William a check for the first half of their large order. The recollection of her buggy ride with Katie the day before prompted a wide smile.

Rebecca took in Natalie's high heels and tight-fitting jeans. Rebecca had never dreamed of changing her faith or what she wore, but for the first time in her life, she felt a bit frumpy in her long, solid-colored dress and tennis shoes. She gritted her teeth.

In fact, when she'd first met Natalie, she'd experienced that same insecure feeling. Rebecca hadn't missed the disapproving look the girl had darted her. But she strongly suspected that Natalie's negative attitude involved much more than Rebecca's ways.

And Rebecca sensed that William was the cause of the animosity. She noticed the sparkle in Natalie's eyes when she stared at him.

And this wasn't the first time Rebecca had noted that look. She rolled her shoulders to rid the uncomfortable tenseness. Natalie liked William. Was there reason to be concerned?

As the ceiling fans whirled, Rebecca pushed a rebellious strand of hair back over her ear and considered her relationship with William in the most logical manner she could. First of all, she was certain of his feelings. Secondly, they'd known each other forever. At least, since they'd started school. And not only did they love each other, but they were best friends.

Suddenly she was too warm in her long sleeves. Her chest tightened, making it more difficult to breathe.

William's love for her was as solid as an oak table. Tight jeans and high heels couldn't steal that, could they?

As William and Henry lifted a box and loaded it into the back of a white pickup, Natalie stepped to Rebecca. Automatically, Rebecca forced a friendly smile. Natalie glanced at Rebecca's head and frowned.

"I'm curious about your head wrap. Is it something like the Muslim women wear?"

The question was asked politely enough, but Natalie's tone was edged with sarcasm.

Rebecca raised her chin and responded, "It's called a kapp; it's worn by Amish women."

Natalie's voice hinted frustration. "You have to be different, don't you? Why don't you dress like the rest of us? You're not in your Amish town, Rebecca. This is the real world. And this is the way *real* people dress." She pointed to her jeans.

Rebecca tried to stay calm. Getting upset would get her nowhere. Besides, what Natalie said was true. Rebecca wasn't in an Amish community, and she was the one out of place.

"Not everyone practices the same beliefs, Natalie."

Natalie wrinkled her nose. "I wouldn't be caught dead in something like that. Couldn't you find something a little more stylish?"

"We stick to our beliefs. No matter where we are."

Natalie smiled mischievously. The look forced an uneasy trickle up Rebecca's spine. "You think William will always stick to those ridiculous Amish rules?" She shook her head with certainty. The sparkle in her beautiful blue eyes wasn't kind. "Rebecca, can't you see the light? I overheard that William wants to get a driver's license. And can you blame him?"

Before Rebecca could get a word in, Natalie went on. "The grapevine also says Daniel wants him to stay here and become his business partner."

Rebecca's jaw dropped. Of all that Natalie had blurted, the last statement was the most potent. The force of its significance nearly knocked Rebecca to the ground. She considered the source of the information. She probably shouldn't believe anything this girl said. But this was the second time she'd heard mention of a partnership. Was it true?

That night, a noise awakened her. Startled, Rebecca lay very still, listening. A breeze whistled through the window screen. She could hear Daniel snoring in the room down the hall.

The cool breeze made shivers dance up her arms and legs. To keep warm, she pulled the covers closer to her body. A storm brewed. Thunder rumbled.

Lightning bolts brightened the sky. She heard the noise again, but couldn't identify it. What she did know was that there had been a considerable drop in temperature since she'd gone to bed.

She decided to close the window. But before leaving her soft blankets, she enjoyed the warmth a little longer. Her thoughts drifted to her simple home, her comfy bed, and the beautiful quilt her mother had spent months making for her. Although she enjoyed this house and what it offered, it didn't measure up to those all-too-familiar comforts of the place she'd lived her entire life.

As her heart pumped to a lonely beat, she considered Katie and their buggy ride. She'd loved meeting someone of her own faith. Rebecca looked forward to next Tuesday when Katie would stop again. She was a much-needed blessing God had sent her way.

The unidentified sound interrupted her thoughts, and Rebecca focused her attention on the open window. More alert, she sat up. The room was dark except for the small area under the skylight where the moonlight slipped inside. She breathed in the scent of newly mowed grass.

When the soft fluttering began again, she quietly tiptoed to the screened window. It was then that she glimpsed an envelope. The corner was wedged into the space where the screen slightly separated from the sill.

The breeze lifted the other corner to create a flapping sound. With great hesitation, Rebecca slowly plucked the envelope.

As she closed the screen, the sun began to rise, providing enough light to see her first name handwritten in black ink. Her pulse zoomed into fast gear. For long, uncertain moments, she stared at the envelope. Finally, she inhaled a shaky breath and tore it open.

Two questions nagged at her. First of all, what was the letter doing in her window? It wouldn't have been difficult to place it there, since Rebecca's room was on the ground floor. Secondly, who had placed it there?

An unsettling sensation filled her chest as she removed a piece of cream-colored stationery. She pulled out the small paper and regarded the contents with keen interest.

As she read the short, direct message, her heart nearly stopped. She caught her breath and froze in place.

Go home.

Chapter Three

The following morning, Rebecca related to William what had happened as they stepped from the house to the woodworking shop that was some distance away. Above, the sun illuminated the sky. Not a cloud in sight. It was the perfect day for a picnic, a wedding, or anything.

Under normal circumstances, Rebecca would enjoy the beautiful weather. But not today. She stopped and turned to William. Without replying, his lips curved downward. His jaw tensed.

As their gazes locked, she handed him the simple message. In silence, he stared at the paper. As she waited for a response, her hands shook and she clasped them together.

As he regarded the two words, his brows furrowed in concern. Tiny creases made their way under his eyes. The last thing Rebecca wanted was to worry him. He already had enough on his plate, but she couldn't keep the words a secret. Long moments later, he met her gaze and returned the paper.

"What do you think?"

"It's hard to say." He shrugged. "This has to be a sick joke."

"I've never had anything like this happen."

He raised his voice a notch. "Why didn't you come wake me up?"

"That would have been selfish. Besides, I wasn't in harm's way. It's not as though someone was trying to break in."

"That's my Rebecca. Always thinking of everyone but herself. But you should have awakened me right away. That's what I'm here for."

For several blissful moments, Rebecca thought of only William and how he looked out for her. She remembered the time he had rescued her in a winter blizzard. There were other memories, too.

She'd never forget how he had walked her home from school and carried her books. Each afternoon as she stepped inside her house, he had proudly dipped the brim of his hat while saying good-bye.

William was strong. He was her shield. God had given him to her. But right now, Rebecca wondered what he would do about the note. The situation was real. Rebecca hadn't dreamed the message.

She gazed into his eyes. Her heart melted when she noted their warmth and concern. "William— obviously, I must have offended someone."

His fierce expression told her that he would be at her side. As the intriguing metallic-gray flecks danced in his blue depths, she was reminded that there was nothing they couldn't overcome together. She smiled a little and let out a breath of relief.

"I'm better already. I'm so glad I shared this with you."

His voice took on a firm tone. "Rebecca, I want you to make me a promise."

"What?"

"That you'll never keep anything from me."

She nodded. "Deal."

He gave a doubtful shake of his head and rolled his eyes. "The note baffles me." He threw up his hands in a frustrated gesture. "I can't imagine who would want you to leave. It's troubling. I'd like to handle this and be done with it. But how can I? We don't know who sent it."

A tense silence went by. Finally, William cleared his throat.

"When I think of someone at your window during the night, it sends chills up and down my spine. Just think, someone was here, and we didn't know it. That's almost as disturbing as the note."

Rebecca considered the warning. "The message is plain and simple. Someone doesn't want me here."

"Who?"

As soon as he asked the question, Rebecca recalled her recent conversation with Natalie. Rebecca pressed her lips together in deep deliberation. She certainly didn't want to accuse the girl if she was innocent.

At the same time, Rebecca had promised William to never keep anything from him. Relief swept through her as she decided on a direct approach. Besides, Mamma had always told her that hiding things got a person nowhere. The only way to solve problems was to talk honestly. "It could be Natalie."

William frowned. "Henry's daughter?"

Rebecca gave a firm nod.

"Why do you say that?"

"She likes you, William."

He grinned. His cheeks reddened a bit, making him appear younger than his age. "For heaven's sake, I just met the girl." He raised a curious brow. "You must know something I don't."

Rebecca folded her arms over her chest. "I caught the way she stared at you."

"Maybe she was interested in my suspenders." He touched the brown strap.

Again, Rebecca shook her head.

"How can you be sure?"

"Because her eyes . . . sparkled. Not only that, she made it clear she disapproves of me. Well, the way I dress, anyway. She was interested in my kapp and asked if it was the same headwear that Muslim women wear."

He laughed. "You're joking."

"No, William. You have to trust me on this one. I'm not delusional."

She yearned to broach William about becoming Daniel's business partner. She decided to wait until there was more time to discuss it.

William looked up at the sky, tapping the front of his shoe against the ground. As Rebecca thought about what she'd just disclosed, she wrung her hands. It was amazing they were having this conversation. Even more interesting was that every word she'd said was true.

Never had she dealt with anything like this. In Arthur, her world had been a safe haven. She'd been secure and protected in her tightly knit Amish community. But this was the real world. And things were different. God must have surely planted her at the

Conrads' home to educate her. But she was learning
more than she wanted to.

"So you think Natalie left this?" He pulled the
note from Rebecca's pocket and held it in front of
them.

As Rebecca took in his curious expression, she
shrugged. "I certainly can't rule her out." She hesitated. "William, we haven't been here long, and
during this brief time frame, I've met only a handful
of people. Unless the sender is someone who hasn't
even met me, there's a very short list of people who
could have done this."

She ran her hands down the front of her dress
and looked down at the ground. When she looked
up, she said, "I suppose it could be one of the shop
workers. Who knows? Maybe someone didn't like
me stepping in." She hesitated. "To be honest, Natalie's the only person who has made her dislike
obvious. She wrinkled her nose at me."

"Wrinkled her nose?"

Rebecca nodded and squared her shoulders. She
stepped forward so her face nearly touched William's
chin. "I told you that she doesn't care for the way
I dress."

William grinned. "You know what?"

They were so close, she smelled the woodsy scent
of his clothing. She loved the way his eyes lit up
when he smiled. She couldn't believe that later this
year, she would be his wife.

She remembered his question and blushed a
little. Her voice softened. "What?"

"*I* like the way you dress." As he eyed her up and
down, heat rushed to her cheeks. William always
made her feel good about herself. "In fact, there's

not one thing I'd change about you, Miss Rebecca."
He put a hand on his hip. "No one looks as good as
you." He winked. "And there's absolutely no one in
the world with more beautiful chestnut-colored
hair."

Rebecca sometimes wished that she could wear
her hair down. She recalled Natalie's comment and
lowered her gaze a bit. "But . . . but do I look plain?"

He closed his lids. When he opened them, moisture glistened like morning dew on a leaf. As they
looked at each other, her heart sang a happy little
tune.

"There's something, Rebecca, that makes you
stand out from the rest. And it has nothing to do
with what you wear."

"What is it?"

He thought a moment. "A lot of things. Your
logic. The way you look at things. And your smile. I
remember learning in church school that a person's
smile helps us see into his soul. And when you smile
at me, I see everything that's good and honest."

"Thanks, William."

His voice took on a firm tone. "And Natalie?"

Rebecca raised a curious brow and waited for
William to continue.

"She doesn't hold a candle to you."

She loved William. There was something about
him that made her feel safe and secure. Somehow,
she'd always known that they would marry. They had
never discussed it until recently, but all along, it had
been sort of an unwritten thing.

Couples in her Amish world didn't really have
what the English referred to as an "engagement."
But taking wedding vows was a different story.

Amish weddings were a huge affair with feasts of fried chicken, dumplings, and delicious homemade dishes.

Everyone in the community participated. Usually, the celebrations took place in the home of a family member. Or under a large tent. In fact, the last wedding she'd attended had been held at the house of the groom's best friend and had lasted over half a day.

As sweet memories filled Rebecca's thoughts, a breeze pushed a loose tendril of hair from her bun. Blissful moments passed while she looked into his dark depths where she saw pure contentment.

Outside of the shop, the intimate moment was quickly shattered by a scream that seemed to come from the home. At the same time, she and William startled. Without hesitation, they turned and re-traced the path back to the house.

Inside, Beth was touching her husband. Rebecca gasped in shock as she glimpsed Daniel on the living room floor. His eyes were closed.

"I called for help."

The moment Rebecca and William began to shake Daniel, two paramedics bounded inside of the front entrance, shouting their arrival. William quickly went for them.

Automatically, they stepped aside for the ETs to do their jobs. Rebecca's frightened heart pounded hard. As one uniformed worker shook Daniel, the other checked his pulse. Rebecca grabbed Beth's hand and squeezed it for reassurance.

Beth's desperate voice cracked with emotion as

she related what had happened. "He complained of pain in his left arm. Then he collapsed. Oh, please help him. You've got to save him."

Rebecca blinked back tears and said a quick prayer. Daniel couldn't die. "Please, God. Let him live. William needs to know his father."

The older tech motioned for Beth, Rebecca, and William to step back. They complied. Rebecca's heartbeat catapulted to an uncomfortable pace as they continued unsuccessfully to revive Daniel.

Rebecca's gaze shifted back and forth from Beth to William. Beth's eyes had doubled in size. William's jaw was set. His face was filled with horror and disbelief. In silence, they watched the crew work on Daniel.

As soon as a technician announced that he'd found a pulse, Rebecca and William let out deep, drawn-out sighs of relief. Beth cried, "Thank you, God."

While the rescue crew lifted Daniel onto a stretcher, Beth exclaimed, "I'm coming with you."

The younger tech responded with a quick nod. "Take the front seat." At Daniel's side, she walked to the passenger door. Beth's eyes never left Daniel until the workers shoved the stretcher into the back of the emergency van. In a split second, the men jumped inside and the double doors were pulled closed.

"Call when you know something!" William's words were silenced by the loud bang of the heavy metal slamming shut. When the vehicle pulled away, red lights flashed. Not long after, a loud siren whistled.

Ironically, the bright sun slipped behind a cloud. The brightness disappeared, and the sky turned several shades darker.

Rebecca and William stood in silence as the ambulance disappeared. The dramatic scene that had just taken place would stay with her forever. She wished she had the power to save Daniel. But only God could do that. She breathed another quick prayer.

Then she glanced at William. "He'll be okay. God will watch over him."

She said the words with conviction. Because she believed them. She couldn't bear the thought of William losing his dad. They didn't even know each other. God had finally put them together. Surely the Lord would give them enough time to bond.

William's chest rose and fell at a quick pace. Concern covered his face like a white sheet. When the dust from the ambulance settled, Rebecca motioned him back inside, where they sat on the living room couch. The cream-colored leather felt cool against Rebecca's palms. The air-conditioning was a sharp contrast to the warmth of the outdoors.

William extended his long legs and leaned back onto one of the cushions. He spoke in a shaky voice, "As I watched Dad on the floor, I felt totally helpless. He could have died, and there wasn't anything I could do for him. There's got to be a way for me to help. Otherwise, I'm not much of a man."

She leaned toward him so that their elbows touched. "William, you *are* a man in every sense of the word. Don't ever underestimate your self-worth. You're doing so much."

"You mean by running his business?"

She nodded. "As soon as you heard Daniel needed you, you were on your way to help. You came unselfishly and without hesitation. Think of all you've accomplished! Without you, he'd be in trouble."

William rolled his eyes in frustration. "Your glass is always half full, Rebecca. And I adore that about you. But making cabinets won't keep him alive."

"You can't save him. Neither can Beth. Keeping him alive is up to the doctors. And God."

She paused and took a deep breath. "You must realize how fortunate we are to have been raised by such strong, Christian people. Remember all we've learned at church. Now we're being tested. Have faith. And pray. It's only through prayers that we communicate with God."

He leaned back and reached his arms behind his head. His knuckles made an imprint in the leather when he clasped his hands together. Rebecca watched him squeeze his eyes closed, revealing tiny worry lines.

When he opened his lids, the expression on his face was a combination of pain and hope. He sat up straighter.

In an upbeat tone, he asked, "You think Beth will call soon?"

Smiling a little, Rebecca nodded.

William grinned. "A phone should be mandatory in every Amish household. What would we have done without one today?"

Rebecca agreed. "They certainly come in handy. Especially in emergencies."

Everything was happening at once. Her stay at the Conrads'. The anonymous note. Daniel's failing health. Crucial things that required serious thought.

Rebecca focused on Daniel's condition. The rest would have to wait. Right now, William needed her. He came first.

The phone made her startle.

She went to stand by William as he held the receiver to his ear. When he hung up, his eyes filled with uneasiness. "It was Beth."

Chapter Four

Daniel had suffered another heart attack. Rebecca glanced at the small calendar on the fridge that showed it was already the last of June. She ran a damp dishcloth over Beth's granite kitchen countertop. She stood on her tiptoes to reach the other side. Out of breath, she landed back on her feet.

Beth was staying at the hospital until Daniel was out of intensive care. He was in fragile condition, but his doctors were hopeful. The cleaning lady was on vacation, so Rebecca would give Beth a boost with the chores. Somehow, she'd help in the cabinet shop *and* make sure the house was taken care of.

Laundry wouldn't be difficult with Beth's Maytag. And thanks to the grocery delivery service, Rebecca didn't need to shop.

As she watered the bright red geranium plants in the kitchen, she stopped to gaze out of the large bay window. Since yesterday's conversation with William, she'd noticed moisture under her lids more than usual. The lush carpet of green grass reminded her of a church sermon she'd heard long ago.

The message was that God was in charge of our lives. All that we have in this world belongs to Him, and He has the power to take it away anytime. A million dollars couldn't fix Daniel's heart. But God could.

The sound of the key in the door interrupted her thoughts. Rebecca dropped her dishrag as the front door opened. Beth rushed into the kitchen and tossed her purse on the table.

Rebecca asked, "How is he?"

Beth gave a slight nod. "Fragile. I came back for a shower and change clothes."

Rebecca didn't miss the dark, hollow circles under Beth's deep blue eyes. Or that her voice shook. Rebecca motioned to the pitcher by the window. "How 'bout some tea?"

Beth smiled a little. "Thanks, Rebecca. That's the best offer I've had all morning."

Rebecca grabbed a glass from the nearest cabinet and held it under the automatic ice maker. Small cubes clinked as they hit the sides. She repeated the motion with another glass and poured the tea. Beverages in hand, Rebecca joined Beth at the table.

Beth took a sip and smiled satisfaction. "Delicious."

"Thanks."

"When do you think he'll come home?"

Beth shrugged. "I'm not sure. The doctors believe he'll be okay, but to be honest, Rebecca, I don't know what to think. It scares me to see Daniel so helpless. His face is void of color, and he doesn't talk much. I keep praying for God to work a miracle."

Rebecca looked away, trying for comforting words. To her chagrin, she was at a loss. "Oh, Beth. I'm so sorry. Somehow I just know he'll be okay."

Rebecca's heart ached. She went for a tissue to give Beth time to compose herself. All the while, she considered the right words to say to her. Rebecca handed Beth a blue Kleenex.

"I've never been in your situation, but I pray for Daniel every night. Surely, your church is praying, too. Prayers will heal him."

Beth blew her nose and nodded. "Several support groups have Daniel on their lists. And believe me, no one's praying more than me."

Rebecca gave a reassuring nod. "Then you're doing all you can. If we just knew what the future held."

"But only God knows."

Beth caught her breath, wiping a tear with her tissue. "Your belief is genuine, Rebecca. I could tell that when I met you. I know what you risked coming here. It took a bold woman to do what you did. There must have been opposition from your community. Yet you followed your heart. What's your secret of staying so strong? And how do you maintain such faith?"

The questions took Rebecca by surprise. She was astonished that Beth saw her as a strong person when Rebecca battled such fears. She'd thought a lot about the partnership rumor. She wanted to ask Beth if it was true. But this was hardly the right time. Besides, if Daniel was going to invite William to partner in his business, she'd find out soon enough.

In the meantime, there was no need to borrow trouble. That's what Old Sam always said.

Rebecca's mind returned to her current conversation with Beth. Rebecca did have faith. She'd never really considered where it came from. She just knew it was there. After giving careful thought, she leaned forward.

"I don't know. What I am sure of is that God looks after me. I don't have control over everything. But He does. And I trust He'll guide me to make the right decisions. Even though it might not seem best at the time." She paused a moment and added, "Sometimes it can be scary when we don't understand what's happening."

Beth took another drink and returned the glass to the table. "I'm from a Mennonite family, Rebecca. Although we use electricity and have different interpretations for certain scriptures, we still believe in the resurrection and the forgiveness of sins, just like the Amish. The fundamentals of our church are the same as yours, really."

Rebecca went to refill their glasses before rejoining Beth. "There are so many religions, Beth. I've always wondered which one God would prefer."

"Me too. And to be honest, I never understood how one denomination could believe it was better than another. In the whole realm of things, we know so little. I don't get too wrapped up in specifics. Scripture interpretation is just that. God knows how He wants us to practice our faith." She lifted her hands in a helpless gesture. "We're only human. We do our best and hope to please Him."

Rebecca considered what Beth had said. Rebecca

had never really given much thought to other faiths. She'd always assumed that the Amish interpretation of the Bible was right. Did that make her like those who believed their faith was "the one"? Maybe she needed to open her eyes.

"Daniel and I never really gave much thought to being tested. It wasn't something we even discussed. But looking back, believing and having faith was easy because everything was fine. We were healthy. Daniel's business did well. We didn't want for anything." She squeezed her eyes closed for a moment and opened them. "Until Daniel's first heart attack. My goodness, Rebecca, it was so unexpected. Daniel hadn't even complained about not feeling well. When a crisis arises, you really find out how strong you are." She paused and shook her head in dismay. "I'm going to tell you something. And I want this to stay between the two of us."

Rebecca leaned forward. "I'm a good promise keeper."

Beth lowered her voice to a mere whisper. "I'm sure God must be disappointed in me. I'm ashamed to say this, but I'm scared. I love Daniel so much. He's my sun, moon, and stars. People tell me I'm strong and that I'll be fine. But I don't believe I can survive without him."

Beth's voice shook as she flung her hands in the air in frustration. "If I could trade places with him, I would do it in a heartbeat. What's happening . . . It just isn't fair."

"Beth, I'm sure God isn't disappointed in you. Anyone in your position would feel the same way."

Their gazes locked. Beth was regarding Rebecca

with a hopeful look on her face. Rebecca suddenly realized Beth was waiting for reassurance. She swallowed. She wanted to offer hope and encouragement. But there was no guarantee Daniel would get well. Rebecca wished she could promise Beth that he would. She couldn't.

Rebecca could see that Beth, too, was fragile. She wasn't in a hospital bed, but her mind was in a state of doubt and denial. How could Rebecca reassure her and at the same time, help her to face reality? What would Old Sam say?

She searched for the right words. Finally, they came. Rebecca cleared her throat. "Beth, let's take one step at a time. I think the best we can do for Daniel right now is to support him, let him know we're there for him. And definitely, the prayer chain should be encouraged. We should ask for prayers from everyone we know."

Rebecca turned her chair to better face Beth. The legs squeaked as they ran over the floor. "In the meantime, William and I are here to help. We're trying to keep Daniel's business going." She grinned. "I know it's not the same as fixing his heart, but at least it's something we can do."

Beth's smile was warm and thankful. As she set her glass of iced tea on the table, the ice cubes clinked.

Beth touched Rebecca's wrist. Her hand was cold. A few goose bumps trickled up Rebecca's arm. At that moment, she had an idea. She stood and pointed a finger. "I'll be back."

She went to her room and returned, handing Beth the scripture book she read from every night.

"Mamma made it for me. In fact, she told me to share it with you."

In silence, Beth opened the pages and began turning them. She looked up. "Scriptures?"

Rebecca gave a proud nod. "They help me to deal with my worries. They'll comfort you, too."

Beth's voice softened. "Do you mind if I borrow this?"

"Keep it as long as you like."

With a small sigh, Beth flipped the cover shut. To Rebecca's surprise, William's step-mamma set the book on the table and threw her arms around Rebecca. Then Beth released her and held her at arm's length.

"Rebecca, you're such a sweet girl. Daniel and I appreciate everything you and William have done for us. You're so young to take on such responsibility. But I feel uneasy. You've worked much too hard. When Daniel's well, I promise to repay you. I'm not sure how we can make this up to you, but we'll figure something out."

Rebecca let out a breath of relief as she darted Beth an appreciative look. "All we want right now is for Daniel to recover. And when he's well, we'll celebrate."

Beth pressed her hands together in prayer and looked up at the ceiling. "I thank God for sending you and William. How could we have done without you? Not only do you work, but you provide moral support. I needed a lift, Rebecca. You gave me that strength to go on."

The compliment boosted Rebecca's spirits. She nodded in appreciation. "Thank you, Beth."

"You know, when things are good, people don't

realize what they have. I guess you could compare life to a car. When it's up and running, you don't give it much thought. But when the battery goes dead . . ."

Rebecca considered the statement.

Beth laughed a little and raised a hand in apology. "Forgive me. For a moment, I forgot that you wouldn't know about vehicles."

"It's okay."

"I guess what I'm getting at is that now I realize the small problems I fretted over should never have made even a small dent in my life. Car repairs. Electric bills. Things that can be easily fixed. We had it all, Rebecca. Daniel's heart condition has given me a loud wake-up call. I never dreamed how my life could change."

As she walked to the window and looked out, her heels made a light clicking noise against the over-sized mauve tiles. Several moments later, Rebecca joined her. Beth turned and motioned to the four corners of the room. "Look at all of this. It's wonderful." She paused. "But I can live without it. I've never considered myself materialistic, but now that I'm faced with keeping Daniel alive, I realize I've placed too much importance on the house."

Tears welled in Beth's eyes. "I'd give up everything with a snap of the fingers to have Daniel well. In fact, the only thing I care about is his recovery, Rebecca. He's all that matters. Because without the man I love"—she lowered her voice so that Rebecca barely heard her—"none of this matters. He's my life. And I'm so scared of losing him."

Before Rebecca could respond, Beth broke down and cried. As she threw her head back, tears rolled down both cheeks like a waterfall. She pressed her fingers to her face.

Rebecca took her hand and led her back to her chair. "Here. Sit down."

Beth did so. Rebecca pulled up a chair next to her. She wanted to let Beth know her husband would be fine. That he would recover and that they would spend many more years together. As Beth cried for Daniel, Rebecca struggled to think of something to say.

She patted her on the back. "You'll be okay. Please don't cry." But Beth's tears continued. Certainly, Rebecca was short on experience in this field. How could she console William's step-mamma? As she listened to Beth mumble something between sobs, Rebecca knew she had to say something. But what? She decided to use her reasoning skills. She'd learned a lot from Old Sam. And her schoolteachers had always told her she possessed good common sense. Where was it when she needed it?

Finally, an idea hit her. She leaned forward to grasp Beth's shoulders. "Beth." Rebecca's voice was gentle but firm. Beth met her gaze.

"When I used to have problems, Mamma always told me there's nothing that can comfort a person like the outdoors."

She released her hold on Beth and stood in front of her, lending a friendly hand. "Let's go outside."

Beth didn't respond.

Rebecca nudged her arm. "Come on. We're going to breathe in some fresh air and between the two of us, we can surely figure out how to cope with Daniel's health."

Without arguing, Beth let Rebecca lead her to the

front door. They left the house and proceeded across the vast yard of velvety grass to the quiet black-top country road.

The warm, balmy breeze rustled the leaves on the tall oaks. Above, large clouds that looked like fluffy mashed potatoes floated lazily in the light June sky like life rafts on an ocean.

Rebecca raised a confident chin. "I've never been in your situation, so I can't speak from experience. But if I were in your shoes, here's what I think I would do."

Letting out a breath, Beth dabbed a tissue over both eyes and straightened her shoulders. She cleared her throat. When she glanced at Rebecca, the lost expression in her eyes had been replaced with a mixture of hope and curiosity.

"You're a good thinker, Rebecca. What would you do?"

"First of all, I would look at what we know. For instance, Daniel's condition. What we're sure of is that it's touch-and-go."

Beth squeezed her eyes closed as if she were in pain.

Rebecca jumped in. "But the doctors are hopeful."

Beth's lids flitted open.

"That means Daniel has a good shot at recovering. So . . . we should be optimistic and do our utmost to ensure he has the best chance to make it."

"How?"

Rebecca pursed her lips in deep deliberation. "By focusing on prayer. By getting as many people as we can to pray for him."

As they walked quickly, Beth nodded. "I think we're on top of it in that department. And according to our church friends, Doctor Stern is one of the best cardiologists in the U.S."

Rebecca raised a skeptical brow. "Friends?"

"Yes. He comes highly recommended by other physicians, too, and I've confirmed his credentials on several medical websites."

Rebecca nodded approval. She'd seen computers in the library and in businesses and knew what a website was. Rebecca was intrigued by the Internet and the tons of information it provided.

"Okay. We're confident in his doctor."

A long silence ensued as they walked. The midday heat made tar bubble on the narrow blacktop road, and they stepped to the side to avoid getting sticky black stuff on their shoes. The smell of freshly mowed grass in the ditches reminded Rebecca of home. An ache filled her gut.

Rebecca's brain cells worked in high gear as she struggled to remember everything she could about her cousin's hospital stay. She recalled a nurse saying something about a patient's attitude being the most important factor during the healing process.

The tone of her voice was etched with a newfound enthusiasm. "Beth, we have to find a way to help you deal with your stress. It can cause illness. Right now, Daniel needs you. He can't afford for something to happen to you. Besides, if you're worried, Daniel will know. I'm sure he senses your concern."

"True."

"If you're certain he'll get well, he'll pick up on that. When we visited my cousin in intensive care, one of the doctors told Mamma that a person's recovery can be affected by their mental attitude. The power the mind has over the body is amazing."

The tense expression on Beth's face finally relaxed a little, and Rebecca was relieved their conversation might finally produce results. A gentle breeze caressed Rebecca's face. For a moment, she lifted her chin to enjoy the feel of the warm air.

"Your mother must surely be one special lady. I'd like to meet her."

Rebecca smiled. "I'd like that too, Beth. I'm sure the two of you would be instant friends."

Beth gave a friendly nudge to Rebecca's arm. "She must be proud of you. There's nothing that makes a mom happier than raising a thoughtful child."

Rebecca's heart warmed at that thought. "I think so. But she worries about me, too."

Beth's eyes filled with surprise.

Rebecca grinned. "She's always told me I'm too bold. For an Amish girl, that is."

"Is that bad?"

"I'm not sure. I try to please my parents. At the same time, I like to think for myself and make my own decisions. Sometimes, it's hard to do both . . . if you know what I mean. I think the best thing for Daniel is to pray and have faith he'll get well. Start making plans so he'll have something to look forward to. What's most important to him?"

"Umm . . . Let me think." Long moments passed as they walked side by side. A mosquito buzzed in front of Rebecca's face, and she swatted it away. The hot, muggy air seemed to stand still until a comfortable breeze fanned Rebecca's eyelashes.

She turned to Beth. "What are his hobbies?"

"That's a tough one."

"He doesn't have a pastime?"

"Daniel's such a hard worker, he hasn't had much energy for other things."

"But if he had a vacation, what would he do?"

Beth laughed a little. "That's easy. Fish. When he was a kid, he did it all the time. I don't know if you've noticed, but he subscribes to every fly-fishing magazine that exists."

"That's a man thing."

"Mm-hmm. He pours over and over those pages. Fishing is his number-one passion, I think." Beth paused and in a more serious tone said, "But his first love is William." Her voice cracked with emotion.

"William?" Rebecca couldn't hide her surprise.

Beth hesitated. "You don't believe me, do you?"

Before Rebecca could respond, Beth went on. "And I don't blame you. After all, why would you think William was the most important part of Daniel's life when he left him with his aunt and uncle?"

"Are you sure he loves William so much?"

"I couldn't be more certain."

As Rebecca walked, swinging her arms, she digested what Beth had told her and recalled her last conversation with William about Daniel.

Beth said, "I never realized the deep pain Daniel has carried over the years at leaving William behind. No doubt, it was a difficult choice; I just didn't know how much he agonized over it."

After a brief hesitation, she continued. "I thought he was comfortable leaving William with his aunt and uncle. That way, William stayed Amish. And Daniel did what he was sure Miriam would have wanted. It seemed like a win-win situation . . . until two years ago. That's when he began expressing huge regrets about leaving William behind. Daniel had nightmares. I think he harbored the pain inside so long, he finally couldn't stand it. I wish I had known what he was going through. Now he suffers terrible guilt for not having raised William."

Rebecca spoke in a soft voice. "Of course, it must haunt him. After all, William's his own flesh and blood. But if Daniel loves William as much as you're saying, why doesn't he show it?"

As Rebecca and Beth increased their pace, Rebecca caught her breath. Sometimes she thought that sporting shorts and a tank top would be a nice change to her long dress.

"In his own way, he tries. But Daniel isn't a good communicator, Rebecca. He keeps things to himself. That's the way he is. But he has a heart the size of the State of Texas."

Beth stopped and turned to her. Rebecca put a hand on her hip, and Beth went on in a defensive tone. "Did you know that I offered to adopt William?"

Rebecca shook her head in surprise.

"But Daniel was so adamant about him being Amish. Because of William's mother."

As if on cue, they started walking again. A long silence ensued before Rebecca responded. "You can't blame yourself, Beth. It was Daniel's decision. But he loved you. And he loved William enough to do what was best for him. It must have been terribly difficult to know what to do. When you think about it, there wasn't a perfect solution. When Daniel recovers, I wish he'd have a heart-to-heart with William."

Beth rolled her eyes. "Like I said, Daniel isn't the best communicator."

"But it's important to explain his actions to William. Urge him to do it, Beth. It's the only way the two of them have a chance to be close. William regrets not growing up with Daniel. From the day he left William with his aunt and uncle, William resented Daniel . . . but when we came here, I finally realized how deep his feelings really went. To be honest, William didn't discuss it much until we moved in with you."

"What kind of regrets?"

"He feels abandoned. Surely you can understand why. I mean, he was so young when his mom died. That's a lot for any kid to deal with. To make things worse, less than a year later, Daniel left."

Rebecca gave a sad shake of her head. "I can't even begin to imagine the suffering William went through. His faith is strong. So is his determination. But even for the toughest person, losing a mother *and* a father . . . that's an awful lot to cope with."

"It is. Oh dear. And to think that I'm responsible." Her voice cracked with emotion. "I feel awful."

Rebecca let out a deep sigh. "On one hand, he loves Daniel and seeks his approval. On the other, he resents his dad for not raising him. He's sure that his mother never dreamed his dad would leave him. I have no doubt that Miriam had planned for William to grow up Amish, but because of the circumstances, Daniel probably should have taken him."

"I agree. But how can we fix it?"

Rebecca pressed her lips together and considered the question. Beth wanted to help William be close to Daniel. That realization prompted a new hope in Rebecca.

She thought out loud. "We can't change what happened. What's done is done. Like they say, hindsight's twenty-twenty. At this point, their relationship can probably never be perfect. But there's got to be a way to bridge the gap."

"I hope so. We would have raised William if Daniel hadn't felt such tremendous obligation to his late wife."

"But wasn't raising William Amish important to Daniel, too?"

Beth shrugged.

"Obviously, Miriam didn't consider Daniel remarrying outside of the faith."

"I'm sure she didn't." Beth held up a hand in defense. "Don't get me wrong. Daniel's a good man. But despite his strict Amish upbringing, he's very open and accepting of other religions. To be honest, I don't think all of the picky details of living Amish are important to him." Beth took a deep breath and put her hand over her mouth as if to unsay what she'd said. "I'm sorry, Rebecca. I didn't mean it to come out that way. What I *meant* was that to Daniel, it's a person's heart that counts. Not whether or not he uses electricity." She let out a sigh. "Do you get what I mean?"

"Of course. Daniel must have known that marrying you would cause controversy. The Amish are good people. They're also cut-and-dried about their way of living. They don't make exceptions to the rules."

"Don't I know it. Being shunned used to bother Daniel a lot. Especially when we were first married. But time heals all wounds. I really think he's moved past that. If only we can mend his relationship with William . . . I'll be so happy."

Rebecca smiled a little. "I'm glad you're with me on that one. With the two of us working to bond them, we're bound to succeed." She stopped to consider the situation. "To be honest, I'm glad I had the opportunity to grow up with William and to love him. It's hard to imagine life without him. At the same time, I regret what he's gone through."

"Me too. I carry such huge guilt, Rebecca." She paused. "Please pray that God will forgive me."

Rebecca squeezed Beth's hand. "You can't take all of the responsibility for what happened."

Rebecca ran her fingers over her damp forehead. The temperature had risen since they'd started their walk. She thought of how good it would feel to remove her kapp and tie her hair up in a ponytail.

When a breeze finally fanned her face, she closed her eyes a moment in relief. When she opened them, her thoughts drifted back to the situation between William, Daniel, and Beth.

She felt sorry for all three. When Daniel had fallen in love with Beth, he had faced a no-win situation. Either he gave up Beth, or he left William. With the strict Amish rules, he couldn't have both. In the end, William got the short end of the stick.

"Oh, Rebecca. If only life were easy."

"It's never perfect, is it? But let's plan that fishing trip for Daniel. It might give him the positive outlook he needs to recover. I'm sure I won't have trouble convincing William to go. If Daniel thinks about something so wonderful, how on earth can he not recover?"

Beth's eyes sparkled with joy as she let out a sigh of relief. "Rebecca, you're a special girl. You're wise beyond your age. And kind. I think you could do whatever you set out to do. You'd make a marvelous teacher. Or counselor."

"I've learned a lot from my friend, Old Sam. I'll tell you about him some time." Rebecca put a firm hand on her hip. "As far as being a professional, that's not likely to happen. I'm expected to continue the family business."

"The woodworking shop?"

"Yeah."

Beth raised a skeptical brow. "Just out of curiosity, though, let's imagine that you could be whatever you wanted." She touched Rebecca's arm. "What would you choose?"

Rebecca thought a moment and frowned. She wasn't crazy about their subject. Imagining things that could never materialize would only lead to disappointment down the road. Rebecca didn't have the option to do what she wanted to. So why go there?

She tried to be realistic. It was much simpler to accept life as it was. If she accepted what was within her reach, she'd be happier. And she preferred it that way.

She glanced at Beth and realized that Beth awaited an answer; her eyes sparkled with hope and excitement.

"Think about it, Rebecca. Imagine the world at your doorstep."

Beth's excitement was contagious. It didn't take Rebecca long to inhale a hopeful breath and allow her mind to wander.

If she had the freedom to do anything . . . She pictured herself as a nurse. A teacher. Even a businesswoman. The last thought prompted a grin.

She wondered how her parents would react if they saw her with a briefcase. She pictured herself in a knee-length skirt and dress jacket. She suddenly wondered how she'd look sporting a short, professional haircut.

"I've never told anyone this . . . not even William. In fact, I'm not sure it's a good idea to even think that . . ."

Beth nudged her. "What, Rebecca?"

She threw Beth a hopeful glance and giggled. "I'd love to have a floral shop."

"Oh, Rebecca. That would be wonderful! You must really love plants."

Rebecca lifted her gaze to the sky. "My favorites are purple irises. And nothing in the world can match the exotic smell of gardenias." Looking down at the road, she clasped her hands in front of her.

She darted Beth a helpless look and lowered her voice. "But it won't happen, Beth."

"Not if you don't let it."

They continued in silence. Relieved that the subject had been dropped, Rebecca relaxed a little. A rabbit darted in front of them. They stopped a moment and laughed.

As soon as the road began to veer to the right, they turned around. Rebecca considered their conversation. Even if her dream never materialized, it had been fun talking about it. When she had confessed her idea, it hadn't really sounded unrealistic. Could she dare hope?

She breathed in the smell of freshly mowed grass. Large white fluffy clouds hovered protectively in the sky.

As she took in the cornfields on both sides, she thought of home. She enjoyed doing the family garden. The fresh smell of tomato vines when she picked the ripe vegetables.

She yearned for her mamma's love and reassurance. The sense of belonging and acceptance—the feeling that whatever happened, she'd be okay. She missed talking with Old Sam.

But there were other important things to tend to. Daniel. William. And Beth. The anonymous note. At the thought of the warning, Rebecca's heart pumped a little harder. Although she had no proof Natalie had written it, common sense told Rebecca that was the case.

She had been taught to give others the benefit of the doubt. She wasn't proud of herself for believing Natalie was guilty without proof. But Henry's daughter had definitely made her feelings about Rebecca clear, as well as her interest in William. Would Natalie actually harm her?

She yearned to tell Beth about the message. She'd love to confide how worried she was. Her fears of losing William, and about William changing. But how could she dump her problems on a woman who faced losing her husband?

There must be another way to get information about Natalie. To learn a bit about the girl who liked William.

Rebecca slowed her pace. At the same time, they moved to the side of the road and waved to a man passing on a green John Deere tractor. All Rebecca could hear was the loud noise of the machine's engine. When it was finally in front of them, they moved back to the center of the road.

The noise finally evaporated, and Rebecca decided

to pursue the subject on her mind. "Beth, do you know Natalie well?"

Beth's voice was edged with curiosity. "Henry's daughter?"

Rebecca nodded.

"Just bits and pieces about her. She's an only child. Her mother tried for years to have children. Finally, Natalie came along. Her parents adore her. From what I hear, the sun rises and sets on the girl. She owns everything from a new car to a closet full of designer handbags. She's even traveled all over Europe."

Rebecca realized how different she and Natalie were. Rebecca didn't own a designer purse. And she'd never even driven a vehicle, let alone owned one. And Europe? Rebecca couldn't begin to imagine flying to another country. Or even flying.

"You must have met her," Beth said.

"Yes." After a slight hesitation, Rebecca went on to confess her concerns about Natalie's interest in William. Afterwards, she threw her hands in the air in a helpless gesture.

Beth thought a moment. "It must be disconcerting when another woman goes after your man." She paused. "But you know what?"

"What?"

"I wouldn't worry about William. He's totally smitten by you, Rebecca. It's so obvious."

Rebecca's spirits rose. "What makes you say that?"

"His eyes light up when you're around. And the tone of his voice lifts several notches when he talks about you."

"Really?"

Beth nodded. "Natalie could never steal William

from you, even if she tried." Beth cleared her throat. "Just between the two of us, I think that Natalie would be a tough girl to please. I've never had children, so I can't speak from experience. But I don't think it's a good idea to set unrealistic expectations."

"What do you mean?"

"I'd want my kids to have a nice life, but it's important for them to also take on an honest view of the world. I understand why Natalie's parents spoil her; they do it out of love. No doubt about it. But, Rebecca, when you have everything, what is there to work for?"

Rebecca shrugged. "Good question."

"It's important to make your own way. Or at least to know how to do it."

Beth let out a small breath before continuing. "In this world, you have to prepare yourself for the 'what ifs.' Even when the world's at your doorstep, things happen. Without warning, life changes like night and day. You've got to roll with the punches. Otherwise, you won't be able to fight the battles. Just look at me. I had it all. Then Daniel suffered a massive heart attack, and those wonderful material things couldn't help me. My perfect world did a flip-flop."

She let out a painful moan and gave Rebecca a friendly nudge. "Just listen to me rattle on. I'm not usually this talkative. But Daniel's touch-and-go condition has forced me to take a deeper look at things and see their real worth."

Rebecca nodded in acceptance. "It's okay to talk about it. In fact, it's probably good therapy. I wish I could make things better."

Beth sniffled. "You have, Rebecca. Thanks for listening." Beth's voice went hoarse with emotion.

"Daniel's the center of my universe. I'll do anything to get him through this. Please pray that he makes it."

"I do. Every night. You're a strong person, Beth."

Beth gave a sad shake of her head. "Not as tough as I'd like. Every morning, I wake up afraid of losing him. When I'm tired, it scares me even more."

Beth took a deep breath. "I want to make him the happiest man in the world. And there's something else."

Rebecca glanced at Beth.

"You know William better than anyone, Rebecca. Can you think of a way for the two of us to be close?"

Chapter Five

The early July sun was setting as Rebecca stuck Mamma's letter in the mailbox in front of the Conrad home. As she closed the lid, William pulled up the red flag.

In silence, they made their way up the winding sidewalk to the front porch, where they sat on the oversized swing. As they started swinging, Rebecca closed her eyes while the warm, gentle breeze caressed her face. When she opened her lids, she let out a small, satisfied sigh and smiled at William as the iron chains holding the swing to the porch ceiling creaked.

"When's Katie coming back?"

Rebecca told him. The comments from Katie and Natalie concerning Daniel wanting William to stay in Indiana to help with the business loomed in her thoughts like a heavy dark cloud on a sunny afternoon. Rebecca had thought and thought about that potent piece of information. She wanted to know if it was true.

The only way to know was to ask William. She'd

put it off long enough and decided a straightforward approach. "William, you and I have always been open with each other."

He turned so that their gazes locked. Surprise flickered across his face. His jaw was set as they regarded each other in silence. In front of them, the setting sun slipped farther into the vast area of gray until a kaleidoscope of colors melted into a haze. Crickets chirped in the bushes behind them.

William's eyes took on that metallic appearance that Rebecca loved. When he spoke, his voice was soft. "What's on your mind?"

Rebecca related the rumor. "Is it true?"

William gave a firm shake of his head. "That's the first I've heard of it." He hesitated. "It's a strange comment."

"Why do you say that? You certainly wouldn't be the first father-and-son team to work together."

"To be honest, I can't imagine my dad even thinking about inviting me to be his partner." He raised his arms in frustration. "We can barely discuss the weather. The last thing I feel toward him is that father-son type of relationship I've always dreamed about."

He paused. "I'm glad he's okay. I can't wait till he's out of the hospital. Maybe we can get a new start when he comes home."

"We haven't been here long, William. Have you really tried telling your father what's in your heart?"

"Not really. We've been so busy."

"We've been here over two weeks. Now that we've settled in, I think you should sit down with your dad and talk to him. When he's a little better, of course."

Rebecca added, "I mean really discuss what's on your mind. Like you do with me."

William paused. "And tell him what?"

Rebecca giggled. "It will come to you, William. It can't be that difficult. Just be yourself. Be honest. That's the only way for your dad to get to know you."

"It's a little late for that." Resentment edged his voice.

She shook her head as their feet met the porch floor before they pushed the swing back into the air. Rebecca pressed her palms against her thighs as she considered William's comment. She glanced at him. "It's never too late, William. Be happy for this opportunity to start over. Maybe his heart attack will turn out to be a blessing in disguise."

William cocked an amused brow. "I wish I had your positive outlook."

"I'm fortunate to have spent time with positive people."

"Like Old Sam?"

At the thought of Old Sam, Rebecca's heart warmed. She could almost hear him grumbling while he built beautiful hope chests.

"You miss him, don't you?"

Rebecca gave a slow, thoughtful nod.

William chuckled. "I'll bet he misses you, too. Between you, Rachel, and Annie, he's one spoiled man."

Rebecca paused as she considered William's question. "I enjoy being with Old Sam. It's funny, but he inspires me to dream."

"Don't I inspire you?"

Rebecca squeezed his hand. "Of course." Several moments later, she went on. "I feel sorry for Old Sam."

"Why?"

"Because he misses his wife."

"Jah. I'm sure he does."

"That's why he busies himself in the barn."

"It's a good thing. He supplies most of the town with hope chests."

Rebecca laughed. "I suppose. You know what I really love about him though?"

"What?"

"Listening to his advice."

"He must know every proverb that ever existed."

Rebecca nodded in agreement. "He's a wise man."

"Have you put anything in the chest yet?"

Rebecca pursed her lips thoughtfully. "Just notes."

"Notes?"

For some reason, Rebecca didn't want to refer to it as a diary. That word sounded too secret and confidential. "I write down my thoughts at night. It helps me to reflect on the day."

The breeze turned a notch cooler. They turned at the sound of the front door opening.

"I thought you'd like some iced tea." Beth stepped out onto the front patio and handed each of them a glass.

"Thanks." Rebecca took a drink. "This has got to be the world's best-tasting tea."

Beth winked. "It's China Mist. Shipped straight from Arizona."

William had already downed half of his. "Arizonans sure know how to make tea."

Rebecca glanced up at Beth. "Any word on Daniel?"

Beth gave a half nod. "He's hanging in there." With a light laugh, she added, "I just know that one of these days, he'll be back in the shop. And I'll breathe a sigh of relief when that time comes."

She stepped back inside. The door clicked shut.

"It must be frustrating for her. She loves your dad so much."

William finished his tea and placed the empty glass on the ledge next to the swing. "I won't argue that." He turned to her. "How about we check out the Conrad property. Are you up for a walk?"

"Sure."

They stood at the same time. William motioned ahead of him. "After you, Miss Rebecca."

She dipped her head. "Thank you, Mr. Conrad."

As they made their way toward the back of the property, Rebecca considered all of the amenities that Beth and Daniel had. Still, Rebecca missed the simplicity of her home.

In the back of her mind, Katie's comment flitted back and forth, tormenting Rebecca until she could think of nothing else. When she'd asked William about it, he had responded. And she knew, without a doubt, that he was telling the truth.

But if both Katie and Natalie had heard that Daniel was about to offer a partnership, there must be something to it. At that thought, Rebecca's throat tightened.

She hesitated before revealing her thoughts. "William, what if Daniel did offer you a partnership?"

"Here in Indiana?"

She nodded.

The only sound was crickets chirping. As Rebecca awaited an answer, her pulse picked up speed. She clasped her hands in front of her.

She had counted on a future with William. In Arthur. Before coming to Indiana, she'd never even considered anything different. She didn't doubt William's love for her. Yet the uncertainty of what was to come made her very uneasy.

William finally broke the silence. "Rebecca, to be honest, I've never considered partnering with Dad." He pushed out a long, deep sigh. "I suppose it would be wonderful to work together, side by side, if we were close, like a lot of kids are with their folks. But with us, that isn't the case."

The seriousness that edged his voice deepened to border on resentment. "Don't forget that you're talking to a guy who's never even gone fishing with his father."

"I'm sorry." Rebecca darted him an encouraging wink. "There are second chances." When he didn't reply, she dropped the subject. William's relationship with Daniel was a sore subject.

At the same time, Rebecca noted something that prompted a combination of uncertainty and uneasiness in her chest. She'd asked William if he would like to partner with his dad. And in the end, he hadn't answered.

Three days later, Daniel was home from the hospital. On a lawn chair, William watched Rebecca plant tiny petunias in a row. Yesterday's conversation played in his mind. A partnership with his dad? He eyed the man next to him and smiled in relief. It was good to have him back. According to the doctors, time was the key to recovery.

With a proud grin, William nudged his father's arm. "She's the most meticulous person I've ever met. Look. She even uses a yardstick to measure the distance between the holes."

Daniel gave a slight nod. "She's a fine girl, William. She'll make a good wife."

Daniel's voice was weaker than usual. William had hoped the warmth and sunshine would help him to feel better. But sadness filled his eyes.

"She's been looking forward to doing this for you. Even if it is already the middle of summer."

William turned his attention back to Rebecca and smiled as she tapped her garden spatula against the soil. As he took in her soft features, he thought about their future together and of the children they would have.

But a sudden concern prompted him to frown. He pressed his lips together for a moment and considered the circumstances. He turned.

There was so much he wanted to tell the man he'd spent a large part of his life missing. Things he'd yearned to say for years. But how could he? He really didn't know his dad well enough to bare his soul.

Perhaps the truth would please him. William cleared his throat.

"I'd like to stay close."

For long moments, they stared at each other. William felt an embarrassing blush in his cheeks. His heart pumped a little harder than usual. Salty moisture stung his eyes, and he blinked back tears. No expression from his dad. A combination of disappointment and uncertainty fought inside of William's gut until it ached. For years, he'd kept his thoughts to himself.

With a newfound determination, he squared his shoulders and continued in a low, emotional voice. "I've been without you too long. I want you and Beth to move back home." He hesitated. "Where you belong."

Daniel gave a slow shake of his head. "Can't . . . can't do it, son. I'm an outcast." He paused. "Shunned." He stumbled over his words. "They, well, you know . . . that . . . they don't forget things like that."

"But Arthur . . . it isn't all Amish." William, too, fell over his words. Why was talking to his dad so difficult?

William knew the answer. It was hard because he wanted his father's love and approval. Sought it with all of his heart. In spite of what his father had done, William would give anything to know his dad loved and cared for him.

"It wouldn't work."

William raised a brow. "What did you say?"

"You heard me, son. It . . . it just wouldn't work."

William fought the bitterness that filled his chest. He sat up a little straighter. "I always wanted to be like the other kids and have a dad."

"You had me." His tone was defensive.

"No, I didn't. We didn't live in the same house. Not even in the same state! In fact, I barely saw you."

Daniel squeezed his lids for a moment and shook his head.

William suddenly recognized he'd made a huge mistake. Daniel was ill. Now wasn't the time to discuss regrets.

William tried a more gentle approach. "When Rebecca and I raise our family, how can you play an active role in the lives of our children? Don't you want to be with us?"

Long moments passed. Finally, Daniel placed his palm on William's thigh. "Why don't you stay here and be my business partner?"

Three goals. It was already the end of the first week of July, and Rebecca hadn't heeded the bishop's request. There was so much to do. How could she decide which things were the most important?

As she sat on her bed, the cool night breeze floated in through the bedroom screen. She loved summer evenings. There was something soothing and comforting about crickets chirping and tiny lightning bugs blinking in the dark.

She enjoyed sleeping with the windows open. The Conrads kept the house cooler than Rebecca preferred. But Beth had given her permission to open her window at night.

Rebecca frowned as she recalled her advice to Beth. Rebecca didn't know if Beth could ever win

William's approval, but Rebecca had offered a suggestion. She'd recommended that Beth teach William to drive. William definitely had expressed an interest in the BMW.

Who knew? Maybe there was a chance for Beth and William to be close. It gave Rebecca a warm feeling inside to know that Beth intended to make an effort.

Smiling satisfaction, Rebecca pulled out her scripture book and crossed her legs. Beth had read Mamma's gift, front to back. Mamma would be pleased.

Getting comfortable, Rebecca lay back with two pillows supporting her. She bent her knees and clasped her hands behind her head as she looked up at the ceiling.

The air smelled of eucalyptus. She breathed in the sweet smell and closed her eyes in enjoyment.

Although she loved Beth and Daniel, she couldn't wait to go home. But Rebecca realized that this experience was helping her to grow as a person. She had already learned that life was more complicated than she'd ever imagined.

She now faced issues she'd never experienced in Illinois. For instance, the strained relationship between William and Daniel. Beth's regrets and concerns. Natalie. The anonymous message. Beth's encouragement to pursue a profession. And Rebecca's forbidden desire to do it. The rumor that Daniel wanted to partner with William.

"Oh." Rebecca moaned in distress. All of these issues had materialized from living with the English.

An uneasy feeling swept through her as she considered Beth's confession that she couldn't survive without her husband.

She sympathized with William's step-mamma. The doctors had released Daniel, but he was still fragile. What if Daniel didn't make it? His doctors hadn't sent him home with a warranty.

Frustrated, Rebecca rolled her eyes and silently scolded herself. She shouldn't think that way. Her mother had raised her to focus on the positive. Old Sam stressed looking at her glass half full. To pray and to have faith.

But she was fully aware that prayers weren't always answered the way a person wanted. At least, that's what the bishop had said. It was important to believe, but it was also necessary to have enough strength to deal with reality. And there was no denying that Daniel was very ill.

Rebecca sighed as she held her handmade book. While she flipped through the pages, her thoughts drifted to Beth. And William.

She hadn't known Beth long, but Rebecca felt a strong bond with Daniel's wife. Beth was an open, honest woman who spoke her mind. Rebecca admired the way Beth struggled to accept obstacles and deal with them.

In a way, Rebecca did the same. She considered the changes in her own life and her longing to do what was right. She imagined herself in Beth's position.

Their situations were similar, really. Beth worried about losing Daniel. And Rebecca fretted about losing

William. But why? Even though he hadn't indicated a problem with their relationship, circumstances had driven him to change.

Needless to say, being English certainly wasn't a hardship. Rebecca admitted a liking to the amazing round porcelain bathtub that oozed warm, bubbly water from the side jets.

But Rebecca was an Amish girl, heart and soul. She still planned to follow in her mother's footsteps. Even though she had been exposed to easy-to-get-used-to comforts, she would eventually leave them behind, and they would become nothing more than nice memories.

But could William let them go? The question nagged at Rebecca. She frowned as she shifted her weight and rested on her elbow. Thoughtfully, she placed the prayer book in front of her.

After dinner, William had played with the television remote to find the ESPN channel. Rebecca hadn't missed the happy expression on his face as he had flipped through the channels.

And his interest in Beth's car was obvious. He hadn't said so, but Rebecca had watched him check out the interior on more than one occasion.

She couldn't stop his interest in these un-Amish amenities. But what if he began to like the English way of life too much? What if they grew apart?

Desperation swept up her arms and landed in her shoulders. She rolled them to rid herself of the uncomfortable sensation. What would she do?

She shifted onto her back and rested the book on her stomach.

She'd calmly assured William's stepmom that Beth would find strength to carry on. By the same token, if Rebecca lost William, she would need to heed her own advice. But how? She was expected to marry, bear children, and work side by side with her husband. Amish rules weren't etched in stone, but she knew them by heart.

Rebecca planned to marry the man she loved. But what if circumstances forced them apart? Would she replace him?

She didn't believe she could marry someone just for the sake of producing children. She needed love.

Her shoulders tensed as she thought of Daniel possibly asking William to become his business partner. As she considered William and what he wanted, that familiar scripture about love being unselfish once again came to mind.

Nonetheless, the thought still brought an ache to her chest. Not because she was selfish, but because of the significant change in their lives such an offer would cause if William accepted.

Rebecca directed her attention to the book. Holding it, her gaze landed on Mamma's neat printing. Rebecca whispered the reassuring words. Those very phrases she had read in church so many times. But she'd never really taken them to heart. Until now.

She contemplated the bishop's instruction to accomplish three unselfish, important goals at the Conrad home. Rebecca smiled a little.

This made her trip here more of a mission. Creating the goals gave her purpose. A way to serve God.

She decided on her first. It was to support and comfort Beth. To encourage her to rely on the faith she so desperately needed to see her through Daniel's illness. Rebecca felt a passionate desire to help William's stepmom.

Rebecca considered the task at hand. Stretching her legs, she frowned. Definitely, this objective was unselfish and important. But how to accomplish it?

She was only human. Unlike God, she couldn't work miracles. And Beth was in dire need of emotional support. What could Rebecca do to keep William's stepmother strong?

She shifted down on the pillows. She wanted to help Beth, but lacked experience and education.

She recalled their conversation. What a wonderful blessing it would be to give helpful advice to those in need. Offering support to Beth made Rebecca's life more purposeful and meaningful. But how to provide that much-needed encouragement?

While the question lingered in her mind, she switched her attention back to the small book. In a low, soft voice, she read the scripture in front of her. "'To the one who pleases him, God gives wisdom, knowledge and happiness.'" The verse was from Ecclesiastes. Rebecca raised her chin and digested the potent words.

In Arthur, she'd never given them much thought. Because she'd been secure. There had been no serious concerns. Nothing more than getting the chores done.

But now that she was exposed to new challenges, she realized how much she craved God's holy word. She sought His guidance like never before.

Mamma had once told her that every answer to life's problems lay in the Bible. That said, this must surely be the right scripture. What it meant was that God would help Rebecca to help Beth. At least, that's how Rebecca interpreted it.

She relaxed. Maybe she shouldn't worry so much. She was trying to take on something only God could direct her to do. In the meantime, she searched for her own answers.

She had told Beth that she was expected to follow in her mother's footsteps. That meant being a good wife and mother. Heeding the faith. But what if she could also have a career? Rebecca's heart picked up speed. She began giving that question serious consideration. Was it wrong to pursue a career that was conducive to her faith and Amish lifestyle?

There must be rewards in life besides being a good wife and mother. A nursing profession? Teacher? Counselor? Maybe even owning a floral shop. Couldn't there be opportunities for a career, and at the same time, serve the Lord?

In deep thought, she laid the book down and folded her hands over her chest. Question after question flitted through her mind until she stood and went to open her hope chest. It was inside this work of art that she had placed her concerns. Her dreams.

She gently traced her finger over the carved bouquet as she thought of Old Sam. What would he say if she told him her worries?

She got comfortable again against the bed frame and removed her notepaper and pen, wondering which proverb he would recite. She jotted the date at the top right-hand corner.

She poured out her heart and her soul on the

lined paper. How she wanted to help Beth find comfort and strength. That she wanted Daniel to live, and for him and William to be close. That she missed her family. And Old Sam.

"I'm sure that God sent me here to fulfill many needs. I want to come through for Him. What if William chooses to remain in Indiana? Will he actually become Daniel's partner? Worse, what if he decides to become English?

"I love him. I also love my faith. But if it boils down to William or faith, which would I choose? Love or loyalty?"

Chapter Six

The following evening, dusk set in as William and Rebecca traversed the long, scenic trail behind the Conrad property. How could he tell her about Daniel's offer? It wasn't something that could be ignored. Because William yearned to be close to his father. But the more he thought about how to explain his wants to Rebecca, the harder broaching the subject became.

Old oak trees loomed ahead of them as they made their way down the hill. Large green leaves flitted back and forth with the warm breeze.

Being next to Rebecca provided him with a strong sense of security. Something he'd especially appreciated since his arrival in Indiana. He let out a deep, satisfied sigh as they walked the beautiful undeveloped land.

Ahead of them, the setting sun displayed deep, rich colors of orange and purple. The fading ball of light lingered in the western sky.

"Aenti Sarah always told me that each day's a miracle from God and that I should go to bed blessed to have been given an opportunity to serve Him. That the next day would hold even more blessings and another opportunity to live for Him."

Rebecca darted him a quick glance. "Your aunt is a wise woman. I always admired her for her strength and wisdom. She's very much like Mamma."

"And you."

"I would be proud to be half as good as either of them."

William thought of Aenti Sarah and wondered what advice she would give him now. Was he serving the Lord? William pondered the question. He worked hard to help his father. That must be for God. At the same time, William struggled to win his dad's long-awaited approval.

When Rebecca smiled, his heart fluttered. Rebecca always made him feel better. Even in the worst times.

William definitely wasn't proud of his bitterness. He tried to hide it. Cover it up. After all, there was no point in revealing his feelings. They would only add to an already damaged father-son relationship.

Changing the past was impossible, but he *could* create a better future for himself. Couldn't he? He struggled to forget all of the times he'd missed his dad.

William was sure Aenti Sarah loved him dearly. Treasured him like a son. She'd never said so, but she'd shown it by making sure he was well fed and tucked in every night. By ensuring that he'd done his homework. He missed her. An ache formed at the back of his neck.

William frowned. He was weak. Uncle John would be ashamed of him. He should be brave and strong. Unafraid of the unknown.

"I remember when I was seven."

"What happened?"

"I was bailing hay with Uncle John." William shook his head and blew out a breath. "It must have been a hundred degrees that day. I told him I needed a break."

"And?"

"What I got was a nice lecture on how a man doesn't complain about being tired. Or about lifting something heavy. Or about being hot."

Rebecca pressed her lips together.

"A man does what he has to do. And that's that." A grin tugged at William's lips as he recalled those words. He pictured his tall uncle running his hand through his long, gray beard as he spoke. In fact, William could almost hear the gruff timbre of his uncle's voice.

Rebecca giggled. "Your uncle's one tough man. I don't think I'd want to bale hay with him. Knowing him, he'd never get tired."

William nodded.

While he remembered his uncle's words, he wished he could be what everyone expected of him. But he couldn't. Not right now, anyway. Because he was scared. And homesick.

The realization prompted blood to rush to his cheeks, and he hoped Rebecca wouldn't notice. He had never really realized how much he loved Aenti Sarah who'd waited after school for him at the front door.

His thoughts drifted back to her small kitchen, where he chatted with her while she set the dinner table. He missed being reminded to drink his milk. William cherished those motherly good-night kisses on his cheek. The sparkle in her eyes as she folded his socks.

"I wish Aenti Sarah owned more sophisticated things to make her chores easier. She does it all the hard way."

"So does Mamma."

"They both work so hard. But I can't help but think of how much more Aenti Sarah could accomplish if she owned Beth's appliances."

"True. But she's tough, William. About as strong-minded as your uncle. And as stubborn. If she owned English things, do you honestly believe she'd use them?"

William shrugged and furrowed a doubtful brow.

Finally, he chuckled. "That'll be the day when Aenti Sarah tosses a load of towels into a Maytag, adds detergent, pushes a button, and goes about her other business while the machine works."

He imagined her with a television set and grinned. "I could never picture her watching soaps. Or driving an automobile."

A breeze caressed the back of his neck. As they stepped down a hill on the trail, Aenti Sarah stayed on his mind. He appreciated what an amazing woman she was. He considered himself fortunate to have her. She was the most conservative person he'd ever met. A strict Amish woman who didn't deviate from the rules. She loved her horse and buggy. And he'd never heard her complain.

She was his second mother. His gut ached. He realized his main problem. He had been trying to figure out the source of his grief. Now he knew.

A great wave of acceptance came over him. His father's illness wasn't the true root of his sadness.

"I miss Mom." His voice cracked.

Pressing his lips together in agony, he stopped and turned to Rebecca. He searched her face for comfort. "I really miss her, Rebecca. I feel such a huge void in my life. I'd give anything to have her back."

To his dismay, salty tears stung his eyes. His bottom lip quivered. He silently scolded himself and fought to stop the sadness that hit him. Determined to act like a man, he bit his tongue.

Rebecca sighed in sympathy. "I'm so sorry, William. Of course, you miss her. And I'm sure that being here with Daniel has brought back memories of the three of you together. It must be an emotional time. And I feel helpless that I can't bring her back for you. If I could, I would. Because I wish she were here, too."

William struggled to compose himself. "If she hadn't died, we would still be in Arthur."

"Yes."

"And I wouldn't be fighting the resentment I feel for Dad and Beth." He swallowed and continued in a hoarse voice. "If Mom were alive, things would have been different. So different. Why did God take her? I wish He'd taken me instead."

Their gazes locked, and sympathy emanated from her eyes. Right now, he needed more than medicine. He needed a mother. And she was gone.

"Oh, William."

They stood in silence. He watched as she gently pushed a strand of hair behind her ear.

"I love you, Rebecca."

She looked up at him. "I love you, too, William. More than you could ever know."

He sighed, then smiled a little, and they continued their walk. The dry brush crunched under their shoes. Tall pine trees scented the air with a fresh, Christmassy smell.

"William, your mother wouldn't want you to hurt."

"But that doesn't take away my pain. She's not here, and I need her. It seems like she's been gone forever. If only I had a picture. At least I'd be able to look at her. But we don't take photos. So there's nothing but memories."

"At least, they're good ones, jah?"

"Oh yes. Do you realize that it's been nearly a decade since she passed on? I'll never forget her."

Rebecca hesitated before lowering her voice a notch. "You're a lot like her."

He glanced at her and raised a curious brow. "How?"

"You inherited her best traits." Rebecca stopped and turned to William. "I was little when she passed, but Mamma says you have her eyes. Her smile. Even her brows. But more importantly, William, you have her tenacity. That's something to be proud of."

"What do you mean?"

They continued their walk. Every once in awhile, William's hand brushed Rebecca's. Even though touching her wasn't exactly appropriate, William savored the much-needed comforting sensation.

"Her strength. Her perseverance. When she fought cancer, the doctors wrote her off, but she refused to give in. She always had faith, William. She fought hard to stay alive. I remember her telling me that she would fight till the end. And she did. I'm sure it was a battle because she must have endured terrible pain. I admired her so much, William. She was an amazing role model."

William gave a sad shake of his head. "I'm so sorry I couldn't have done more for her. At the time, I didn't realize how tough things were." He shrugged. "Because she never complained. And to be honest, I don't think I wanted to acknowledge that she was terminally ill. I'm sure she didn't want to focus on cancer. In fact, she probably wouldn't have lasted as long as she did, if she had."

"You've got a point. Remember, you were only a child. Kids usually don't understand the pain their parents go through. How can they? They're not mature enough. Or experienced. I think you did the best thing you could have done for her."

"What?"

"Just being there. Talking to her. And helping her get through each day. It's probably best that you didn't focus on her illness. Old Sam told me that Miriam was the kind of woman who didn't want to worry anyone, especially her own son. That was one of her remarkable traits."

"I still wish I had helped more."

"You were wonderful. You did your chores. I'm sure your folks couldn't have made it without you. You never disobeyed them. You were there day in and day out. Remember that scripture about love being the greatest gift?"

Lowering his head, he nodded slowly.

Rebecca lifted her chin. "Never underestimate the value of memories. They get us through life. And they can also serve as important teaching tools." She paused.

"William, you couldn't have had a nicer mamma. When I visited, she always managed a smile."

William grinned. "She was happy."

"Jah. In fact, I don't even recall her mentioning her illness. Instead, she asked about me." Rebecca smiled a little. "She was always interested in what we learned at school. I think she would have made a great teacher. She made sure we did our homework."

William rolled his eyes. "I remember."

"And she loved talking scripture. Be proud of your mamma, William. I saw a bumper sticker once that said, 'How many years you live doesn't matter. It's how much life you put into those years that's important.'"

"That makes sense. Obviously, whoever said it never lost someone. It's easy to give advice when you have everything."

"Just think of all your mamma did. Even when she was sick. It's pretty amazing, really. Old Sam mentioned that she packed more into her short life than most eighty-year-olds. And in a sense, you're carrying on with her wishes."

"What do you mean?"

Rebecca's voice reflected surprise. "Just what I said. She had a life full of goals. But her efforts didn't die. Because when she passed on, you continued fulfilling her wishes."

William thought about what Rebecca said.

"She loved Daniel, William. Just like she loved you. She spent her life taking care of the two of you. Now that she's not here, you've taken her place. Just look at all you've done for your dad. I can honestly tell you that she would appreciate you being here for him. But it's not only that. I won't forget when you told me about coming here."

They turned to each other. Rebecca smiled. William's heart warmed as the light in her eyes helped fill the emptiness. When he looked at her, his pain lessened. With her, he could endure almost anything.

He considered Rebecca's take on him helping his father. "Anyone else would have done the same thing."

Rebecca shook her head. "Don't be so sure about that. I think you're not giving yourself enough credit for what you've done." She laughed a little. "You've got to admit that this was a pretty bold move for someone who had never even left Illinois."

He couldn't hold back a grin. "You've got a point."

"Leaving your aunt and uncle was brave, William."

Rebecca's tone was upbeat. They stepped to a faster pace.

"And you didn't hesitate. As soon as you got that call, you decided to come. You made up your mind to do what was right. You stepped right into Daniel's shoes and took over for him. And did an excellent job, I might add. Especially when you think about how far behind he was in his orders."

Exhaling a satisfied breath, William raised his chin. "You know what?"

"What?"

"I have no regrets about what I'm doing."

"Good."

"But I'm not sure I want to fill my father's shoes."

Rebecca glanced at him.

"Most boys want to be like their dads. Not me. I

would never have left my son." He raised a hand. "No matter what happened. There are no circumstances that would excuse deserting your own flesh and blood. I don't think he realizes how I suffered. And to be blunt, it was a selfish move on his part. And Beth's. What they did affected my whole life."

Rebecca let out a small, helpless sigh. "I agree. But it just goes to show that life certainly isn't perfect. And neither are your folks. But take lessons from the past. There's no use fretting over what happened, because you can't undo it. You've said that yourself. Unfortunately, there's no opportunity to ask Daniel to go back in time and change things. This situation isn't like retaking a math test."

"I know."

"It's a lot of baggage to deal with, but can you make yourself push on?"

A long silence ensued while he considered her question.

"Be like your mamma, William. Even in her sickness, she made the most of her time. She'd want you to do the same. Forgive Daniel. And Beth. They did the best they could at the time. I'm sure that it's not easy for them to live with what they did. And while we're on the subject, you're not the only one with regrets."

"What are you talking about?"

Rebecca cleared her throat. "I had a lengthy discussion with Beth about you and Daniel. She feels awful about what happened. So does Daniel."

William stiffened. He straightened his shoulders and raised his chin. "They should. What did Beth say?"

Rebecca explained.

Afterwards, they slowed their pace. Darkness was setting in. They turned around on the trail and headed back to the house. As the sun began to fade into the darkening sky, the temperature dropped. The sudden coolness prompted a shiver up William's arms. But his mind was on what Rebecca had just told him. He bit his lip while he digested that Beth had offered to keep him after she married Daniel. He'd always believed she didn't want him. Had he misjudged her?

"You think she's telling the truth?"

Rebecca nodded. "Absolutely. She's not perfect, William. But she's a good, honest woman. Her heart's in the right place. And there's no doubt in my mind that she loves Daniel." Rebecca lowered her voice. "She'd like to be close to you."

William gave a frustrated shake of his head. "She should have thought about that when she and Dad left me with Aenti Sarah and Uncle John."

"I'm sure she did. But it was a complicated situation." Rebecca threw her arms in the air in a frustrated gesture. "Apparently, your mom's expectation that you be raised Amish weighed more than taking you with him."

William shoved his hands into his pockets and stared straight ahead. A mélange of colors faded into a dark shade of purple. Locusts started making their nightly sounds. Lightning bugs glittered in the distance.

"I'm so confused."

"I understand. But give it time. And it'll be okay. You know what they say about time?"

"That it's the healer of all wounds."

She nodded.

William bit his lip and pointed. "Look at the sunset."

"It's amazing."

"Exactly. But if God can create such a beautiful sunset, why couldn't He have given me a dad?" Before Rebecca could respond, he corrected himself. "I mean, a *real* father. Surely everyone deserves that, don't they?"

Rebecca nodded.

As they continued their walk, William squeezed his eyes closed in a moment of grief. As soon as he opened them, a whoosh of pain filled his chest until he thought it would burst. But he couldn't cry. At the thought of his uncle, William straightened his shoulders and composed himself.

Moping wouldn't help matters. He knew that. And he wouldn't be a baby. But he had to talk. And Rebecca was the best listener he could have.

He cleared his throat. "Why did God take both of my parents away, Rebecca?"

She spoke in a soft, reassuring tone that helped to ease his troubled mind. "William, I wish I could give you an answer." She gave a helpless shrug. "But I can't. Only God knows why He does what He does. There's a purpose for everything. I think we have to explore the positive side. Daniel's still alive. You've got a second chance with him. Take advantage of it. There's no guarantee how much longer he'll be here. So make the most of what you have. Is life perfect?" She shook her head. "No. But we have to make the best of the time we have here on earth. Our lives are short. It's a shame to be angry or upset. To be happy, we must forgive and move on."

William didn't respond. Her advice made a lot of

sense. But talk was easy. Carrying it out would be difficult.

Their steps slowed as the sun took another dip into the horizon. "I'm not as good as you, Rebecca. You're the one who's like my mother. Not me. You could forgive Daniel, couldn't you?"

Rebecca gave a slight nod. "I think so."

"I'm not sure I can."

"But you have to try. Otherwise, you'll never forgive *yourself*."

She paused and caught her breath. "When Daniel married Beth, he was forced to make a very difficult choice."

William frowned. After a lengthy pause, he raised a brow. "And he chose Beth."

"Yes, he did."

As they continued in silence, the pain in William's chest grew worse. So did the oversized lump in his throat.

Rebecca straightened her shoulders and lifted her chin. "William, I believe God did what He did for a purpose."

"What purpose?"

"There's only one explanation."

William looked straight ahead, waiting to hear it.

"He wanted you to be with me."

William took in a deep breath. "Maybe you're right, Rebecca." He paused. "Listen to me complain. I should be ashamed of myself. My mom would expect me to be better."

"I'm so proud of you."

"You are?"

"Of course. Don't you realize everything you've done for Daniel?" She went on before he could answer. "Just look at what you've accomplished. It's a considerable feat."

"But right now, I'm not happy inside. I feel guilty about my feelings." He threw his head back to glance up at the sky. It had turned a dark bluish-black color. The dismal shade reminded William of a sweater he'd watched his aunt knit for one of his cousins.

He realized that he was just a small slice of the large world. In fact, he played such a miniscule role, he wondered if God even heard his prayers.

He nudged Rebecca's elbow. "Thanks for listening. I'm glad I talked."

"I'm always here. And I love for you to share your concerns with me. It means that you trust me. Someday, I might need you to listen to my problems."

He frowned. "Do things bother you?"

Rebecca shrugged. "Of course." She sighed. "I don't imagine there's anyone alive without worries. But to be honest, mine aren't worth mentioning. Not when I think of how Daniel's suffering. And when I consider what you've gone through. Right now, I just want Daniel on his feet. That should be our main focus."

Discussing his relationship with his father wouldn't make things better. In fact, he decided not to bring up his dad's offer this evening. William was ready to change the subject.

"Your dinner was delicious. Tonight, Rebecca Sommer, your chicken dumplings were even better than Aenti Sarah's." He laughed. "Did you see how many Dad ate?"

Rebecca nodded. "I'm glad he liked them. And thank you for the compliment, even though I think you're stretching the truth a bit." She raised an amused brow. "Everyone knows that Sarah makes the best dumplings around. It was fun using Beth's kitchen. It's a woman's dream."

"Rebecca!"

"What?"

"I'm surprised to hear you talk like that."

"Why?"

He shrugged. "I thought you didn't like the English ways."

"Did I say that?"

He hesitated. "No. I just took it for granted, I guess."

Rebecca put a hand on her hip. "Who on earth wouldn't enjoy Beth's kitchen? It's a cooking wonderland, and I'm not ashamed to admit that. At the same time, I guess I'm lucky because I can do without it. I have no problem returning to Arthur and getting back to my roots. Living here makes me appreciate what I have. It's also forced me to think."

He waited for her to go on.

"I've learned to not judge others for the way they live. Time here has provided me with a bigger picture of the world. Now I better understand that all religions serve the Lord. Not just the Amish. When Beth and Daniel used to visit, I'm embarrassed to say I thought they were all about material things."

When he eyed her, she held up a hand in defense. "I'm certainly not proud of that. But I couldn't help it, William. They drove a nice car. And Beth wore beautiful clothes. I really misjudged her."

"You did?"

Rebecca nodded. "Jah. Beth's far from Amish, but she worships the Lord. She does it in a different church. And with a different set of standards.

But that's okay. Not everyone interprets the Bible the way we do. Not everyone has to think like us. That would be impossible. Beth has good values."

William shrugged. "She also has plenty of conveniences. Aenti Sarah would love the air-conditioning. In fact, I feel the English have an unfair advantage."

"Because of their modern-day appliances?"

"Of course."

"William, your aunt shops at Walmart and Sears. She's fully aware that these things exist. But what makes her so special is that she's happy with her life as it is. Have you ever heard her complain?"

William shook his head and rolled his eyes. "But she'd never whine, even if she was unhappy. She makes do with what she has. That's how she was raised. Beth has it too easy."

When he glanced at Rebecca, he caught her look of disapproval. "Just ignore me."

"I'm not going to."

William walked in silence. Rebecca was so perfect. Her thoughts were pure. Unlike him, she didn't feel malice toward anyone. The last thing he wanted was to burden her with his problems.

"William, never keep anything from me. I'm your best friend."

He smiled a little. "I know. If anyone can help me, it's you. I don't like what I feel. I want to change. To tell the truth, I would love to forgive Dad and Beth and be close to them." He lifted a shoulder. "But I don't know how to do it."

He dropped her hand and clenched his fists. "Bad thoughts clutter my head, and I'm not sure who I am anymore."

"Because of Daniel?"

"I suppose so." He cleared his throat. "I wish I were more like you. You never want more than you have. You're satisfied."

She nodded. "Yes. I guess I'm fortunate in that way. But our situations are different. I'm not in your shoes. And I'm worried." She paused. "How do I get my old William back? The carefree William who joked and teased me. The William who made me laugh."

He grinned.

"If only life were simple."

"It is, really. The problem is, you're making it harder than it needs to be. Daniel isn't perfect. Neither is Beth. But they love you. Daniel may not love you the way you want to be loved. But just accept that. Your expectations are too high. I've no doubt he deeply cares for you. Beth, too. William, now's not the time to be bitter. Daniel needs your support. He's fighting for his life."

William blinked away the burning sting of salty tears. His heart ached. A combination of shame, guilt, and sadness struggled within him. Why couldn't he be happy?

"Enough about me. I want to know something."

She lifted an inquisitive brow.

"How do you get past your problems?"

"I can't say that I overcome my fears, but I pray

about them. Every night before I go to bed, I read Mamma's scripture book. It gives me strength to know that God will take care of me. And I write down my most troubling and joyous thoughts. Seeing them on paper actually helps me deal with obstacles. It also makes me appreciate all that I have."

"Your faith is stronger than mine."

"Pray, William. God will give you power to overcome your bitterness. He'll provide you with the strength and wisdom you need. You'll see."

William hesitated. He lowered his voice to a more serious tone. "What do you think about living like the English?"

Rebecca let out a small sigh. "Honestly, I could never be English. I'm an Amish girl, inside and out. That's not to say that I don't enjoy some of their amenities. Who wouldn't?"

"Like?"

She pulled her arms over her chest. "The jets in the bathtub. The way the water sprays against my feet." She turned to him and slowly rolled her eyes in delight. "Hmm. There's nothing like it, really. It's so relaxing and soothing. I could stay in there for hours."

William paused. "What else do you enjoy?"

He watched her with amusement, loving the dreamy look that emanated from her eyes while she thought.

"Besides the fancy tub?"

"Uh-huh."

She shrugged. "Beth's double oven, I suppose. It's great to bake everything at once instead of waiting for one dish to finish before putting another in."

She sighed. "How 'bout you? What do you like most about Daniel's house?"

"That's a no-brainer. The television. ESPN, in particular."

"What are your favorite sports?"

"Football and soccer. I confess that I'm really going to miss watching that big screen." He cleared his throat. "If you want the truth, it won't be easy going back to the Amish world." He winked. "In fact, you wouldn't have to pull my arm hard to convince me to live like this."

William noted the tense, heavy silence as they continued. Disappointment welled inside of his chest. For some reason, he'd expected her to agree. He wished she would.

Finally, Rebecca spoke in a low, uncertain tone. "You'll join the church, won't you?"

Silence ensued while he considered the question. The more he pondered, the less certain he became. Finally, he realized she had stopped and looked at him for an answer. "I think so."

He caught Rebecca's immediate sigh of relief.

To his disappointment, Rebecca changed the subject as they continued their walk. "What a beautiful evening. I love sunsets."

"How 'bout those awesome colors?"

She nodded approval. "There's a kind of magic when the sun starts to disappear. Actually, there's so much more to a sunset besides the kaleidoscope of beautiful colors. When I watch the sun go down, I think of what I've accomplished during the day. Sometimes, I wish I had done more. In fact, when I see the sun slip away, a rush of emotions hits me."

She giggled. Her cheeks reddened. "It sounds silly, doesn't it?"

"Not really."

"Sometimes, I can't help but feel a bit sad that the day is gone."

"But there's always tomorrow."

She paused and lowered her voice to barely more than a whisper. "Not always, William. That's something we take for granted. The jets in Beth's fancy tub and the double oven are nice amenities, but seeing another day is a miracle. Something that can't be bought."

A chaotic rush of emotions tugged at William's heart. "I like the way you look at things."

"The world is amazing. We're fortunate to be here. Life is a miracle. And I don't want to waste a minute. In the end, if I'm happy with how I've spent my time here . . ." She shrugged. "I'll have no regrets. What more can a person want?"

As William considered her statement, he rolled the kinks out of his shoulders. He didn't like wasting time, either. He wanted to rid himself of resentment. How could he be happy when he was drowning in a pool of regret?

He eyed her. It was time to put his worries aside.

She stopped to face him. "What?"

"Remember what we used to do when we were in the fields picking tomatoes?"

Rebecca threw her head back in laughter. "How on earth did we jump from such a serious conversation to picking tomatoes?"

"That's my point. We made a vow. A long time ago."

She nodded slowly. "To never let life get too serious.

And to not work so hard that we don't have fun." She smiled a little. "Remember?"

He nodded. His gaze drifted to the tall oak that hovered over the creek. "We're breaking our deal." Before she could respond, he held up a hand to stop her. "But we can fix that."

She lifted a suspicious brow. "And just how do you propose to do that? We're not in the tomato field, so we can't just sit down between the rows and talk about Old Sam. Or about Martha Wagler's pies."

"No. We can't do that. But starting right now, no seriousness. And if either of us says anything serious . . ."

"Then we have to take a bite of Martha's gooseberry pie!"

William made a face. "Now that is severe punishment!"

They laughed.

Several heartbeats later, William wiped a tear from his eye. "She's such a good woman. Tries to do for everyone. I remember when she used to bring get-well pies over to my mom."

Rebecca put her hands on her waist. "She didn't eat them, did she?"

"Are you kidding? My mother was a good sport, but not good enough to eat Martha's pies! She couldn't take a bite without making a face."

Rebecca giggled. "Your poor mamma. I can imagine how tough it was for her to explain that she'd save the pie for dessert! And poor, dear Martha."

Rebecca gave a sad shake of her head. "Her intentions were good. We have to give her credit for that. But baking just wasn't her area of expertise. I'll never forget when she used to try to sell her pies to the town bakery. They wouldn't buy from her."

"Jah. Because she never added sugar! Didn't anyone ever tell her that?"

They laughed together. As the sun slipped another notch into the horizon, William wished he could stay with her and talk to her all night.

"I guess not. But someone should have," Rebecca said. "You know the pies aren't edible when Old Sam won't even touch them."

William's jaw dropped. "You mean Martha tried them on him, too?"

She nodded. "When Rachel and I were in his barn once, Martha brought him a pie. She said something about him working too hard on an empty stomach. To be honest, I think it was just an excuse to chitchat."

William raised a mischievous brow. "She had a thing for Old Sam?"

Rebecca shrugged. "She likes him, William. Who wouldn't? And when you think about it, they'd make a great pair. Both of them love to talk. And they're both widowed. Of course, you know Old Sam."

"He'd never look at any woman. He'll always love Esther. And I've no doubt that he has no intention of replacing her." He nodded. "That's true love."

Rebecca agreed.

As William pictured Martha trying to get Old Sam to eat her pie, he grinned. Suddenly, he couldn't get the amusing image out of his mind. "What did Old Sam say to Martha when she delivered the pie?"

"He thanked her, of course. He invited her in to chat while he worked on a hope chest."

"I'm sure he did. But you know Martha. She's the persistent sort. Didn't she want him to try it?"

Rebecca nodded. "I recall her asking. But Old Sam is too smart to be talked into gooseberry pie that he knows will make his mouth pucker." Rebecca's eyes lit up. "If I remember correctly, he assured her that it looked too good to eat. That he was busy. That when he finally sat down for the night, he wanted to make sure he enjoyed it. That he'd save it until before he went to bed." She winked. "That was smart thinking on his part."

"And?"

"There was no argument. As I recall, Martha left with a smile on her face." Rebecca put a hand over her mouth to stop a giggle. "Then, as soon as she was gone, Rachel nudged Old Sam and asked him if he was really going to eat that pie."

"What did he say?"

"With that wise grin of his, he told us that he'd learned the hard way not to ever take another bite of Martha's pie. But that this was one time not to be truthful. Because he'd never want to hurt Martha's feelings. And besides, what good would it do?"

"Old Sam. He's too much. It might do me good to sit down with him sometime and shoot the breeze."

"Just listening to him is so refreshing. He takes on the world with such a pragmatic view."

"I wonder what he would say about my issues with Beth and Daniel."

Rebecca pointed a scolding finger. "I know exactly what he would tell you."

William arched a curious brow while he waited for her to continue. He loved it when she was on a roll.

"He would advise you to put them out of your mind and to enjoy your life. That something good always comes from something bad. And that Daniel's heart attack was meant to happen so the two of you would become closer."

Rebecca leaned toward William and whispered, "And that if anything were to happen to him or Beth, you'd realize you'd made a huge mistake in being upset with them." She raised her palms in a helpless gesture. "But by then, it would be too late for a second chance."

William finally nodded agreement. "You're probably right."

Rebecca pressed a firm hand against her waist. "Of course I am."

"Are you ready?"

Rebecca's eyes reflected confusion. "For what?"

Before she could interrupt, he squared his shoulders. "Get ready. 'Cause I'm going to close my eyes and count."

"Wait! What am I supposed to do?"

"Hide."

She stepped forward. She was so close to him, he could feel the warm caress from her breath. The gleam in her eyes told him she was ready to take him on.

"How many seconds do you have to find me?" she asked.

He appeared to give the question serious thought. "Ten."

She stepped closer. "What's my prize if you don't find me in ten seconds?"

He shook his head. "Oh no you don't. I set the rules for this game. The purpose isn't what you win. It's what I get if I find you."

She gave a slow nod. "I see. And what might that be?"

Time stood still while she awaited his answer.

Rebecca whispered, "William, you didn't answer my question. What's your reward if you find me?"

"I'll tell you when I catch you."

"That's not fair."

"Why not?"

"Because if I don't know the prize, I have no idea how hard to run and hide. The whole purpose of the game is to win, right?"

"Of course."

"And I need to know what's waiting at the finish line so I can determine how much effort to give this."

"Miss Rebecca, this is only a game. And you're making too much out of it. All I can say is that you'll want to be caught. Now"—he straightened—"I'm going to turn around and close my eyes."

Before she could argue, he began counting. He smiled as he listened to the crunching of dried brush under her shoes. In fact, the sound told him which direction she headed. While he shouted the numbers as loud as he could, he tried to ascertain her path.

"Ten!" He opened his eyes and turned. "Here I come!"

He made his way to where he thought she'd gone. No sign. He stopped when he heard her giggle.

Raising an amused brow, he made a dash for the colony of raspberry bushes. Rebecca jumped up from her squatting position and rushed to get away. He caught her.

She nearly lost her balance as he steadied her. He didn't want to ever pull away from their tight embrace, even though it wasn't proper.

"You told me I'd like the prize if I got caught," she teased. "Thank goodness, I'll finally know what it is."

"I'm going to give you a choice."

Together they sat on the ground. As they held hands, a lightning bug blinked between them.

"What are my options?"

"You can choose . . . a piece of Martha's delicious homemade gooseberry pie."

Rebecca threw her head back in laughter. "You said I'd like the reward. That's no fair."

He pointed a finger and shook his head. "Uh-uh. Let me finish. Or . . . a kiss."

Chapter Seven

Rebecca was at ease in Katie's buggy as her horse trotted out of town on the country road. As the horse's hooves clicked against the blacktop, Rebecca thought of last night's kiss.

For one blissful moment, she closed her eyes and relived the feel of William's mouth on hers. It was the first time he'd kissed her on the lips. It was also forbidden; still, she'd never forget that magic sensation. When she opened her eyes, an excited shiver danced up her arms.

They weren't married; yet she didn't feel as if they'd done anything wrong. She loved William. And he loved her.

As the horse trotted, Rebecca considered what he'd said about the English ways. She frowned. With her permission, he'd leave the Amish faith in a heartbeat. No doubt about it. But what could she do?

Deep down inside, Rebecca was uneasy. Scared. Afraid that William would become so attached to the

English amenities, he would decide against joining the church.

If that happened, she would lose him. Becoming English was something she would never do. As much as she loved him, she would be a faithful Amish girl forever.

She turned to her new friend. "Katie, have you ever been tempted to give up your heritage?"

Katie darted Rebecca a surprised glance. "Never. Why do you ask?"

Rebecca touched on her concerns about William. Afterwards, she gave an uncertain shrug of her shoulders. "I can certainly understand how difficult it is to return to the simple life after experiencing so many frills."

Katie nodded. "I know."

"You do?"

"Of course. When I did Rumspringa, I tried different things." She darted Rebecca a rebellious wink. "I even drove a car." She rolled her eyes. "Can you believe it?"

Rebecca sucked in a surprised breath. "You did *what*?"

Katie nodded proudly. "You heard me. And I don't have a single regret. I looked at it as an opportunity to find out what I wanted. Of course, I'd planned on joining the church, but it was important to make sure I wouldn't regret doing so. I loved the English perks, but realized my upbringing was so strong, I could never leave it. After the test period, I didn't doubt who I wanted to be. Or how I wanted to live."

Rebecca nodded in agreement. "That's how I

am. I enjoy a number of things about the English lifestyle . . . How could I not? But in my heart, I'm a simple Amish girl. I guess all of those church sermons stuck."

Katie turned to lift an inquisitive brow. "Then you'll stay Amish?"

"Of course."

Katie hesitated. "Then why did you ask if I had been tempted?"

Rebecca recalled her disturbing conversation with William. Should she discuss it? She wasn't sure. She couldn't betray William's confidence, especially his feelings about Daniel and Beth.

But if she kept her concerns to herself, how could she get an honest opinion? What she needed was another point of view.

Maybe Katie could help. After a pause, Rebecca related her concern about William's bent toward the English ways. She went on to tell her that there had been no partnership offer yet, but that she feared the outcome if Daniel actually did approach William with the idea.

A thoughtful look crossed Katie's face.

Rebecca put a hand on her hip and turned to Katie. "So . . . if you were in my shoes, what would you do . . . if you had to confront the issue of William becoming Daniel's partner? Would you encourage it? William wants a relationship with his dad. A partnership would bond them."

Katie frowned. "In my opinion, what William likes isn't what's most important. Honey, this isn't only about him. It's about you, too. And a partnership with Daniel would mean a huge compromise on your part. Just think of what you'd be giving up. What do *you* think about them running the business together?"

Rebecca pressed her lips together in deep deliberation. "I'm not sure."

Katie lowered her voice to a more confidential tone. "It would mean not spending the rest of your life where you grew up."

What Katie said was true.

"You'd be without your family. Your roots, Rebecca. Is that what you want?"

Rebecca clasped her hands in frustration. "Of course not. My parents will need me when they're old." She smiled a little. "I've always planned to build a 'grandpa' room."

Katie hesitated. "Let's say that you *did* stay in Indiana. You think you'd become one of them?" Before Rebecca could respond, Katie went on. "I'm not passing judgment on William's parents, but you have to admit their way of life is a far cry from ours."

"I'm aware of that. My parents have instilled strict values in me, and I intend to keep them. If I had my druthers, I'd stay in Arthur. But what you said is true."

Katie raised an inquisitive brow.

"You know. You said this isn't only about William, but it's about me, too. If you turn that around, it's not just about me. William's happiness is important as well." Rebecca sighed. "Even if the partnership offer doesn't materialize, he still loves living like the English. If I deny him the type of life he wants, that would be total selfishness on my part, wouldn't it?"

Katie pursed her lips and sat up straighter.

Rebecca shifted positions and went on. "The situation is complicated. I love my family."

"Of course you do. And you have an obligation to them."

Rebecca nodded. "On the other hand, I sympathize with William. I've had the luxury of being raised by my parents. God has blessed our family with good health. William wasn't as fortunate. He lost his mother. Shortly after that, his father left him."

Katie shook her head. "It's sad what William went through. And I certainly understand his wanting to bond with Daniel. Every boy wants to be close to his dad."

Rebecca agreed. "It's strange. The Amish church shunned Daniel for marrying outside of the faith. As a result, Daniel shunned his own son. But he paid a heavy price. He must carry tremendous guilt. I feel sorry for both of them."

"Not me, Rebecca. My sympathy goes to William. After all, Daniel was the adult. William's fate was in his hands. And we can't forget that it was Daniel's choice to marry Beth. He could have chosen a widow within the Amish community."

"But he fell in love with Beth."

"I know. But poor William had no say in the situation. The ideal solution would have been for Daniel to marry one of his own. Then, this mess wouldn't have happened."

Rebecca dropped her jaw in surprise. "True. But I understand why Daniel loves Beth. I respect and admire her. She truly adores her husband. He means the world to her."

"But she's not Amish."

"That's okay, Katie. She's a Christian woman."
Rebecca paused. "How do you make yourself fall in
love with the right person?" Before Katie responded,
Rebecca reworded her question. "What if the guy we
fall in love with isn't of the same faith?"

"It's our responsibility to make sure he is. That's
why we meet people in our church."

"It sounds simple. But I don't think it is. Because
the heart chooses. Not the mind."

"You don't believe we have control over our
hearts?"

With a smile, Rebecca shook her head. "Not
always."

"Maybe there's some truth to that." Katie shrugged
her shoulders. "I don't know. Fortunately, it's an
issue I don't have to deal with. While we're on the
subject, how's Daniel? I haven't heard much about
him for a while."

Rebecca was quick to notice how Katie changed
the subject. Unlike Katie, Rebecca didn't believe
that everything was black-and-white. Gray areas had
to be dealt with. And she certainly didn't blame Beth
for falling in love with Daniel. Or vice versa.

"Hanging in there. He's fragile. At this point, his
recovery's in God's hands."

Rebecca longed to talk to someone about William's
resentment toward Daniel. She'd love to get Katie's
input. Maybe if Rebecca had a second opinion, she
could offer better advice to William.

But she couldn't ask. Because William had con-
fided in her. He trusted Rebecca enough to confess
his feelings, and she owed it to him to keep his issues
in confidence.

"So what would you do, Katie? About encouraging William to partner with Daniel. If it comes to that."

"I can't imagine that happening."

"But if it does?"

"It's difficult to answer. I know you love William. But you also love the Amish church. I can't see you without your family, Rebecca."

"It's hard to imagine."

"Any man I loved would have to be from here. I'm not flexible enough to live elsewhere. Maybe I could manage living out of state a couple of months. But permanently?" She shook her head.

"But fortunately," Katie continued happily, "I don't have to choose. Pray about it, Rebecca. God will tell you what to do. It might not be tomorrow. Or the next day. But in time, you'll know. And in my heart, I believe you'll decide against a partnership between William and Daniel . . . if you're confronted with it."

Rebecca nodded in acceptance.

Katie laid a reassuring hand on Rebecca's arm. "Promise me one thing."

"What?"

"If you and William decide to stay here, don't give up who you are."

Rebecca let out a small, uneasy breath. "If William decided to join Daniel, there are plenty of Amish communities in the area. Yours, for instance. There's no reason William and I couldn't be Amish."

Katie raised a doubtful brow. "Right now, you're living like the English."

"That's because we're staying with William's parents. When we marry, we'll have our own home. And you can be sure it'll be in an Amish community whether we're in Illinois or Indiana."

"You sound certain of that. *Gut* for you. That's what William wants too, right?"

Rebecca hesitated. "I think so."

Katie glanced at Rebecca with skepticism.

"I confess I'm concerned that William has taken such a liking to certain things in the Conrad home."

"He's addicted?"

"I wouldn't say that. But he loves television. Air-conditioning. I've especially noticed how large his eyes grow when he looks at Beth's car . . . Of course, I have a temptation of my own."

"Oh?"

Rebecca giggled. "I'd love to wear blue jeans for a day."

Katie joined in the laughter. "I hate to tell you this, but the longer William lives with them, the more difficult it will be to break him of those pleasures."

Rebecca frowned. She bit her lip and digested what Katie said. But she couldn't dispute the facts. What Katie said was true. "Do you plan to marry, Katie?"

A long silence passed while Rebecca awaited a response.

"I'd like to." Katie sighed. "I used to dream of it. There was this boy I grew up with. His name was Amos. We were an item from the time we started school together, just like you and William."

Rebecca smiled sympathetically.

"When we got older, I expected we'd marry. I dreamed of having a family. Of growing old together.

It didn't materialize, Rebecca. God didn't intend it to work out."

"What happened?"

"When we went through Rumspringa, Amos took advantage of everything he could. It didn't take him long to decide that he was happier not being Amish."

"But what about his feelings for you?"

"His love wasn't as strong as I'd thought. In a short time, he changed. Before I realized what was happening, I had lost him, Rebecca. And there was absolutely nothing I could do."

"I'm so sorry, Katie."

"Me too. But that experience made me realize just how important Rumspringa is. It was a painful thing to go through, but realistically, it was better to lose him when I did. Fortunately, most of the time, those who are raised Amish end up joining the church. Not in his case."

Rebecca laid a reassuring hand on Katie's arm. "There will be someone else for you. I'm sure of it."

Katie's lips lifted a notch. "I hope so. My dream is to be a mother. I'd love a house full of little ones."

They laughed.

As the warm air floated in, Rebecca breathed in the scent of freshly mowed grass. Blades of dark green grass cluttered the edge of the road. Soybean crops in the field were growing fast.

She turned to Katie. "Did you ever walk beans?"

Katie quirked a brow. "Walk beans? What on earth are you talking about?"

"You know. When you go through the fields and cut out the weeds with a hook."

Katie's eyes widened. "You did that?"

"Every summer."

"It sounds grueling."

"It is."

The subject prompted Rebecca to recall a certain conversation she'd shared with Beth. "Katie, do you ever dream of having a career?"

Katie eyed her and grinned mischievously. "Funny you should ask. I've given serious thought to running my own business."

"Really?"

Katie nodded with confidence. "Right now, I help my parents with their shop." She shrugged. "By no means am I unhappy. They have a fairly large clientele, and the business pays the bills and then some. And I have to admit that I enjoy making quilts, sweaters, and other knickknacks for the shelves. In fact, right now I'm working on the biggest project I've ever done."

"What is it?"

Katie's eyes widened with excitement. "A quilt."

"Hmm. I bet it will be beautiful."

"Beautiful, yes. But this is a particularly special quilt, Rebecca."

They glanced at each other.

"I'm making it out of handkerchiefs that belonged to my grandmothers and great-grandmothers."

"Wow. That's going to be one special piece. When you finish, will you give it to your mother?"

Katie hesitated. "I would love to. I've given that a lot of thought. But I've decided to contribute it to the auction in September to raise money for the new schoolhouse."

"That's certainly a generous contribution."

"I'm happy to do it. Everyone who wants to contribute will offer something unique to bring in a good donation. Hopefully, when it's all said and done, we'll be able to afford the materials. Of course, the work will be contributed by everyone as time permits."

"You must be pretty proud of what you're doing. What a great cause. The new school will be around for years to come."

"That's why I'm investing more time and care in this quilt than I've ever put into any project. As I cut and sew, I think of my grandmothers and wonder if they'd enjoy watching me create something that really belongs to them."

She hunched her shoulders. "Sometimes it gives me the chills because I feel such a connection with them. I wish they could see the end result. My grandmothers were strong women, Rebecca. I wish I could be everything they were. As far as the quilt, I would hope they'd love it."

"I'm sure they would."

"If you want the truth, it will be difficult to let go of the work."

"Of course. Because when it's finished, it will be much more than just a beautiful piece of art. It will be a part of your family heritage. An heirloom, really. Maybe someone in your family will buy it."

"We'll see." Katie let out a contented sigh. "I wonder what my grandmothers would say if they knew I dream of running a day-care center."

Rebecca smiled a little. "I'm sure they'd give you the thumbs-up."

"You think so?"

"Of course. Caring for children is part of God's plan for all of us. What would we be like if we hadn't experienced the love of our parents and teachers? Just imagine trying to raise a plant without water."

Katie grinned. "That's a nice analogy."

"You must really love children."

"I teach them. Watching them is so fun. Most of all, I love telling them stories. They hear the same story over and over, and every time I tell it, it's like they're hearing it for the first time."

"Isn't it wonderful to be young and innocent?"

Katie gave a firm nod. "There's nothing like glimpsing the excitement on their faces." She frowned.

"Is something wrong?"

"My day-care center won't materialize. There are too many obstacles standing in my way." She paused. "But it's okay to dream, right?"

"It will happen if you make it happen. It doesn't have to be just a thought."

Rebecca considered her own advice. What she'd just said applied to her own dream to run a floral shop, didn't it?

She touched Katie's arm in a reassuring gesture. "Katie, your day-care center doesn't have to stay in your imagination. I'll bet you could thrive in that field. These days, there are so many single parents who look for responsible, caring adults to watch their youngsters. I would think there'd be a high demand for quality child care."

Katie let out a hopeful sigh. "I'm aware that there's

a demand for it." Several moments later, she shook her head sadly. "But I don't think God planned for me to run a center."

"Why not?"

"Because carrying out my wishes would interfere with what my parents have in store for me. I can't let them down."

"You think they'd be disappointed in a career that could help so many children and mothers?"

"It's not that. It has to do with their business. All my life, I've listened to how they've arranged for me to carry on in their footsteps. How I'll have a steady income. I'm an only child. I don't have brothers and sisters who can take over their shop. It's mostly for coffee, but there are knickknacks, too. There's only one candidate for the job, and like it or not, it's me."

Rebecca laughed.

"What?"

"I'm sorry. But the way you said it was so funny." Rebecca cleared her throat and approached the subject with a more serious tone. The expression on Katie's face told Rebecca that she was concerned. "I can see where you're put on the spot. What I can't believe is that you're the only person to carry on their trade. There must be someone else. Cousins?"

"Maybe. But my parents established The Coffee Place for me. And they've done it with so much love, Rebecca. They're so dear. Surely you can understand that as much as I'd like to pursue my own dream, I can't spoil theirs."

Rebecca thought a moment. She crossed her hands over her lap. "Of course, I understand your obligation and your fear of letting them down." In an excited tone, she added, "But maybe there's a way to do both?"

"How?"

Rebecca shrugged. "I'm not sure. Pray about it, Katie. Dreams are precious. If you want something that much, and it's within your reach, you should go for it. Especially if it will benefit others. There's nothing in the world more important than caring for children."

"We'll see. I do pray about it. But I'm sure you know as well as I do that God doesn't always give us the answers we want. And I'm wise enough to understand that sometimes He has His own plan for us. We have to trust Him because only He knows what's best."

Rebecca considered the statement and realized the truth behind it. Her mind drifted to her imaginary floral shop. But she had an even bigger dream. And that was a life with William. And children. At the same time, she wanted desperately to be with her family and loved ones.

Like Katie, she faced obstacles. If William became Daniel's business partner, Rebecca would be forced to make a choice. She couldn't have both worlds. In this way, she and Katie were in the same boat. She felt an unbreakable bond with her friend and touched Katie's hand.

"It will be okay, Katie." Rebecca squeezed Katie's wrist and smiled. "I'll pray for you."

"Thanks."

Soon, the Conrad home came into view. The ride with Katie was at an end, but the time spent with her had given Rebecca important issues to think about.

As Katie's horse snorted, Rebecca inhaled a satisfied breath. "Thank you, Katie."

"My pleasure. I'm glad you enjoyed the ride."

"I mean, for the talk. It's nice to have a friend with the same interests. I feel like I've known you my whole life."

"What a sweet thing to say."

"I mean it. My stay here has presented challenges. But I've also reaped tremendous blessings." She winked. "You're one of them."

Katie's eyes glistened with moisture. "I'll see you next Tuesday. And as far as you and William?"

Rebecca waited for an answer.

"Everything will work out." Katie cleared her throat. "And by the way, you should try out a pair of blue jeans. That's what's Rumspringa's for."

With renewed faith and energy, Rebecca lifted the bottom of her skirt and carefully stepped down from the carriage. The horse gave an impatient whinny as Katie waved good-bye. Rebecca watched the buggy disappear down the road.

She hadn't disclosed her dream of owning a floral shop to Katie for fear of losing the magic of the mere thought. Rebecca had surprised herself by opening up about it to Beth. Even though Rebecca wasn't in a position to create her business, the fictitious store in her imagination was a wonderful place to visit. She always wanted to have the opportunity to go there.

But what about the advice she'd offered Katie? Rebecca had assured Katie that she needed to make sure her wishes materialize. Shouldn't Rebecca heed her own words?

She made her way up the front steps and frowned

as she recalled Katie's thoughts on William. But Rebecca agreed: The longer William enjoyed the English life, the more difficult it would be to tear him from it.

She wanted with all of her heart to marry her childhood sweetheart and live forever in her beloved Amish town. But would that desire become reality? Or would it merely stay a dream like her imaginary flower shop?

It was already mid-July. William had postponed telling Rebecca about his dad's offer long enough. While he finished paperwork in the shop office, William considered how best to broach her with the subject. As he added a column of numbers, he thought of last night's walk. He recalled their kiss. For several blissful moments, he closed his eyes. When he opened them, he let out a small sigh.

He had been leading up to the subject of the partnership by talking to her about becoming English. But the moment Rebecca had made it clear that she could never be anything but Amish, he'd stopped. There would be another opportunity, wouldn't there?

He wrote in the total in the bottom right-hand corner and raised a brow. Would there ever be a good time to tell her? While he considered the question, he shook his head slowly. Even the noise from the electric saws couldn't stop the probing question from repeating itself in his mind.

Pursing his lips, he tapped the pencil point against the ledger and stared straight ahead. The sound of the door opening interrupted his thoughts.

Rebecca smiled. "Thought I'd better check on you. You've been in here quite a while."

He nodded. They were alone. He took a deep, decisive breath and motioned to the small bench in back of the shop.

She put a hand on her hip. "Something wrong?"

"There's something I need to share with you."

In silence, they sat next to each other. Long moments passed while he noted the puzzled expression on Rebecca's face. How could he explain the offer?

She leaned toward him. "What's going on? Is it Daniel?"

William shook his head. "No. But we had a conversation." He sat up straighter and faced her. "While you were planting flowers the other day, I had a heart-to-heart conversation with my dad."

Her lips lifted into a beautiful smile. "That's wonderful, William. You've got to tell me all about it."

"I was honest, Rebecca. I didn't mean to hurt him, but I told him how I had always wanted a father."

Rebecca paused. "What did he say?"

"That I had one."

"Oh."

"But I responded that he hadn't been there for me." William lowered his head. When he raised it, he shrugged. "And it's the truth." He pulled in a deep breath. "Oh, Rebecca. I wonder now if I should have kept my mouth shut."

"Why?"

"Because of his heart condition. The last thing I want is to make things worse. He's struggling to survive as it is."

"Did you argue?"

"No. In fact, I went on to say how I wanted to stay a part of his life."

Rebecca sighed in relief. "Good. Then you shouldn't be on a guilt trip. He must have been happy to hear that you wanted a relationship with him."

"But I regret my comment about not having a dad. It was thoughtless, especially under the circumstances."

Rebecca thought a moment. "William, I really don't believe you were out of line. Life isn't perfect, and you certainly can't pretend it is. While your aunt and uncle raised you, Daniel didn't even try to be your father. In fact, you can count his visits on both hands. You barely know him. But I believe the two of you will become close."

William raised a doubtful brow.

"I really do. At least, that's what I'm hoping for. To develop a relationship with him, you have to start somewhere. That means talking and being upfront about your feelings. Obviously, it's impossible to pretend everything's normal when it's not."

"I know."

"As long as you spoke without malice and from your heart, you surely can't hold yourself responsible for what happened. I hesitate to give advice on something I've never dealt with, but it would seem to me that if Daniel wants to be close to you, he has to accept responsibility for leaving when you were young. I've never worn your shoes, but I'm sure many others in your situation wouldn't give him that opportunity."

She put a hand to her hip and posed another

question. "What was Daniel's reaction when you told him you wanted to stay in his life?"

William bit his lip. As Rebecca regarded him, he stared straight ahead. The pulse on his neck picked up speed.

He watched Rebecca clench her hands together on her lap and interlace her fingers.

Tell her. An inner voice prompted him to go on. Why was relating this so difficult? He knew the answer. He wanted to partner with his dad. And he wanted Rebecca. Was it possible to have both? He was about to find out.

An uncomfortable tingle floated down his arms and landed in his fingertips. He flexed them to rid himself of the strange sensation.

"William?"

He cleared his throat.

She patted his arm in reassurance. "Talk to me. We've always been honest with each other. Just because we're not in Arthur doesn't mean that changes." She paused. "How did he respond? He surely didn't tell you he didn't want to be with you."

William's voice suddenly took on a very serious tone. "No."

Rebecca let out a small, nervous laugh. "That's a relief. So what's the problem?"

"I asked him to move back to Arthur where he belongs. To bring Beth."

"And?"

William shrugged. "He said it wouldn't work."

"Oh."

Several heartbeats later, William said enthusiastically, "He invited me to become his business partner. In Indiana."

The rumor had come true. As the words rang through her mind, Rebecca found it difficult to remain calm.

While William looked at her for a reaction, she stared straight ahead. An uncomfortable sensation made her shoulders tense, like when she was young and had done something wrong that she hadn't wanted to tell her parents about. That ache she'd experienced before standing in front of her classmates and presenting her assignment on the large green chalkboard.

Time seemed to stand still while she sat and digested the statements. As she thought, William continued.

"So what do you think?"

As her pulse accelerated to the speed of a race horse at the finish line, she silently ordered herself to stay calm. Mamma had always told her to consider things carefully before responding. That even though she would face difficult issues, there was nothing she couldn't handle. Because God was her protector.

There was no sound of saws. No voices. The room became unusually quiet. Rebecca knew she could have heard a pin drop. For the first time in her life, she questioned her mother's advice.

William stood and paced to the door and back. But Rebecca barely noticed the movement while she considered all that was at stake. She contemplated

Daniel asking William to move to Indiana to become his business partner. She wanted William and his dad to be close. But a partnership was complicated.

Deciding to do that would mean that if Rebecca wanted to marry William, she would need to leave her family. Daniel's business was in Indiana. Not in Arthur, Illinois. And she treasured her Amish world more than anything.

Of course, there were Amish communities nearby. She thought of Katie. But it wouldn't be the same because Rebecca's family was in Illinois. And right now, she missed them more than ever.

She'd never planned on being without them permanently. She couldn't fathom seeing them only on holidays. She missed talking to her mother every day. Rebecca frowned.

William stepped in front of her and crossed his arms over his chest. When he spoke, his voice was soft and apologetic. "Rebecca, I'm sorry. I didn't want to say anything."

She looked up at him and tried to control the shakiness in her voice. "You had to tell me. I'm going to be your wife, William. We need to think about this. Ignoring it will get us nowhere."

"Trust me, Rebecca. It was the last thing I expected him to say. I know it isn't what you wanted to hear, but you've always told me to be straightforward."

She took a deep breath to calm herself. "I expect honesty from you, William. Nothing less. I have a question." She paused. "How did you respond?"

William's cheeks took on a light shade of pink like they always did when he confronted something he didn't want to discuss.

"I told him I was flattered." William raised a hand.

"But I didn't commit. You know I'd never make a big decision like that without consulting you."

What had happened to her simple life? What Rebecca had just learned was not like anything she'd ever had to deal with. She had mixed feelings. She was sure she should be happy Daniel had offered William a partnership. And she'd been warned that this was coming. Katie had mentioned it. So had Natalie.

Finally, William had an opportunity to build a relationship with his dad. After all these years, Daniel was making an effort to be close to his son. And winning Daniel's approval and attention was William's dream. How could she deny him that?

On the other hand, granting him that opportunity forced a huge sacrifice on her part. One that would affect the rest of her life and the lives of her beloved family. How could she live away from them on a permanent basis?

"There's so much to think about. Of course, it would be great for you to work with your dad. On the other hand, our children would miss out on growing up with their cousins. My parents would have to travel out of state to see their grandchildren."

Suddenly, Rebecca wanted to cry. Her whole life revolved around her family. Not only did she help Mamma with household chores, but her parents expected her at the woodworking shop.

She was sure that the business ran much more smoothly when she did her part. Her mother and father had made a huge sacrifice in allowing her to come here. In fact, the only reason she was in Indiana was because of Daniel's heart condition. She couldn't stay forever. That wasn't what she had agreed to.

Her parents would need her when they got old. In their community, the younger generation took care of their elders. She pictured the grandpa-house she'd always planned behind her home. She loved her brother and sister. Their cousins. Aunts and uncles.

William was looking at her to go on. The expression on his face was a combination of uncertainty and hopefulness. She had to say something. But what? As usual, she decided on a straightforward approach.

"William, how wonderful that Daniel offered you a partnership. That means he truly loves you. Maybe you can put the past behind you and start over."

She inhaled on a shaky breath. "But move to Indiana?"

She gave a skeptical shake of her head. "It's something we didn't plan on. I'm a little surprised right now. Forgive me. I . . . I just wasn't prepared for that, I guess."

"Oh, Rebecca. It would be a huge adjustment for you. For both of us. I haven't forgotten how close you are to your family. And of course, I would miss Uncle John and Aenti Sarah. They've made so many sacrifices to raise me. Done their very best to make sure I knew I was loved. And the way they feel about Dad, well . . . They certainly wouldn't approve of me becoming his partner. Their opinion is so important because I want to please them for all they've done. But if I did take this offer . . . I'd be an outcast, just like Dad." William smiled a little. "There's a lot to think about. But fortunately, this doesn't need to be settled today." He nodded. "But at some point, we'll have to decide. And we'll make the right choice."

What William said was true. She could tell by the look in his eyes that he wanted to accept. She loved William. She adored her family. If he partnered with his dad, she'd have to give up one. Which would it be?

Chapter Eight

That night, Rebecca flipped her room light on and sat on the floor next to her hope chest. As she traced her finger across the engraved flowers on the lid, she thought of Old Sam and let out a small sigh. In barely more than a whisper, she asked, "Old Sam, what would you tell William? I wish I could talk to you now. More than ever, I need your advice."

She pressed her lips together in a thoughtful manner and pulled open the lid, removing the notepad and pen inside. Leaning back against the bed, she bent her knees and put the paper on her lap.

She recorded the date in the upper right-hand corner and considered Daniel's invitation to become William's business partner.

She began to write. *Never before have I faced such strong challenges. Before I came here, I thought life was simple. It's not. It seems like circumstances are pulling William and me apart. I love William. And he loves me. But he also yearns for approval from his father. I want him to be happy. At the same time, I long to grow old around my folks. I'm not selfish, but giving up my family would be so hard for me to do. It wouldn't be fair to them.*

She sat up a little straighter. She adjusted the pad on her lap and inhaled the pleasant scent of eucalyptus as she considered the bishop's request for three goals. At the same time, Daniel's offer to William rang in and out of her thoughts.

She stared at her pen and wrote. *How did life suddenly become so complicated? I'm still the same person I was before coming here. My passions haven't changed. The most important things in my life are William, my family, and my faith. I've always believed that I would live to be very old with all three. Now I realize that I took that for granted.*

For several long, thoughtful moments, Rebecca focused her attention on her diary. As she continued to write, a lone tear slid down her cheek. She didn't bother to stop it.

If I offer William my blessing to join his father, I give up my family. I don't know how I would survive without them. At the same time, I can't imagine breathing without William. What should I do?

The next afternoon, Rebecca's thoughts lingered on the tough decision she was about to make.

"It's quittin' time."

William's voice startled her. As she looked up, she accidentally brushed her thumb against a piece of oak she was holding.

"Ouch." She squeezed her eyes closed and dropped the board.

William grabbed her hand. "I'm sorry. Didn't mean to surprise you." He held her fingers close to his face while he scrutinized the wound. "That looks like one wicked splinter."

She didn't protest when he motioned her into the office. With quick steps, he made his way to a small cabinet and returned with tweezers and a Band-Aid. He laid the Band-Aid aside and darted Rebecca a mischievous wink.

"Good thing I have some medical training."

She laughed. "You don't have any medical training. And I'll be fine. Really. It's only a splinter. Not a bullet casualty."

He took her wrist and gently lifted her hand for a better look. "You're much too brave, Miss Rebecca. You're underestimating the severity of your wound."

As he carefully scrutinized the swollen area, her pulse picked up speed. The serious look on his face made him appear older. His jaw was set. She could feel his warm breath caress her skin.

"Hold real still."

She did so as he placed the tweezers next to her thumb. He quickly pulled out the splinter and proudly displayed it in front of her.

"Would you look at that?"

She smiled a little. "Thank you, Doctor. What would I have done without you?" she teased, but inside she was shaking. She loved the way William took care of her. His concern. At the same time, the heavy decision she had to make loomed over her like a dark cloud.

He winked. "There's no charge for my services, ma'am, since the splinter was my fault."

They returned to where she'd been working. Careful to not put pressure on her thumb, she placed her brush in a can of paint remover and motioned to her piece. "What do you think?"

Together, they eyed the long cabinet board. William gave a satisfied nod. "It's beautiful. Miss Rebecca. No one applies stain like you do."

"Thank you."

He pressed his lips together and blew out a breath. "But no more shop talk today. We're done."

Rebecca paused to motion to the clock on the wall. "It's only one o'clock."

Pressing his palm against the small of her back, he motioned ahead. "You've been working much too hard. And did I tell you how much I appreciate all you've done?"

She nodded.

"Now, I have a surprise for you."

Rebecca's heart jumped with excitement. "A surprise? What is it?"

He winked. "Come outside, and you'll see."

They made their way to the door and stepped outside. Once the door clicked closed, Rebecca glimpsed the horse tied to the nearby pole. Her breath caught in her throat. She pulled her hands over her chest in amazement. "Oh, my goodness!"

"This afternoon, we're taking a horse-and-buggy ride." He pointed to the carriage. "Would you be my guest?"

Before she could answer, he put a hand up to stop her. "And I won't take no for an answer."

An excited laugh escaped Rebecca's throat. "I'd never turn down a horse-and-buggy ride! Especially with you. Where did you get . . ."

He arched an amused brow. "Let's just say Beth helped me to borrow these. Now, no more questions.

The afternoon is for fun." He held out his hand. "After you."

He helped her to step up into the "black box." After she moved over to the passenger side, William joined her.

In silence, they proceeded onto the blacktop. As the hooves clicked against the road, Rebecca closed her eyes a moment to breathe in that familiar woodsy smell of the bench. The thick cotton blanket on her seat was soft against her hands. When she opened her lids, a smile tugged at her lips.

She turned to William. "To what do I owe this pleasure?"

William darted her a grin. "The pleasure's all mine. I wanted to offer you something nice for all you've done." He gave a low whistle. "Believe me, I gave serious thought to what you'd like. After deep deliberation, I decided this ride would be the perfect gift."

"You've got awfully good instincts."

He raised a finger. "The afternoon is just starting."

Rebecca breathed in a happy sigh. As the buggy creaked, her spirits lifted. While the bright, warm sun shone down on them, all she thought of was the bliss of this simple afternoon. The smell of freshly cut grass. The bright orange sun overhead. How wonderful life was.

"It seems like an eternity since we've ridden in one of these together."

He nodded. "If I remember correctly, the last time we did this was after the singings. It was a couple of nights before we left Arthur."

Rebecca paused. "Oh yes. It started to rain just when you pulled up to my house."

She recalled the blissful evening. She missed the singings. She longed to be in Arthur. "Don't you miss them?"

"The singings?"

"Uh-huh."

He shrugged. "To be honest, I haven't given them much thought. We've been so busy in the shop."

Rebecca considered his response. She sat up straighter. "Every night, I imagine what I'd be doing if I were home." She crossed her arms against her chest in a wistful manner. "Sometimes I can almost smell Mamma's homemade butter. And I can even hear my brother and sister screaming as they chase each other in the yard."

"Beth has butter in the fridge. Doesn't it smell the same?"

Rebecca shook her head. "Not really. And the taste can't compare to Mamma's. Besides, there's something about making it yourself."

William lifted a casual shoulder. "I suppose. But I can tell you this. You know what I like most about Arthur?"

She was pleased that William missed something from home. That she thought of Arthur day and night and that he seemed content in Indiana prompted an uneasy feeling in her chest.

"What?"

He grinned. "Aenti Sarah's butterscotch pie."

He laughed. Rebecca joined him.

Suddenly, William's voice dropped. "Honestly, Rebecca, I could live here."

Rebecca closed her eyes a moment as she digested the words she'd been halfway expecting for some time.

A long silence ensued before Rebecca spoke. "What about your aunt and uncle? Don't you want to see them?"

"Of course." William cleared his throat. "But we're still in touch. Aenti Sarah calls once a week. It's not like I don't talk to her. And as far as day-to-day work, that hasn't changed. I'm basically doing the same trade here. Building cabinets."

He chuckled. "The difference is that when I'm off, I kick back in the air-conditioning and watch the sports channel. I have no complaints about how Dad and Beth crank the air down to get the house cool at night." He blew out a satisfied breath. "I sleep like a log in that king-size bed."

Rebecca's throat went dry. She wasn't sure what to say. While the buggy gently rocked, she knew she should enjoy being alone with William. Moments together like this were rare. She should love talking with him.

She looked down at her lap. Her hands were clenched together and her knuckles were pale. It wasn't difficult to understand why the initial happiness of this ride had suddenly evaporated.

The defeated feeling was due to changes in William. Unlike her, he had developed a bond with the English way of life. And unlike her, he didn't appear to long for the things in her hometown that were so very dear to her.

He softened his voice. "Hey, don't look so serious."

She sighed and smiled a little. Why worry? She

couldn't control William's preference for his dad's lifestyle. So she might as well enjoy the sunny afternoon. Relaxing, she crossed her legs at the ankles and turned to face him.

She giggled as she drifted back in time. "Remember when we used to sell homegrown vegetables at our stand on the street?"

"That seems like a long time ago. We were just kids."

"And you used your profits to treat me to lunch at Yoder's Kitchen."

William's eyes lit up with enthusiasm. "Now that's one good memory."

"And it should be. You practically ate them out of their home-made dumplings."

"I'm sure we'd never find a restaurant here that could match Yoder's Kitchen. Their fried chicken is the best."

As they proceeded down the road, Rebecca's tense shoulders began to relax. Why on earth should she worry? Next to her was the same William she'd known her entire life. The William she'd grown up with and knew like the back of her hand. There had never been an issue they hadn't been able to work out.

A field of wildflowers loomed in the distance. William pulled over to the side and tied the horse to a tree.

"We can't end the afternoon without a bouquet."

They got out of the buggy and talked while they took slow steps. Sometime later, Rebecca watched in silence while he bent to pick a handful of yellow and purple flowers. With a proud smile, he stood in front of her and handed her his freshly picked arrangement.

"For you."

She took them and breathed in the light, sweet smell. "They're beautiful. Thank you."

They returned to the buggy. Inside, Rebecca got comfortable and took in the smell of the bouquet. The temperature dropped a notch as they made their way home. When the Conrad property came into sight, William darted her a glance. "A penny for your thoughts."

She turned to better face him. "I was just thinking about us and all that we've accomplished since we've been here."

"It's hard to believe, isn't it?"

She nodded. "When we get back home, we can honestly be proud of all we've done."

"You really miss Arthur."

She gave a firm nod. "Don't you?"

He paused. When he finally spoke, his voice cracked with emotion. "I know what you'd like to hear. And I wish I could tell you that I do. But we've always been honest with each other."

He breathed in. "Rebecca, I like it here. Everything is at the tip of your fingers. Don't you think you could get used to this? You've admitted to enjoying Beth's double oven. And why would you want to wash towels by hand when you're used to her washer and dryer?"

Rebecca thought a moment. "I've enjoyed our time here. And I'm thankful for the opportunity to help your folks. But when I'm back in Arthur, I won't miss these amenities."

She lifted her hands in a satisfied gesture. "I guess you could say that I'm happy with the simple life."

"Rebecca, this *is* the simple life. Don't you see?"

Rebecca considered his question. The back of her neck tensed as she and William locked gazes. At that moment, she confirmed what she had really known but not wanted to admit. William wanted to become English. As she looked at him, she realized he was waiting for an answer.

She didn't mind speaking her heart, even though she was fully aware that William wanted to hear otherwise. "No, William. To me, the English life is not simple. In fact, it's much more complicated than the Amish ways."

His eyes reflected his confusion.

Rebecca went on in the calmest voice she could muster. "There are more decisions to make in this world. Yes, living Amish requires more physical work. I'm not denying that. But mentally, the English life is more complicated. I understand why you might prefer living like your father, William. And I don't begrudge you that. But I'm the same Rebecca I was before coming here."

She gave a helpless shrug. "I still prefer to stay the girl I've been the last eighteen years."

In silence, they looked at each other. Rebecca noted the sad expression on William's face. Obviously, he was disappointed that she had failed to be taken in by this newfound life. But she, too, was equally disappointed. Because the man she loved had changed.

She wouldn't be concerned if this change didn't affect their future. But right now, she wasn't sure if William would return to Arthur.

After they arrived at the Conrads' home and William tied the horse, they walked in tense silence toward the house. She didn't bother to ask how the horse and buggy would be returned to the owner. Her future with William weighed heavily on her mind. She needed guidance. She needed Old Sam.

The month of July was going by quickly. Letter in hand, Rebecca quickly stepped to the mailbox in front of the Conrad home. If she couldn't walk to Old Sam's red barn and talk to him in person, she'd settle for asking his advice the second-best way she knew. The good old postal service. She couldn't call because he didn't have a phone.

All night, Rebecca had agonized over her conversation with William. Finally, at two in the morning, she'd flipped on her lamp and had written to the wisest person she knew.

As the white chunks of gravel crunched under her shoes, she smiled a little. As she did so, a small yawn escaped her. Why hadn't she thought of contacting Old Sam before?

As she anxiously stepped away from the house, the grinding noise of electric saws from the shop filled the air.

She reached the mailbox, where a small yellow butterfly hovered gracefully. While the warm breeze nudged the bottom of her long skirt, Rebecca pulled the letter from its unsealed envelope and read the contents out loud. She wanted to make sure she'd made her concerns clear, so he would know how to best counsel her. And if anyone could tell her what to do about William, it was Old Sam.

"'Dear Sam, I hope you're doing well and that you're not working too hard. I wanted you to know that I love the hope chest you made me and that I look at it every night before going to bed. It's a treasure. I'm doing okay in Indiana. But I miss coming over to talk to you. I'm dealing with an issue that requires your expertise. That's why I'm writing this letter.'"

She glanced away a moment and took a deep breath. "'William is becoming comfortable with the English. Actually, he loves their ways more than I ever anticipated. I'm so afraid I'm losing William, Sam. He loves me. That I'm sure of. But I don't know that he'll want to return to Arthur when his father recovers from his heart attack.'"

For a moment, Rebecca looked away from her neat printing and bit her lip. With a frown, she returned her attention to the letter. "'Sam, I long to marry William. But I want to go home and raise our children Amish. For me, life wouldn't be the same anywhere but Arthur. It's my greatest fear that I'm losing him. Is it selfish of me to expect him to join the church if he decides not to? I know what's in my heart; at the same time, I have an obligation to respect his wishes, too. I'm sure you'll know what to tell me. Right now, I'm uneasy. I can't wait to hear from you. Love, Rebecca.'"

With newfound confidence, she refolded the letter and sealed it in the envelope. She shoved it into the mailbox and pulled up the red flag.

She smiled. Soon she would hear from Sam. It was just a matter of time until she would know what to do about the different directions she and William were headed. With a deep sigh of relief, she made

her way to the house. As she approached the front
patio, Beth pushed the front door open and waved.

"Rebecca! Your mother's on the phone."

Excited, Rebecca rushed to the house. She couldn't
wait to talk to her mamma. Everything would be okay.

That afternoon, Rebecca squinted as the bright
sun illuminated the light blue sky. She looked down
at her flower garden. Her geraniums boasted bright,
beautiful colors. The hot pink petals were her favorites.

As she admired her work, she thought of her
mamma's disturbing call. The words weighed heavily on Rebecca's mind as she rolled up her sleeves to
her elbows and put her hands on her hips. Flowers
grew fast. So did weeds. And so did the weeds of life.

Rebecca wrinkled her nose. Her parents were
concerned about her longer-than-intended stay in
Indiana. They wanted her home. People were talking. Rumor had it that Rebecca and William would
leave the Amish community, just like Daniel, and
that Rebecca's parents were at fault for allowing
their daughter to go out of state. To Rebecca's chagrin, her poor parents were taking the flack for her
absence.

She gave a sad, frustrated shake of her head, adjusted her work apron, and squatted to pull butter-
print from the soil. One by one, she tossed the thick
green stems into a plastic bag.

As Rebecca continued removing the unwanted
plants, she tried to focus on the positive: Daniel's
business was back on track. She'd already decided
on one goal for the bishop. She had a new friend,

Katie. Beth had been wonderful to Rebecca. Soon Rebecca would be back in Arthur.

But would William be with her? She considered that ominous question. At the same time, she thought of her parents. A dull ache formed in her chest.

There weren't many phones in the Amish community, but it didn't matter. Rebecca knew all too well that once gossip started, it spread like wildfire.

Facing the truth was difficult because she truly believed she was making the right choice by extending her stay. How could she leave when Daniel's condition was touch and go? In spite of the turmoil at home, she believed with all of her heart that God wanted her here until Daniel was on his feet again.

Besides, William needed help with the shop while Beth counted on her for moral support. More importantly, Rebecca could influence William to make the most important decision of his life. Whether or not to join the Amish church. How could she go home when so much was at stake?

She considered William. Usually, he was decisive. But right now, he was as fragile as a feather in the wind. He hadn't hesitated to express his love for the English ways. Right now, he could go either Amish or English.

Rebecca's presence could influence him to make the right choice. A decision that would affect the future. For both of them.

She looked inside her bag of weeds and raised a thoughtful brow. To remove unwanted plants, she merely yanked them out of the ground. She smiled a little. If only getting rid of life's problems were that simple.

But how could she possibly destroy the verbal

weeds bothering her folks? Could she stop rumors? If only there was a way.

Rebecca yearned to end the gossip. How could she justify staying in Indiana when her mother was paying the price?

In the small, tight-knit community, approval was important. Rebecca bit her tongue as she thought of others judging her. If only everyone would mind their own business. But they didn't. And Mamma didn't deserve this stress.

She needed to come up with two more goals. She couldn't leave without carrying them out. She had taken that instruction to heart. And she would be a better person after she left here.

At the same time, William was still the reason she was in Indiana. If she returned to Illinois before Daniel recovered, what would happen to William?

He was her true love. And she had no intention of bailing on him, even if they weren't married. How could she leave him when he needed her most?

Rebecca stood and rubbed her hands together to rid them of dirt. Catching her breath, she focused on her task at hand and bent to lift her heavy metal watering can. Slow, steady steps took her to the end of the row, watering each flower, one at a time.

As soon as the liquid touched the plants, the green leaves became more alive. The stems took on a darker, more vibrant shade. Rebecca recalled the scriptures her mother had sent with her and realized that water to the plants was similar to scripture to the soul.

She stopped a moment, watching the moisture glisten as it clung to the soft, velvety-looking petals of the pink petunias. Turning, she made her way down the next row.

She returned to the spigot on the side of the house to refill her watering can, still worrying about her parents. And about William. About their future together. Would she lose him? For a moment, the dreaded problems flitted through her mind until she shook her head to rid herself of them.

She recalled the story of Adam and Eve. Of course, weeds were a part of life. And she knew from a long-ago sermon that a person's success was dependent on how he or she dealt with obstacles. For every problem, there was a solution. She couldn't let negative issues get the best of her. She must pray for a way to remove the sinful plants.

And if she couldn't rid herself of them?

She would work around them.

The lesson about measuring success stuck with her. She had listened with interest when the preacher explained how trials made us stronger and that challenges force us to grow as human beings. In a deep, low voice, he'd explained to the small, attentive congregation that without pain, a person's faith isn't tested.

Therefore, it is impossible to know what we could overcome. When obstacles are thrown at us, our personal success is measured by how we cope with them. When all is said and done, facing battles strengthens our faith.

Rebecca enjoyed her life without obstacles. But she definitely had taken the first step by addressing whether or not to give William her blessing to become Daniel's business partner.

She prayed about what to do. She thought about

her future with William twenty-four-seven. Salty tears stung her eyes at the thought of telling Mamma she must leave them for good.

She remembered her special scripture book and yearned for home. That would have to wait. But how long? In the meantime, what would Rebecca tell William? Should she give him her blessing to partner with his father and forfeit everything so dear to her?

She let out a faint moan of distress and came to a decision. She wouldn't do anything until she was confident of her choice. Either way, she would suffer a huge loss.

She robbed William of his opportunity to go into business with his father, or she abandoned her family. Which was worse?

As Rebecca stopped a moment to look up at the large white clouds in the light blue sky, she thought of Mamma's advice to deal with the negative and focus on the positive. Rebecca sighed contentment as she took the advice to heart. Even with weeds, there was still much to be thankful for.

Family. William. Her newfound friend, Katie. Her health. Faith. And her dream.

Other enjoyable things that made her life special. Being outside. The warm sun shining down on her back. Birds chirping. Horse-and-buggy rides. Old Sam. She grinned.

She stopped to study a tiny hummingbird as it hovered over the cannas. If only her decisions were as simple as the bird's.

But human life involved complex issues like beliefs, religion, pleasing others, making difficult choices, and living with those decisions.

It was amazing how these beautiful, fragile-looking plants survived and grew under the hot sun as well as occasional downpours. If God watched over her plants, He would certainly protect her. And William.

Surely, he would guide her down the right path. He was omniscient. There was nothing God couldn't deal with. Was there a way to make everyone happy? She thought hard.

Rebecca dreamed of her flower shop and lifted her chin in determination. The thought prompted a big grin. It was a wonderful, happy dream.

She imagined arranging flowers and watching people smile when she delivered them. She pictured herself in a room filled with exotic plants. She envisioned herself clipping long, green stems and arranging them in terra-cotta bowls and crystal vases.

She imagined smelling sweet scents all day. Of setting deep green leafy plants into earthy-looking bowls of different shapes and sizes.

At least she had a dream. Even if her flower shop never materialized, the very thought brought happiness. A bright spot in her life.

She thought of Katie's ambition to run a day-care center and smiled. In more ways than one, she was a lot like her new Amish friend. Both had big dreams. At the same time, they faced obstacles.

As Rebecca pulled another weed from the moist earth, she thought of her conversation with Beth and realized she was passionate enough about plants to make selling them a career. She'd read books on different species. She was aware of which genera required little water and those that needed a lot. She could mix compatible plants into the same pots. She remembered the terrarium of cacti she'd done for her brother for a school project and the bouquet she'd put together for Mamma's birthday.

As a breeze feathered her face, she planted a satisfied hand on her hip. The sun hit the blossoms of her bright red geraniums, making them appear unusually bright.

William's voice made her turn.

"Hey."

She jumped.

He smiled a little. "Sorry. I didn't mean to startle you."

"It's okay." In the same breath, she motioned to her work. "What do you think?"

He furrowed his brows as he appeared to study the garden. Several heartbeats later, he nodded. When his gaze met Rebecca's, he grinned mischievously. "On a scale of one to ten?"

Anxious for his approval, she gave a quick, eager nod.

"Definitely a ten plus."

Rebecca curtsied. "Thank you."

"I don't know what you feed your plants, but they'd win a race. Heck, it's just been little more than a week since they were tiny. This will be great for Dad, Rebecca. How do you always come up with the best ideas?"

She gave a happy shrug.

"I'll never forget when you made Aenti Sarah chicken and dumplings after she pulled a shoulder muscle."

Rebecca laughed. "I'd forgotten that."

William's face turned serious. "Too bad Dad's condition isn't as simple as a pulled muscle. I wish he was healthy and happy again. It would be nice to have an easy fix."

"Yes." Rebecca considered his statement. It would be wonderful to have an easy fix for many things. The partnership, for instance.

She said in a low, confidential tone, "You know my thoughts."

"About something good coming out of something bad?"

She gave a confident nod. "I've said it before, and I'll tell you again. I truly believe that Daniel's heart condition is God's way of bringing you together."

William stepped forward and stared down at the ground. When he finally raised his gaze, he regarded her with curiosity. "Maybe."

Rebecca rolled her eyes. "Of course it is. If it weren't for the heart attack, we wouldn't be here . . . which means you wouldn't have spent time with him . . . which means he wouldn't have offered you a partnership. That's a good thing, William. Don't you see? Obviously, he wants to play a larger role in your life."

The serious look on William's face was so attractive. His eyes took on that intriguing appearance. The small groove in his chin intensified. He was positively handsome.

William stepped closer. The vulnerable expression on his face made Rebecca's heart pick up speed. Their gazes locked.

"I owe you an apology."

Her eyes didn't leave his as she raised a curious brow. "For what?"

"Oh, gee. It's about our conversation about Dad

and Beth . . . I've been thinking, and I was totally selfish."

Rebecca squared her shoulders. "What?"

He shrugged disappointedly. "I don't know what got into me. I can't believe I was so wrapped up in resentment when Dad was in a hospital struggling to live. My mother would be disappointed in me. I was thinking of myself when I should've been focused on him."

With a comforting hand, she patted his shoulder. "It's okay, William. Talking things out always helps."

He nodded and smiled a little. "What's happened to me, Rebecca? Why was I so self-centered?"

She moved her hand to his neck and caressed the tight knot there. She watched him close his lids.

"You're far from selfish, William." She paused. "In fact, you're the most generous person I know."

When he opened his eyes, his expression lightened with hope. "Really?"

"Jah."

"Remember when we used to go to the singings?"

Rebecca grinned. "Those were the good old days. I'm glad we have nice memories. And we'll make more. But right now, it's our responsibility to deal with these issues and get past them. Just think of all you've faced."

He gave a mischievous roll of his eyes. "I guess this is payback for all of those stress-free years."

"Maybe. But we can't let pressure get the best of us. I've read that stress makes a person's mind fuzzy. It wears you out so you can't think straight."

"So how do I clear my head of the fuzz?"

"Good question. I think that if we focus on the

positive, getting through this ordeal with Daniel will be easier to cope with."

He looked at her to continue.

She raised her voice for emphasis. "We completed that entire Kreggs order. That's amazing! William Conrad, you've done a marvelous job."

"I certainly didn't do it alone."

"I'm glad I could help."

William smiled a little and touched her shoulder. "I'm going back to the shop to tidy up. Are you coming?"

"In a few minutes."

As Rebecca watched William walk away, a nice feeling filled her chest. She was proud of him. William was a good, honest man.

On that thought, she hoisted her bag of weeds over her shoulder and picked up the watering can. After giving her garden a satisfied glance, she dropped off her gardening things inside of the garage and washed her hands in the work sink.

As she made her way to the entrance of the woodworking shop, the dream of a floral shop still lingered like the sweet taste of homemade chocolate. But that glimmer of happiness quickly evaporated as she noticed the couple waiting at the cash register. It was Henry Kreggs. And Natalie.

Chapter Nine

It was five o'clock. As William moved the broom over the concrete floor, sawdust floated in the air. The clinking sound of tools filled the building as workers cleaned up. William was pleased about the completion of Henry Kreggs's order.

His dad's business was thriving. Even so, an uncertain ache filled William's chest as he thought of his father. When would his dad be well enough to resume his role at the shop? Would he even work again? If not, William would be forced to decide whether or not to stay and run the company.

Right now, his future with Rebecca seemed dependent on his dad's heart condition. William pushed out a sigh of frustration. He had never been so confused. He was pulled in two different directions.

He'd promised Rebecca their stay here was temporary. At the same time, he felt a tremendous obligation to his dad, even though his father had left him. And then, there was the partnership offer . . .

Aenti Sarah, Uncle John, and members of the church had raised him to be responsible. But what about his commitment to Rebecca? How could he do what was best for her *and* his dad?

Rebecca's voice brought him back to reality. Several feet away, she ran a cleaning rag over a workbench.

"What did the Kreggses want?"

Continuing his task, he glanced at her. "They stopped by to thank us for a lovely job."

As Rebecca made small talk, William's instincts told him that the crux of her interest was Henry's daughter. At the thought of Natalie, William frowned. This afternoon, he'd been attuned to her special attention to him. Rebecca was right.

But William didn't care for Natalie's aggressive nature. She was much more forward than the Amish girls he'd grown up with.

He preferred polite, conservative Rebecca by a long shot. To William, flirting was superficial. He wasn't comfortable with the way Natalie flashed her pretty smile and asked questions about things she surely wasn't interested in.

He hadn't missed the look of disapproval on Rebecca's face when Natalie had talked with him. And he'd taken note of the unusually terse conversation between him and Rebecca following Natalie's departure.

But William couldn't ignore Henry Kreggs's daughter. They were his dad's biggest clients, and their recommendation to others was important. A huge part of the business was word-of-mouth.

Even so, Natalie wasn't high on his priority list. The more William considered the offer to become a partner, the more he wanted it. At the same time, he dreamed of marrying Rebecca and making her the happiest woman in the world. But he knew Rebecca's heart.

She was his soul mate. However, for the first time in his life, there was something he couldn't discuss with her. His father's offer. As soon as he'd mentioned it, the disappointed, concerned look on her face had told him everything he'd needed to know.

Of course Rebecca didn't want to settle down in Indiana. And no one could have predicted his father would have suffered a second heart attack and that William would make so many new decisions on his own. He couldn't ask Beth to take on more responsibility than she already had.

As he glanced behind him, he considered the huge decision riding on his shoulders. He knew Rebecca didn't want to hear about the offer again. And he couldn't bring it up. Because he was in a no-win situation. If he accepted, Rebecca suffered. If he didn't, he'd let his dad down. Himself, too.

He rolled his shoulders to rid them of tension. He didn't like keeping things from her. But how could he discuss the partnership with her if she didn't want it?

As he dumped the pile of sawdust into the garbage, Rebecca's voice startled him. "I'm making your favorite dinner tonight." She paused and darted him a proud smile. "Chicken and dumplings."

He turned to her. "You're an angel."

She stepped closer. When she raised her chin, their gazes locked. The warmth in her eyes emanated like a soft blanket on a cold winter's night. The reassurance in her voice eased his tension. "Anything for you."

"You never cease to amaze me. How do you manage to cook dinner *and* work in the shop?"

"I boiled the chicken early this morning. The noodles are dry. All I have to do is throw everything in a pan of boiling water." She winked. "It's all about organization."

He laughed. "Multitasking?"

She nodded. "You said it."

As he looked at her, guilt filled his chest until he thought it would burst.

She deserved his best. How he yearned to promise her everything she wanted. But how could he? His own dream conflicted with the idyllic life Rebecca wanted.

Her brows drew together in a sudden frown. She lowered her voice. "Something's bothering you, William Conrad. Tell me what it is."

"I'm tired. And worried about Dad."

He was quick to notice the skeptical look she darted at him.

"Is that all?"

Rebecca knew him too well. It was impossible to hide things from her. And he didn't want to. It was just that this time . . .

She took his arm in hers. "Let's wash up. A good dinner will make you feel better."

He agreed. How he wished chicken and dumplings would solve his problems. But his situation wouldn't be easily fixed. And there was no perfect solution. So, he'd have to give up his dream. Or sacrifice Rebecca's. Which would it be?

* * *

When Rebecca opened the mailbox and glimpsed
the envelope from Sam, a happy grin tugged at her
lips. She'd only mailed his letter five days ago.
Without wasting time, she closed the mailbox and
set the pile of mail on the rocky ground. Letter in
hand, she made herself comfortable on the decorative rock beside her. She tore open the envelope and
unfolded the letter.

Beth pulled into the drive and waved. Rebecca returned the gesture. She tapped her foot to a nervous
beat while she skimmed the neat black writing that
lined the page.

*Dear Rebecca, It's good to hear from you. I enjoyed
your note and am happy you're doing well. Your
parents miss you. But no need to worry about me.
With Annie around, I'll never go hungry. She's
keeping me well fed with her sponge cakes. And
Rachel still listens to my horse-and-buggy stories.
I've been giving special thought to your concern
about William.*

Rebecca's heart picked up speed as she pulled the
paper closer to her chest.

*You're a very perceptive girl. But I'm afraid that
a decision of this nature will have to be made from
your own heart. I'm a wise old man. But your
destiny is something that no one can decide but you.*

*It appears that William enjoys the English
amenities, Rebecca, as many Amish youngsters do
while exploring Rumspringa. But realize that
leaving the faith is very different from expressing a
liking for a new and exciting way of life.*

Rebecca paused and considered the statement. As always, Old Sam was right. The thought that perhaps William was merely enjoying a temporary privilege prompted a new spark of hope within her. She adjusted her position on the rock and read on.

> *William loves you. Love is stronger than any problem I've yet to encounter. I have no doubt that the two of you will work this out together. Be strong, Rebecca. Remember that "courage is fear that has said its prayers."*
>
> *Old Sam*

Pensive, Rebecca gazed at the words in front of her, but her mind was on William. She barely heard the hammering sounds coming from the shop. Or the humming of the electric saws penetrating the oak.

The pleasant aroma of freshly cut grass filled the air. The scent reminded her of home . . . and of Old Sam's words of wisdom. Even though it was obvious that he wanted her to make her own choice, he had given her something to think about. His point about Rumspringa was correct.

Perhaps William was merely taking advantage of this short-lived freedom. Rebecca pulled in a deep, hopeful breath.

At that moment, he appeared in the distance. As he raised a hand, he hollered, "I need your input."

In response, she gave a firm nod. He turned and stepped toward the shop. But she stayed put for a few blissful moments while hope spread through her.

When she considered the circumstances, was it really wrong for William to enjoy the ESPN channel?

Or air-conditioning? He had come to Indiana with a goal. He'd had good intentions. Deep down inside, she believed his roots would eventually overcome the temptation to become English.

She returned the letter to its envelope. Bending, she gathered the remaining mail and stood to make her way to the house, where she would lay the bundle on the table before returning to the shop.

Old Sam's letter had been a blessing. A renewed hope stirred within her, wrestling with her doubts until she was convinced everything would be okay.

The next evening, William walked beside Rebecca down the trail behind the Conrad property. Both wore blue jeans. William had left his hat in the house. The jeans and loose T-shirt felt comfortable against his skin. The metal pail in his hand swung back and forth with his gait.

The warm breeze caressed the back of his neck. He smiled at Rebecca. "There's something you should know."

"Jah?"

"You look mighty fine in blue jeans."

She laughed a little. "Thank you. They're comfy. It was nice of Beth to lend them to me, even though I feel a bit on the rebellious side."

"You shouldn't." He cocked a brow. "It is Rumspringa."

"True. And I've been dying to try them."

"This is the only time it's okay to do English things. You wouldn't want to waste the opportunity, would you?"

"I guess not."

"If this is the most rebellious thing you ever do, I think God will forgive you."

She cleared her throat. "William, do you mind if I ask you something?"

"Of course not."

"Do I look as good in jeans as Natalie?"

The question prompted a laugh. "That's the last thing I expected to hear."

"But do I?"

William's voice was firm. "Natalie could never hold a candle to you."

Rebecca grinned as she nudged his elbow.

Rebecca stepped over a tree stump.

"I even confessed my desire to wear jeans to Katie."

"You did?"

Rebecca nodded.

"What did she say?"

Rebecca gave a casual shrug of her shoulders. "That I should try them. And . . . that she had even driven a car."

"Good for her. That's next on my list."

Rebecca stopped a moment to run her hands down her thighs.

"Something wrong?"

"No. I'm just not used to slacks. But no complaints. How does that T-shirt feel?"

"I could wear it every day."

"It wouldn't be hard to make me put these on again."

"Then will you?"

Rebecca hesitated. "I doubt it."

"Why not, if they feel right?"

She rolled her eyes. "Because I'm who I am in my

dress and kapp. You know me, William. Rebecca
Sommer belongs in her Amish attire." She sighed. "I
suppose I'm too much of a creature of habit to
change."

The statement prompted William to think. What
she said was very true. Rebecca's upbringing was
more engrained in her than anyone he knew. And
during the month they'd spent here, he'd clearly
seen that she hadn't been tempted by the English
ways like he was.

As he glanced at her, he saw a stubbornness that
wouldn't allow her to change even if she wanted to.
In many ways, he wished that he was as strong in his
beliefs as she was in hers. He kept his thoughts to
himself, though.

There was enough conflict between them already,
and it wouldn't behoove either one of them to focus
on their differences. Especially with the business
offer weighing heavily on his mind. He deliberately
changed the subject.

"I hope we can find those raspberry bushes Beth
talked about."

Rebecca smiled a little as she walked at his side. "I
have an eye for raspberries. In a few hours, I'll be
baking pies for Daniel in Beth's wonderful double
oven." She giggled. "And unlike Martha Wagler, I'll
add sugar!"

They laughed.

Several steps later, William looked ahead and took
a deep, satisfied breath. So many things flitted through
his mind as the sun flooded the sky with a mixture
of colors that seemed to morph into one shade:

Daniel's condition. The shop. The offer. What William would do if his father didn't recover.

He shrugged his shoulders to rid himself of the cumbersome worries. "It feels good to be outside, doesn't it?"

Rebecca nodded. "July's my favorite month. There's something so comforting about the middle of summer. Old Sam always says that there's nothing like a warm day to soothe the soul. As usual, he's right."

William arched an inquisitive brow. "Does your soul need soothing?"

He noted a slight hesitation and frowned. Of course, she was going through difficult times of her own. And he was to blame. He had burdened her with Daniel's offer. And now Rebecca carried that burden on her own shoulders. William didn't deny that this offer had put a barrier between them. Yet, he felt the need to get it out in the open, hoping Rebecca would be able to offer advice as wise as Old Sam's.

But it was a dilemma without an easy solution. He wanted to erase the tension between them. But how?

She stepped into a dip in the ground and lost her balance.

He was quick to steady her. "Whoa. Are you okay?"

She laughed a little as she stopped and rubbed her ankle. She motioned to the ground. "I didn't see that coming."

As they continued their walk, William took in the beauty of the tall, leafy trees. They created in him an inner peace amid the turmoil he faced.

He lowered his voice so as not to disturb the silence. "It's beautiful property, isn't it?"

She nodded. In a soft tone, she responded, "Everything is lovely." She threw her hands in the air. "The land. The house. The kitchen. All of the rooms. I understand why Beth loves it here."

Rebecca's positive reply prompted a brave response. "Wouldn't you like to live here?"

From his peripheral vision, William noted the quick downturn of Rebecca's lips. Yet, he was glad he'd finally broached her with the question. Because it had been on his mind for some time.

"There's something missing."

They slowed their pace. He raised a curious brow. "Missing?"

"Jah. For me, anyway."

A long silence ensued while they continued down the hill. In the distance, the creek made a gurgling sound. The pleasant chirping of birds filled the air. A woodpecker attacked an oak tree. The sound echoed through the woods.

William waited for Rebecca to continue what she had started to say. When she didn't, he pressed the subject. He wanted to make sure she was at ease. And why wouldn't she be? The English life offered every comfort a person could ask for.

"Tell me what's missing."

She glanced up at the sky as she appeared to consider his question. "To be honest, as much as I love Beth and Daniel, I think what isn't here that's in Arthur is a kind of homespun goodness."

He laughed at the expression on her face when she said those two words.

"Homespun goodness? And what's that supposed to mean?"

She stopped to catch her breath. So did he. They glanced in the distance. An uneasy chill swept up William's back.

She turned to him and met his gaze. As they looked at each other, he swallowed. The reflection of the sun setting in the west highlighted some strands of Rebecca's hair.

He knew he would never tire of her large, beautiful eyes that always reflected goodness and kindness. He loved the rosy glow that colored her cheeks when she was outdoors. And her smile made his heart pick up its pace.

They were so close, he could feel the warmth of her breath. "Homespun goodness is like when Mamma hangs towels on the clothesline to dry, and the fresh smell fills the air. It's the sweet smell of butter while she stirs it in the crock. And the feeling I get when I walk into the kitchen to see her making cinnamon bread."

She rolled her eyes. "Just listen to me rattle on."

William swallowed. A combination of sadness and longing filled his chest and created a dull ache. For a moment, he was reminded of that wonderful sensation that passed through his veins when he would step into Aenti Sarah's kitchen and see her taking butterscotch pies from her gas oven.

"I'm sorry. I didn't mean to complain. Sometimes, I think it's the things so familiar to me that make me miss home."

"No apologies necessary. Sometimes I feel the same way."

"You do?"

He was quick to note her hopeful tone. "Of course. Don't you think I miss chatting with Aentie Sarah while she cooks?"

Rebecca nodded.

"And I miss hearing Uncle John grumble."

William looked down at his shoes a moment. When he lifted his gaze, he said, "I wish Dad lived in Arthur."

"He doesn't, William. And I don't think he ever will."

"I'm torn, Rebecca." He turned away. An unfamiliar emotion tugged at his heart.

She stepped in front of him. "I understand."

"It would have been better for both of us if Dad hadn't asked me to work with him. And it would have been best if I hadn't come here."

"Why?"

"Because I was exposed to a way of life that's prohibited to me."

William closed his eyes a moment. It felt good to admit his feelings. At the same time, the realization prompted huge regret.

"But it happened, William. And you'll make the right decisions. Keep praying."

In silence, they started walking again.

"There they are!" She pointed to the bushes.

The enthusiasm in Rebecca's voice was a pleasant contrast to the solemn thoughts in William's head. He smiled. "Looks like there are enough berries for ten pies."

Together, they knelt in front of the bushes and began picking, sharing the bucket between them. It wasn't long before the large metal pail was full.

As they began to make their way back to the house,

their elbows brushed. A smile tugged at William's lips. He was so lucky to have Rebecca.

He was also fortunate that his father thought enough of him to invite him to become his business partner. He wanted both.

In her room that evening, Rebecca once again thought about the three goals for the bishop. She had one. Outside, coyotes yelped. The screeching sound created an eerie tingle that sprinted up Rebecca's back and landed in her shoulders. She rolled them to rid herself of the unwanted sensation.

She yawned and pulled her scripture book from the hope chest. Rebecca stretched her legs in bed and rested her head on two pillows. She changed positions, but couldn't get comfortable. She continued to cross and uncross her legs and shift her weight from hip to hip.

She squeezed her eyes closed a moment and tried to convince herself everything would be okay. When she opened her lids, she shook her head in despair.

Before coming here, she had expected their stay to strengthen her bond with William. But to her dismay, outside circumstances pulled them in opposite directions.

She opened her prayer book to the marked page. The scripture in front of her was from the Psalms. Rebecca loved the Psalms. The passages comforted and reassured.

The deep need for scripture filled her while she read the passage out loud. "'I lift up my eyes to the hills—where does my help come from? My help comes from the Lord, the Maker of heaven and earth. He will not let your foot slip—he who watches over you will not slumber . . . The Lord watches over you—The Lord is your shade at your right hand; the sun will not harm you by day, nor the moon by night. The Lord will keep you from all harm—he will watch over your life; the Lord will watch over your coming and going both now and forevermore.'"

When Rebecca looked up, she imagined arranging her favorite flowers. Gardenias. Irises. Tulips. Baby's breath. As she envisioned the soft pastel colors, she could almost smell the light, sweet fragrances. See the green stems.

Maybe God had planted a purpose behind her dream. How could she serve Him and at the same time, fulfill her hopes? All at once, an idea came to her, and she sat up a little straighter.

A smile lifted her lips as she thought of the cheerful bouquets she could deliver to those who suffered. People like Daniel. She could do arrangements for those in need of cheer and kindness. Individuals like Beth, yearning for strength and peace.

Poor Beth. Rebecca certainly couldn't work miracles, but there must be a way to show support for William's stepmom and let her know she wasn't alone. A way to make Beth fully aware that God was there for her and assure her that she would survive this most difficult time.

Rebecca frowned. This wouldn't be easy. As she focused on her mission, she suddenly realized how very little she knew about Beth. She lived in a beautiful home, loved her husband, and she made Rebecca feel comfortable; but what were her strengths? Her fears?

Beth believed in God. That was definitely her

strongest point. Rebecca recalled the scripture about God being an ever-present help in trouble.

As Rebecca's dream flitted in and out of her thoughts, more details came to light. She envisioned a Christian floral shop.

Taking a determined breath, Rebecca decided to try her hand at her first project. And Beth would be the recipient. Her smile grew when a second idea popped into her mind. She would attach a short Bible verse to the plants. That would allow her the opportunity to show God's love through beauty and scripture.

Rebecca put down her book and swung both feet off the bed and onto the carpeted floor. The more she considered her idea, the more eager she was to start.

She possessed very little cash, but there was surely enough money to purchase a simple vase. Better, maybe Beth had one in a cabinet. Tomorrow, Rebecca would look.

As far as inventory, she was in luck. During her walk in the woods, she had noted numerous wild-flowers and cattails. Without a doubt, there were possibilities right in their backyard.

She took her diary from her hope chest and began writing. As usual, she jotted the date. Then she put her pen to paper.

I can't wait for tomorrow. Because I know my second goal. It's to brighten the world of people in need, with flowers. Suddenly, I feel like I have a greater sense of purpose. The bishop's request has inspired me to think more of others. I'll start with Beth.

* * *

July sixteenth was a day to celebrate. As William stepped outside of the house, he considered his father's sudden improvement. The doctors were encouraged. In fact, they had given William's dad orders to start light chores.

The house was decorated with banners of bright, colorful ribbon. The tantalizing aroma of pot roast floated through the house.

Rebecca's first floral arrangement was next to Daniel's bed. William had taken in the earthy smells of the colorful blooms that would certainly cheer anyone.

The news had brightened the Conrad home. William had never seen anyone as excited as Beth. She cried with relief every time someone mentioned her husband's unexpected progress. Her eyes had taken on a special light of happiness.

William darted a glance at Rebecca working in her garden. He stepped closer so they were within talking distance. He waved to get her attention.

"Dad and I are going for a walk. Want to come along?"

Rebecca smiled and gave a firm shake of her head. "I'd love to, but I've got work to do." She motioned to him. "Go on. I'll take a rain check."

William nodded in acceptance. He darted her a mischievous grin and glanced back at her. He knew her too well. She could come if she wanted. But his instincts told him that she refrained to allow him bonding time with his dad.

He shoved his hands deep into his pockets. Rebecca always thought of him. But William wished she'd join them. He still wasn't at ease with his father. For some reason, the father-son chemistry just wasn't there. Still, he yearned for it.

As William considered his business opportunity a pang of guilt welled in his chest. He ached for Rebecca as much as for himself. Did he deserve her?

Next to him, his father complained. "I don't know how they expect me to do this."

William took his dad's arm and urged him forward. Obviously, Daniel wasn't the best patient. And William wasn't accustomed to telling him what to do. However, under the circumstances, he'd have to take the lead.

"Remember what the docs said. Walking is the key to recovery. Heart patients who follow their doctor's orders come out winners. You're fortunate you're well enough to do this. And it's not like it's a lot to ask. Not today, anyway."

"Easy for you to say. It might not seem like much. But you haven't had a heart attack."

William rolled his eyes. "We won't go far." He stopped and squinted as he glanced down the road. "How about if we try and make it to that milepost?"

William motioned to the wooden post some distance ahead. The stake was on the Conrad property line.

Daniel frowned. "Do I have a choice?"

William shook his head.

"Everyone's telling me what to do these days. I make my own decisions." Daniel pointed a finger in the air and took small steps forward. "You're forgetting I've run my own company for years. A successful business, too. I can take care of myself."

"I know, Dad."

"Speaking of business, how is the Kreggses' order?"

William's lips lifted into a wide smile. "Finished. And they're happy."

"Glad to hear it. I want to keep Henry satisfied. That man runs every committee in the city. He'll bring me more work down the road."

"That should be the last thing on your mind right now. Concentrate on getting well. Without your health, you can't do anything." He paused. "It's great to see color back in your cheeks."

Their arms brushed as they continued. In the distance, a car turned onto a dirt road. A cloud of dust stirred and then slowly dissipated.

"I broke my back for this company. And heart attack or no heart attack, I'm not going to watch my efforts go down the tubes. You won't let that happen, will you?"

William lowered his voice. "Of course not, Dad."

"Keep it going for me. I'm counting on you, son. Soon, I'll be back to work. And you'll be my partner."

That last statement prompted William to bite his tongue. He considered the impact a partnership would have on him and Rebecca. What should he do?

His father assumed that he would commit. But William hadn't said one way or the other.

Obviously, Daniel was already counting on it. Initially, the offer had excited William. But he wasn't sure if Rebecca would move away from her family.

His dream of being a part of his dad's life had seemed about to materialize. It was what William had yearned for, for many years. But the more time he spent with his father, the more William realized how very distant their relationship was.

In fact, William wasn't sure he wanted to spend huge quantities of time with his dad. It was important to be accepted by him; yet William questioned if they could ever be close. They didn't have much in common.

To William's chagrin, the man next to him seemed cool and aloof. Of course, he didn't feel well. William took that into consideration.

As William glanced at his dad in his peripheral vision, he let out a small sigh. He prayed to make the right decision. There was no need to say anything to worry him. On the other hand, William couldn't afford to offer him false hope.

If that happened, the disappointment in the end would be even worse. William suddenly realized that his father was waiting for him to say something.

When he spoke, William's tone was gentle but firm. "I'm flattered by your offer, Dad. I really mean that. And I'm giving careful thought to it. There are things to consider before I let you know."

Irritation edged his dad's voice. "What's there to think on, son? I've offered you everything I've worked for. I'm handing you your inheritance on a plate."

An uneasy sensation trickled down William's spine. The last thing he wanted was an argument. Especially since his father was finally making progress.

William had never confronted such a situation. His mind drifted to Aenti Sarah. He imagined discussing the partnership with her while she worked on her quilt. How would she suggest handling this dilemma?

Unfortunately, no answer came. William was grateful for the tractor that interrupted them. As the driver waved, William and his dad stepped to the side of the road to allow the red machine to pass.

He yearned to talk to Aenti Sarah. He wanted to

ask her if it was fair for his dad to expect his answer to be yes, when his dad hadn't been around during the critical years of William's life. He was sure her answer would be no.

A tense silence ensued as they continued their walk. In the distance, the sun took on brilliant colors. The hues were so rich, William was sure even the best artist couldn't capture them.

But he couldn't change the past. And he certainly didn't want his dad to suffer a setback. He tried a conciliatory tone. "I'd love to be partners. But it's not my decision alone. Rebecca and I are considering it. Her happiness is important to me."

The lack of response told William that his dad was disappointed.

William spoke tactfully. "I'm flattered you've asked me. But moving out of state is a big decision for both of us. We've always planned on living around her family. And you know Aenti Sarah and Uncle John . . . They'd miss me. Aenti Sarah counts on me to help her out."

"But I'm your father. And Rebecca's the type of girl who would want what's best for you. At first, she might be shy to the idea, but eventually she'll come around." He paused. "A woman's place is with her husband, son. She'll be okay. Besides, Illinois is just a hop, skip, and a jump from Indiana."

William chuckled. "Not by horse and buggy."

"Get a license."

"I thought you wanted me to stay Amish."

Daniel paused. "I did. But now it's time to think of me."

Chapter Ten

The following morning, Rebecca smiled as the light floated gracefully in through the large kitchen skylight. She blinked at the bright ray.

The creamy white walls took on a different shade. The dark grain in the granite countertops sparkled.

Rebecca figured the warm feeling in her heart was due to two things. She'd always loved the natural warmth from the sun and the way it lifted her spirits. The sun was God's way of telling her He'd take care of her.

But today, there was another reason to give thanks to the Lord. The doctors believed Daniel was on the upswing. He wasn't running marathons. Nor was he back in the shop.

But they were convinced that in the near future, Daniel would return to what he loved to do. Rebecca prayed that would be the case.

In the meantime, she would continue helping the Conrads. The housekeeper would be back from vacation next week. It was nice having Daniel home in more ways than one. William was more upbeat and confident. And Beth's smile was back on her face. She was more talkative and positive.

As Rebecca scooped a large helping of scrambled eggs from a skillet and slid them onto a plate, William appeared in the doorway. For a moment, she glanced at him before focusing on the job at hand. "Morning."

"Morning." He came up behind her. "Did Beth hire you to cook?"

She shook her head. "I volunteered. She's with Daniel. I'm giving her a hand."

William's eyes sparkled with affection. His expression alone could give her all she needed to make it through the day. She didn't doubt that William's love could get her through the toughest storm.

She put down her spatula and faced him. Joy emanated from his eyes. Since they'd been in Indiana, she'd missed that sparkle.

He held her at arm's length. "I haven't thanked you enough for your efforts."

Rebecca dipped her head. The pleasure's mine. And I think I've benefited as much as your folks. I've learned a lot about myself."

Curiosity edged his voice. "Oh?"

She motioned to the table. "Let's sit down and enjoy Katie's fresh eggs. I'm starved. And if we don't eat right away, breakfast will get cold."

As they drank orange juice, William asked, "Tell me what you've learned."

Rebecca peppered her eggs. She returned the shaker to the middle of the table and smiled in satisfaction as she took a bite and swallowed.

"I'm more open-minded."

"You mean you've accepted the way my folks live?"

"Yes. Is it for me?" She shook her head. "But it's fine for them. I make it a point not to judge others."

She let out a breath. "What I'm trying to say is that I've been exposed to a much different life than my own. But that's a good thing, William."

"Why do you think that?"

"Because meeting new friends and exposure to different ways are healthy. As a result, I've grown emotionally and intellectually."

When she looked at William for a reaction, he didn't respond.

"Oh, William. There's so much to tell."

He glanced at the clock on the wall and winked. "I've got time."

Rebecca turned toward him as she spread grape jelly on her whole wheat toast. "For starters, God chooses people of all faiths to serve Him."

"Are you talking about Beth?"

Rebecca gave a decisive nod. "Beth is a good wife to Daniel. She doesn't practice her faith like we do, but that's okay because their church has different . . ." Rebecca pursed her lips as she searched for the right word.

"Guidelines?"

She nodded.

"That makes sense. And they have a great life." William grinned. "I've thought a lot about Uncle John and Aenti Sarah. They're missing out."

"William!"

"Even you've admitted there's nothing wrong with different practices. I'm sorry, but it won't be easy going to bed every night without watching ESPN. And air-conditioning helps me sleep better."

Rebecca tried to find her voice. She couldn't.

"Rebecca, I know how strongly you feel about our faith. But surely you could get used to this."

Rebecca's heartbeat picked up speed as she contemplated the comment she'd pretty much expected.

She looked down, hoping to drop the subject.

But he persisted. "Think about it, Rebecca. You've confessed your love of Beth's Whirlpool."

Rebecca took a last bite of eggs, but no longer tasted them. "I admit to enjoying these comforts. But like I've said, underneath it all, I'm a loyal Amish girl at heart. I can't betray everything my parents taught me."

The smile on William's face dropped. "It all boils down to how we're raised, doesn't it?"

Rebecca pondered the statement and shrugged. "Perhaps. But, William, practicing faith takes discipline."

"I guess I'm starting to wonder why Aenti Sarah can't enjoy Beth's conveniences. If they both believe in God, what makes it wrong for my aunt to have an easier life?"

"I can't answer that, William. But it takes a strong person to do what he thinks is right. Just because we enjoy something doesn't mean we should have it."

After a lengthy pause, he shrugged. "You've got a point. Being Amish was obviously important to Mom. But look at how Dad changed. And he doesn't appear to regret it."

"I can't speak for Daniel. I can only tell you how I feel. I understand why you want your aunt to have it easier. There's no better woman than Sarah. I admire her for being who she is."

Rebecca and William regarded each other in silence. All of a sudden, they burst into laughter.

"Just listen to us," William said.

Rebecca grinned. "Next time we're that serious, we have to eat Martha Wagler's pie!"

They laughed.

Afterwards, they sat in silence. Again, the same conflict haunted Rebecca. She knew William loved his aunt. That he would give her the world if he could.

"William, don't forget your roots. They've made you what you are."

"You'll join the Amish church, won't you?"

She gave a confident nod. But inside, she shook like a leaf. Both she and William had been hit with the same bullets when they'd come here.

Rebecca's faith had grown stronger. However, the transition had caused William to question his. Rebecca had to do something. But what?

"I'm only happy with you, William." She lowered her voice to a more confidential tone. "Do you still want to marry me?"

"Of course."

"Even if my dream is to raise an Amish family?"

"Yup. We'll live in Arthur with your folks. Like we planned. Rebecca, I want you to be happy. There's nothing more important to me. And if that means moving back home"—he shrugged—"then so be it."

His admission should have eased her mind. But she wasn't at all relaxed because in her heart, she knew William really preferred to live like his father.

She cleared her throat. "What about Daniel? Have you given him an answer?"

He hesitated. "Not yet. He still wants me to be his partner."

"And you'd love that."

William nodded. "But like you said, we can't always have what we want. I'll give that up for you."

If Rebecca deprived him of joining Daniel, how could she justify her selfishness? Would God approve?

"William, I'm torn."

He stretched his legs. "I know. And I feel guilty for putting you in this position."

She reached over and laid a gentle hand on his.

He scooted his chair closer. "I wish this had never happened."

"What?"

"Dad's heart attack. Leaving Arthur. I would have been better off to never have seen how he lives. Then I wouldn't be tempted."

Rebecca softened her voice. "William, coming here isn't the problem."

"Of course it is."

She shook her head. "It's what I told you earlier. Ignorance is bliss. But it doesn't make us grow."

A skeptical look swept across his face.

"These changes force us to think."

They regarded each other in silence. Rebecca went on. "If God hadn't planted us in another environment, we wouldn't have come across new knowledge. Our belief wasn't tested because we hadn't been challenged."

He gave a sad shake of his head. "Just look at all of the temptations God has shown us. Giving them up won't be easy."

In the shop the following morning, William went through paperwork and crossed off four more orders.

There was good and bad news. His father's business was on track. Revenues were coming in for the deliveries. And new orders were constantly placed.

The bad news was just how serious he was about living like the English. Permanently. As he contemplated his situation, the whirling ceiling fans made a light whistling sound. The strong odor of varnish filled the air. In the distance, a worker swept a pile of sawdust and scooped it into a plastic bag.

William would never forget the uncertainty he'd felt before coming to Indiana. At that time, he couldn't wait for his stint at the Conrad business to be finished. He'd never dreamed how tempted he'd be to leave the Amish faith.

He was comfortable with his new lifestyle. In fact, he really didn't want to return to the old. He bit his lip at that thought. He should be ashamed of himself. And he was.

Yet he could no longer deny a longing so deep inside of him. He wanted his children to have what he should have had growing up. He'd been raised to believe that the Amish life was simple. But he knew of an easier life. The English way. In fact, there was nothing difficult about it. At the tips of his fingers lay so many amenities, they became nothing more than a blur. In frustration, he tried to focus on the papers in front of him. His father would be proud of the accomplishments that had been thought impossible when William and Rebecca had first arrived in Indiana over a month ago.

The grinding of saw blades interrupted his thoughts. He reached for the handheld calculator and added the numbers in the right-hand column. Closing the cover on the paperwork, he let out a low whistle. His father would be darn proud of him and Rebecca.

The business was making a grand profit. He should be happy. William stood and frowned. Hooking his fingers over his pockets, he stared down at the tips of his black shoes.

His inner turmoil wasn't about money. Nor was it about his relationship with his father. An even deeper issue stirred within him. He loved Rebecca. At the same time, he wanted to live like the English. But he knew that convincing her to leave the faith that was so dear to her was impossible.

William had changed. Could his relationship with Rebecca survive?

With a happy sigh, Rebecca ran a dishrag across the sparkling granite. The kitchen smelled of cleaning agents. Beth was in the basement getting peaches from the freezer. Time to go outside. Rebecca stepped to the front hall. But as soon as she opened the door, she stopped.

Her breath caught in her throat as she looked at the note sticking out from under the mat. Tears stung her eyes as she tried to stay calm. But composure was out of the question when she recognized the neat printing with her name on it. With shaky hands, she pulled the note from the envelope.

She wasn't surprised at the message because she'd seen it before. *Go home.*

But there was an additional threat. A hand-drawn picture of an old-fashioned coffin. On the side were two letters. *R. S.*

* * *

In tears, Rebecca nearly stumbled as she ran to the shop.

Inside, she spotted William and rushed to him. She handed him the note. In silence, he looked at it and placed a comforting hand on her shoulder.

As she regarded him in silence, his eyes filled with a combination of concern and anger. "Another warning."

She nodded.

"Where did you find this?"

She spilled her story as tears slid down her cheeks. The drawing stepped up the seriousness of the threat to a much higher level.

"Why is this happening to me? Why does someone want me to leave? And who?"

She caught her breath and explained what had happened. "It was at the door."

He motioned. "Show me where."

Without waiting, she led him to the front entrance of the home where they stopped at the steps and turned when they heard a voice.

Beth's jaw dropped as she looked at Rebecca. "What on earth is wrong?"

Rebecca related the news and showed her the note and the drawing. She didn't want to concern Beth, but had no choice. Rebecca's life was in jeopardy.

"I'm calling the police."

Within twenty minutes, the cops arrived. Outside, an officer asked questions while the other filled out a report.

"Do you have any idea who would do this?" Beth's voice was edged with concern as she directed her attention to the uniformed men.

"No. Any idea when this was left?"

Beth thought a moment. "Within the past few hours."

The officer clipped his pen to the report and looked at Rebecca with a skeptical brow. "Did you tick someone off?"

Rebecca shook her head. She wanted to tell him about Natalie, but didn't. Because Natalie hadn't done anything to her that could be considered a threat, and it wasn't right to bring her name into the ugly story unless Rebecca could prove that Natalie was behind it.

The officer nodded. "It could be someone playing a sick joke. On the other hand, maybe it's for real. In either case, be careful."

"We will," William promised. Beth nodded in agreement.

After the officers left, Beth put a reassuring arm around Rebecca. "Only an unstable person would leave a drawing of a coffin at our door."

"I'm sorry."

Beth and William looked at Rebecca in surprise. "For what?"

"For causing you to worry. I hope Daniel didn't see the cop car. I couldn't bear for him to suffer another heart attack because of me."

"Don't blame yourself, dear."

Rebecca watched the police vehicle disappear. When she thought of the coffin, a cold, eerie chill crept up her spine and landed at the base of her neck. She rolled her shoulders, but the feeling remained.

William frowned. "I can't imagine who would do something like this." He raised an inquisitive brow at Rebecca. "Remember what you told me about Natalie?"

Rebecca gave a quick nod.

William turned to Beth. "You know her better than we do. Would she do something like this?"

When Beth's jaw dropped in surprise, Rebecca related the conversation she'd had with Henry's daughter. "It sounds trivial, doesn't it?"

"You've met other people since you've been here. Like the workers in Daniel's shop. Have you argued with anyone?"

"I had a small disagreement with the girl named Janet over something small."

"What was it?"

"Whether or not to add more stain to a cabinet. I've also asked her to keep her station cleaner."

William sighed. "That's certainly no reason to threaten you."

"No."

"I can't imagine Natalie would be so jealous as to do something like this." Beth's voice was thoughtful as she waved a hand to shoo a gnat that flew around her ear.

William took Rebecca's hand. "Let's go inside. We're taking the rest of the day off."

As soon as they turned, Daniel stood in front of them. "What's going on?"

* * *

In her room, Rebecca collected a small coin purse. As she gathered her belongings, she thought of the coffin drawing she'd found just awhile ago, and worried about William and his parents.

Although the warning had been addressed to her, it wasn't just about her. She didn't want anything to threaten their security. Daniel had seen the police, and Beth had explained what had happened. Of course, the incident had upset him.

She stepped down the stairs where William waited.

She forced a smile. "I'm glad we're spending the afternoon together. Are you sure the shop can do without us?"

He held up a confident hand. "It will have to." He looked at her hands and frowned. "You're shaking."

She drew in a deep breath. "I'm still in shock."

"That's exactly why we're spending time together, Rebecca. What would you like to do?" He reworded the question. "What would help you relax?"

She shrugged. "I'd love to forget about the threat."

"Me too. But we can't ignore what happened." He paused. "How 'bout we discuss it later?"

She nodded in agreement.

"It's a nice day. And it's ours. Now . . ."

Rebecca raised a quizzical brow. "I have something in mind. But I'm afraid it's not your cup of tea."

Outside, as William proceeded to Beth's car, he came face-to-face with his father. Before William could even say hi, his dad took him by the shoulders. "Son, we've got to get Rebecca out of here."

William caught his breath. "You mean, send her back to Arthur?"

Daniel nodded. "ASAP."

"Why? She hasn't done anything wrong."

Daniel shook his head. "We can't have this kind of thing going on at our house. It puts us all in jeopardy."

Heat rushed to William's face. He raised his voice a notch. "It's not her fault. Why should she be punished?"

Daniel released his hold on William. "It's for her own good, son. We've got to protect her. Isn't it obvious that it's too dangerous for her to stay? As much as we'd like to, we can't watch over her twenty-four-seven. And we certainly wouldn't want anything to happen."

William crossed his hands over his chest. "No, but do you really care if she's safe?"

"Why wouldn't I be concerned about her? She's the woman you plan to marry. Of course I want her to be okay."

William swallowed. "But do you really, truly care about her? Rebecca's a wonderful woman. She didn't have to leave her family to help you, but she did. And she came with the genuine hope of saving your business."

Daniel nodded. "I know."

William's voice cracked with emotion. "You've never loved me, Dad. But I want you to care about Rebecca. It's important to me that you treat her like a daughter. And I think sending her home is too harsh. Instead, why don't you press to find out who's threatening her? Offer a reward or something. Don't you want to know who's responsible?"

Daniel let out a frustrated sigh. "Of course. But in the meantime, what if something happens to her? Can Rebecca be happy living here, knowing that someone wants her dead?"

Not long after the conversation with his dad, William watched in amusement as Rebecca shopped in It Can Be Arranged in Evansville. Beth seemed quite fond of the place as she'd gone on about its arrangements and items that were unique to this particular floral shop.

When they stepped inside, William took in the vast array of arrangements. There were live plants. Dried and silk flowers. Balloons. But there were also specialties that Beth had commented on. Gifts from all over the United States. Pottery. Metalware. Printed umbrellas. Displays.

It hadn't taken William long to figure out to leave Rebecca alone to look around. For something to do, he stepped inside of the cooler room and took in the arrangements as well as the single flowers. He looked around and nodded satisfaction.

"Brr." He wrapped his hands around his waist.

As he breathed in sweet, fresh fragrances, he closed his eyes in pleasure for a moment. Rebecca was right. There was something calming and reassuring about plants.

Maybe that's why Rebecca loved growing them. Perhaps that's why his father enjoyed the garden from his bedroom window. William remembered how Aenti Sarah liked to pamper the deep red roses in her backyard.

William stepped back into the main area and closed the door behind him.

"Can I help you?"

"No, thanks." William motioned with his hand. "I'm waiting on the ladies."

The worker offered a nod and proceeded to inventory flowers.

For something to do, William glanced at the small cards attached to vases that were obviously ready for delivery.

They were for weddings. Funerals. Baby congratulations. Get-well bouquets. He took in the combination of bright and subtle petals, glancing with curiosity at some dried roses while he recalled a conversation he'd had once with Rebecca. She dried her flowers upside down, and she'd commented that the hotter the place, the quicker the dry and the more beautiful the hues.

He noticed Beth talking with a clerk who was transplanting a green palm. It hadn't taken much to convince her to drive them into town.

A lady scurried to the register to ring up an order for a customer. But William's attention stayed on Beth. He regarded her thoughtfully.

She appeared to be well-respected by others. Several people in the shop had greeted her and had inquired about his father. William had caught bits and pieces of her explanation of his dad's struggle to get well.

Before he'd come to Indiana, he'd barely known Beth. Worse, he'd hardly known his father. But he remembered his mom. He wished he owned just one picture of the woman who'd been everything to him. Of course, as an Amish woman, she would never have allowed her photograph to be taken. The only images he would ever have of her were in his mind.

As he drifted back in time, he could hear the upbeat tone in her voice. When William had complained about small things, she'd always pointed out the positive and had told him to make the best of what he had. That things could be worse. Her reassurance had always made things okay.

He stood very still and frowned at the tightness in his chest. He finally understood why his dad loved Beth. She, too, had a positive outlook. She also smiled a lot. He liked her laugh.

But she'd never, ever replace his mother. Besides, Beth had caused William to miss out on a life with his father. How could he be close to her?

William bit his lip as he silently chastised himself for thinking negative thoughts. Aenti Sarah would be disappointed in him. So would his mom. But William knew she'd also be disappointed in the man who had deserted William.

A loud noise made him jump. He turned to two women laughing as they pumped air into decorative balloons. The red one had popped.

William's heart beat at a faster pace because of his concern that something could happen to Rebecca. He stuck his hands deep into his pockets. As he glanced at Rebecca, he realized why his mother's death suddenly haunted him.

He was worried about losing Rebecca. He'd always

expected her to be there for him and had taken her love for granted. But what would he do without her?

There was only one solution to the threat on her life. To send Rebecca home.

Chapter Eleven

While Beth and Daniel were at the doctor, Rebecca took advantage of the time alone to create another arrangement. She smiled as she breathed in the sweet, fresh fragrance of the light green eucalyptus branches and stuck them into the sky-blue glass vase. The soft colors blended well with the small cream-colored petals of the baby's breath.

She smiled in satisfaction. Not only because her new project was exciting, but because she'd finally decided on her third goal. It was to bond William and his father. She'd known all along that she'd wanted this; however, the stakes were higher now because she'd set out to mend their relationship, even if it meant losing William. Risking their future made this objective the most difficult of the three.

It was an ambitious goal and difficult to accomplish, but the bishop's request hadn't been intended for easy tasks. By undertaking such an endeavor, she would be reaching for the clouds. But she prayed for help. With God, anything was possible. With Him on her side, she had no doubt that she could move the world.

She heard William's voice and turned. With a nod of approval, he glanced at her project. "It's beautiful."

"Thanks."

"You're amazing." He whistled. "You made this out of those flowers from the shop?"

She nodded. "I've had a little practice."

He arched a curious brow.

"In Old Sam's barn."

"Oh. So that's what you do while he works on his hope chests."

Rebecca nodded with a smile.

He touched a finger to one of the leaves. "Who's it for?"

"Beth."

"Really?"

Rebecca kept her attention on the stems in front of her. She played with them until they looked just right. "This is to encourage and cheer her. She's gone through such a difficult time. The uncertainty of Daniel's condition has been tough. I just want Beth to keep her faith."

Rebecca glanced up at him and smiled. "Hopefully, this will be the right medicine."

William came around to stand opposite her. His smile faltered. The expression in his eyes turned serious.

Rebecca stopped what she was doing. "What's wrong?"

William hesitated and looked down at his shoes as if studying them.

Rebecca waited for an answer. But she suspected

what he was about to say was something she didn't want to hear.

"I've been thinking about yesterday's threat. And the other warning."

She grimaced. A sour feeling filled her stomach until it ached. She'd struggled to put the unpleasant messages out of her mind and concentrate on the good in her life. But as much as she tried to ignore them, they were there.

He took her hands in his. They were cold. The chill spread up her arms and landed in her shoulders. She tensed.

"I'm worried about you, Rebecca. So is Beth. Daniel, too. What happened kept him up the entire night."

"Oh no."

William nodded. "Before we left Arthur, I promised your father I'd look out for you. I'm going to keep that commitment. We're both here to help Dad, but first and foremost, my job is to make sure you're safe."

Rebecca smiled a little. The words comforted her a bit, and the cold sensation began to go away. She rolled her shoulders to relieve the tension.

"As much as I'd like you to stay, the smart thing for you to do right now is to go home."

For a few moments, she was speechless. After giving his statement some thought, she raised her chin and moved her hands to her hips. As she shifted her stance, she remembered her three goals. They were decided. But not accomplished. How could she leave without fulfilling the bishop's expectation of her?

"I can't go. Not yet. You need me. So do Beth and Daniel."

"We'll have to do without you. I won't let anything happen to you, Rebecca. Maybe the letter was a joke; maybe not. In either case, we can't risk it."

She straightened and raised her chin. "I won't allow someone to force me to leave, William. It's not right. Besides, if that person's not even strong enough to warn me to my face, do you think they're brave enough to actually harm me?"

He shrugged. "I don't know."

Rebecca frowned.

William slipped his arms around her and kissed her forehead. "Rebecca, just because you leave doesn't mean you can't come back. For now, there's no other choice. You're much too important to me to take chances. Don't you know I'd be devastated if I lost you?"

He hesitated before continuing. "You're all I have."

As their gazes locked, Rebecca felt his shaky hands on her waist. At that instant, she knew William was afraid. An eerie chill crept up her spine.

When he spoke again, his voice was low and serious. "Please, Rebecca. Tell me you'll leave."

The following morning, Rebecca lifted the hem of her dress and used the two metal steps to get inside of Katie's buggy. Today was the last time she'd be with her friend. At least, for a while. Katie needed to do errands.

Tomorrow, Rebecca would return to Arthur. Beth had already arranged for Rebecca's transportation.

She told Katie about the threat and that Rebecca had finally agreed with Daniel and William. She was no longer safe at the Conrad place.

As Katie took the reins, the horse threw its head back with an impatient snort and stepped in place.

"I'll miss you," Katie said as she closed the door. "But honestly . . ."

Rebecca gave her a curious glance. "What?"

"I'm convinced that going home is for the best."

"You are?"

Katie gave a convincing nod. "That way, you'll be safe." She paused. "I'm sure William will miss you, but hopefully, he'll join you soon."

"That's what I'd like. Of course, he can't leave until Daniel's back on his feet." Rebecca gave a frustrated shake of her head. "Daniel has sure had a hard time of it."

"Any sign of improvement?"

"Jah."

"So when do you leave?"

"Tomorrow."

"Aren't you looking forward to seeing your family?"

"Of course. But I don't like being forced out. I make my own decisions. To be honest, I have huge regrets."

"Oh?"

Rebecca told her about the three goals. "I didn't accomplish them."

"What are they?"

Rebecca ticked them off.

"Well . . . I'd say you've done the first. You've definitely been a support to Beth. And you've got your whole life to help others."

Rebecca glanced at Katie. "But I didn't do the

most important one. I pray every night for William and Daniel to be close. It wouldn't be right for William to go through life looking back and focusing on what could have been. I want him to move forward and make the most of the time he has left with his father. It's only right."

"Don't you think you're asking too much of yourself? You can't make miracles happen."

"No, but I can do my best. I'm not a quitter. The bishop will be disappointed in me."

"I doubt that. Sometimes, circumstances prevent us from having what we want. In this case, there's just too much unknown. But God knows best, Rebecca. He'll guide you."

Rebecca nodded as they turned a corner. "I trust Him. Daniel could suffer a setback."

Rebecca closed her eyes and prayed in silence. *Please, God. Help William to forgive Daniel.* Help them to be close.

When she opened her lids, she relaxed a bit. Even with her struggles, God was still an ever-present force in her life. The evidence was all around.

She took in the breathtaking sky decorated with white fluffy clouds. Tall evergreens that scented the outdoors. A squirrel running in front of them. Beautiful purple and yellow wildflowers springing up beside the road.

Rebecca's thoughts drifted back to their conversation, and she questioned if leaving was really the right thing to do. She wasn't completely convinced it was.

Katie's horse slowed its gait. Within a matter of minutes, they were at the post office. With practiced ease, Katie parked the buggy under the canopy outside and tied her horse to the pole.

She glanced at Rebecca. "I won't be long."

Rebecca waved a hand in dismissal. "No rush."

As she watched Katie disappear around the corner, she let out a sigh of relief. God would help her bond William and Daniel. And He would keep her safe.

At that thought, she glimpsed the corner of a cream-colored envelope between the door and the front mat. Katie had dropped one of her letters. Rebecca quickly bent to retrieve it. But as her hand touched the envelope, she stopped and drew in a quick breath.

She stared at it. There was nothing unusual about the address and stamp. What drew Rebecca's attention was the special marking in the bottom left-hand corner. She'd noticed it before when she'd received the two threats.

But that wasn't all she'd seen on those two frightening occasions. The neat hand printing also struck a familiar chord. It was eerily similar to the printing on her warnings. She stiffened. Her heart pounded as hard as a jackhammer.

Envelope in hand, she plopped back in her seat and stared straight ahead. She barely noticed Katie's horse as she sifted through the facts.

Had Katie threatened her? Rebecca shook her head. No way. Why on earth would Katie want Rebecca gone? Rebecca's hands shook as she tried for an answer. None came. She thought of the worry caused by those ugly warnings.

They had kept Rebecca awake late into the night.

She'd prayed for God to keep her safe from whoever hated her so much.

In the end, those awful threats were the reason she'd finally agreed to return to Arthur before her mission in Indiana was accomplished. Was Katie responsible?

An eternity seemed to pass as that potent, unanswered question haunted Rebecca. In a daze, she continued staring at the emblem and the print. She drew the envelope closer and squinted to get a better look.

But she knew it by memory. The emblem was permanently imprinted in her mind. And the longer she tried to deny the obvious, the faster her heart beat.

She had to find the truth. Needed to know if Katie had indeed been the sender.

Rebecca would ask her. Suddenly, she realized she was clutching the envelope in a death grip. Her fingers ached. She relaxed her hold.

She and Katie were alone. Was a confrontation wise? *If* Katie was responsible, and *if* Rebecca confronted her, would Katie harm her?

After careful thought, Rebecca decided that because they were in a public place, she shouldn't worry. But if anything happened, Rebecca would scream for help.

Why on earth would Katie want her to leave? They hadn't argued. As Rebecca tried for an answer, Katie suddenly appeared from around the corner.

As she walked to the buggy, she waved and met Rebecca's gaze with a wide smile. Confused, Rebecca glanced again at her find and started to return it to where she'd discovered it.

Instead, she held on to it. There was no reason to pretend she hadn't found it. As Katie stepped inside of the buggy, Rebecca turned to her.

"I did my errands."

As Katie slammed her door closed, Rebecca studied her. As soon as Katie turned to her, her smile quickly slipped into a look of surprise when she noticed the envelope in Rebecca's hand.

It was time to get answers.

While Rebecca was with Katie, William helped to steady his dad as he stepped to the front door. Daniel stopped.

"Are you okay?"

With a half smile, Daniel gave a slight nod. "I'm not up to running a marathon, but for the time being, I'll be satisfied with being half a man."

William frowned. "Half a man? Don't say that."

"Why not?"

William shrugged. "Because it's not true."

Daniel gave a frustrated shake of his head. "William, one of my problems in the past was that I wasn't brave enough to communicate with you."

Tears sparkled in the fragile-looking man's eyes as he looked at William. "Your old man never liked to talk about things he didn't want to deal with. And look what happened. From now on, that's going to change."

He motioned to the wooden porch swing. "Let's sit down. I need to clear the air about some things."

Without responding, William joined him on the bench. Their elbows brushed. Sitting side by side gave William a feeling of closeness and reassurance. For the first time in years, he felt a strange and wonderful sense of security.

As they rocked back and forth, the iron chains holding the swing to the roof of the patio creaked. The wooden boards felt hard against William's back. His father's tone was serious. Something was wrong.

He rested a shaky hand on William's thigh and took a deep breath while he glanced at William. "I guess I've got to start somewhere. My apologies for not being the father you deserved, William."

A stressful silence ensued while William waited for his dad to go on.

"They say hindsight's twenty-twenty. Now I see things more clearly than ever." He shook his head and lowered his voice. "I should never have left you. If I could do it again, I would have brought you with me."

William digested the words. "But Mom—"

"I know that Miriam expected you to grow up Amish. That went without saying." He shrugged. "But sometimes, we have to make judgment calls." He hesitated. "Instead of hating me like you should, you came here and made sure my business survived. I don't deserve you."

The admission made William's jaw drop in surprise. He stared at his feet as they moved with the swing. "I could never hate you, Dad. That's not to say I haven't been upset."

Suddenly, William lifted his gaze to stare into the sunset. His voice was hoarse as he drifted back to a time that he would rather forget. "When Mom died, I missed her so much. I cried every night and prayed for God to bring her back to me. Then, you left. I waited for you to come and get me." William shook his head sadly. "It didn't happen. I couldn't believe I'd lost both of you. I thought no one wanted me. That God was telling me I wasn't important enough to be loved. It was so hard."

Daniel blew his nose. William turned and saw that his father's eyes had filled with tears. The color had drained from his face. He looked so old.

William nudged his arm. "Please don't cry, Dad."

"What a mess I've made. I loved your mother so much. I thought I was strong. That I could handle everything myself. I had the world at my doorstep until she died. When I lost her, I turned to mush. Didn't think I'd survive."

William lowered his voice. "But you had me. Didn't I count?"

Daniel regained his composure and cleared his throat. "Son, at that time, Miriam was everything to me. I didn't want to live without her. I'm ashamed to admit that I even blamed God for taking her."

William sat quietly and listened.

"When I met Beth, she wiped away some of my pain." He paused. "But you know what?"

William met his gaze. "What?"

"Even with Beth, as wonderful as she is, I never got over losing your mother."

"You mean you don't love Beth?"

"Of course, I do." Daniel hesitated. "But Miriam was my first love. We grew up together. And even though I did what I was sure she would have wanted,

I let her down. There's no way I can make up the years that you were alone. But I can be good to you in the future. Will you let me try, son?"

William swallowed. He nodded. "Of course."

Daniel dabbed at his eyes with his tissue. "I want a good life for you. Don't make the mistakes I made."

Suddenly, William felt uneasy. "Dad, why are you telling me this now?"

Daniel crossed his arms over his chest. "Let's just say I've had a lot of time to think. Son, I might not be able to continue my business. As you're aware, running the shop takes a lot of work and time." He shrugged. "I know the docs are happy with my progress, but reality is, I'm not sure if I'll ever get the strength to keep the routine I used to."

After a lengthy pause, he sighed. "I'm giving it to you."

William pressed his lips together in a straight, thoughtful line. Had he heard his father correctly? He turned and looked him in the eyes.

As if reading his thoughts, his dad gave a firm nod.

While William considered the statement, Daniel laughed a little. "At least I have something to offer. It can't make up for the years we were without each other, but you'll have a comfortable living. That's more than a lot of people have."

William's thoughts automatically floated to Rebecca and her dream of growing old with her family. *In Illinois.*

He cleared his throat. "Dad, I appreciate your offer. But I can't give you an answer. Not today, anyway. Like I said, a decision this big has to be made between

Rebecca and me. And we haven't decided whether or not to move to Indiana."

Daniel nodded. "I understand."

"Rebecca's very generous. I think she would do whatever makes me happy."

"Then what's the problem?"

"Her dream is to grow old with her family. To raise our children around their cousins, aunts and uncles." He sighed. "How can I rob her of that?"

Daniel shrugged. "I've noticed how you've conformed to our way of life. And I don't blame you for that. But now that you're an adult, you can make your own choices."

Daniel looked down at his folded hands. "Surely you've seen that there's life outside Arthur, Illinois. And you certainly don't have to be Amish to be a Christian. Believing in God is what's important. There's no need to live without electricity, William."

William couldn't think of a response.

"What I'm trying to say is that I'm giving you permission to leave the Amish life."

So many decisions cluttered William's mind, he couldn't think. What he wanted wasn't best for Rebecca.

"William?"

The swing came to a stop. For long, tense moments, William and Daniel sat in silence. Finally, Daniel put a hand on William's shoulder. They regarded each other.

"Son, I don't want to rush you. There's a lot to think about. Like you said, you don't have to make a decision today."

"Yeah, Dad. I'll sleep on it and pray to make the right choice."

Daniel smiled a little. "Whatever you do, know your old man loves you."

"I love you, too."

William hugged his father. At the same time, Daniel's arms came around him like a security blanket. William savored the comforting feeling. He closed his lids.

Finally, he'd heard the words he'd yearned to hear for years. He had what he wanted. His father's love.

As Katie got comfortable in the buggy, Rebecca turned to her. "There's something I need to ask you."

Katie smiled as she laid her purse between them. "Go ahead."

Rebecca lifted her chin and squared her shoulders. "Did you threaten me to go home?"

Rebecca noticed the fast rise and fall of Katie's chest. Several moments passed while Rebecca awaited a response.

When there was none, Rebecca flashed the envelope in front of her. "I found this on the floor." She pointed to the emblem on the bottom corner.

The guilty look in Katie's eyes said everything. A rush that was a combination of sadness and disappointment swept through Rebecca's entire body like a bolt of lightning.

"What about it?"

Rebecca lowered her voice to barely more than a whisper. "I think you know."

"Surely other people must own stationery like that."

"With this emblem?"

Katie fidgeted.

"Katie, be honest. You're the one behind the warnings, aren't you?"

Moisture glistened in Katie's eyes. She spoke in an apologetic tone. "I sent them, Rebecca."

Rebecca leaned toward the girl next to her. She gripped the envelope and waved it in the air. "Why? I thought you were my friend."

A sheepish look covered Katie's face as she looked down at the floor and sighed in defeat. All the while, Rebecca tried to accept what she'd just discovered.

Katie raised her chin to meet Rebecca's gaze. "William was influenced by the English ways. I was so afraid you'd decide to not join the church. So"— she shrugged—"I took matters into my own hands, Rebecca. I didn't know what else to do."

At a loss for words, Rebecca stared at the woman she'd considered a friend.

Katie's voice cracked with emotion. "I saw bad things happening, Rebecca. I believed the Conrads were pulling you in the wrong direction. I know that you assured me you'd never leave the faith. But I knew the only way to ensure that was to force you to move back home. That way, everything would be okay."

She paused and seemed to collect herself. "I did it for your own good."

Throwing her arms protectively over her chest, Rebecca gasped. "*For my own good?* Do you know how frightened I was? How you worried the Conrad family? My goodness, Katie! You put extra stress on Daniel's heart. You threw our lives into disarray."

Katie stuttered. "I-I didn't realize . . ."

"For heaven sake, you left me a drawing of a casket! I was afraid for my life."

Moisture sprang to Katie's eyes. "Rebecca, I didn't mean to cause so much heartache. All I wanted was for you to stay Amish. I'm so sorry. When I wrote those warnings, I didn't consider the harm they would cause. You know I'd never hurt you."

A sarcastic laugh escaped Rebecca's throat. "I can't believe you actually thought that threatening me would ensure I stayed Amish. Where is *your* faith? You of all people must surely realize that I think for myself."

Rebecca caught her breath. She clasped her hands on her lap and cleared her throat. "I'm Amish because that's who I am with my whole heart and soul."

Katie sat as still as an eagle ready to prey on a small animal. Rebecca squeezed her eyes closed in disbelief, still trying to take in what she'd discovered. It was incomprehensible that the reason for her agony had been sparked by someone she trusted.

She straightened. "I'd like you to answer one question for me. When you delivered the threats, where did you park your buggy? We didn't hear your horse."

"Both times, I tied him to a post fairly close to the house. It was far enough away that I knew no one would hear anything." She hesitated. "If only you had stayed in Arthur, Rebecca. You and William would never have been tempted by the English ways."

Rebecca put her hand on her hip and raised her chin. "You still don't get it, do you?"

"What?"

"I have no regrets about coming here. In fact, I'm grateful for this opportunity." Rebecca took in a deep breath. "You know what I've learned?"

Katie merely looked at Rebecca to continue.

"We can't stay isolated all day, Katie, for fear of being tempted. We have to get out and take chances. How will we grow as human beings if we distance ourselves from the world? Goodness. We'd be cowards if we stayed inside four walls for fear of seeing or hearing anything that would make us think. Forcing me to go home would never have accomplished anything."

Katie seemed frozen in place.

"What you did was so wrong. God throws tests at us on a daily basis so when a big obstacle comes our way, we'll have enough experience to deal with it."

"Maybe you're right."

Rebecca let out a sigh. "Look. Being away from my family in a non-Amish environment has been difficult. I admit that. My first nights here were especially rough. And although I appreciate electricity and Beth's fancy tub, I can do without them. The best part of it is that now I know what's out there, and I appreciate my heritage more than ever. I'm accepting of other churches, too. In fact, Beth Conrad is one of the most wonderful people I've ever met. Our conversations have sparked me to think. That's why I'm stronger than before."

"Rebecca, you're so levelheaded."

"You should be, too. And by the way, I'm not

without my own problems. But common sense has always told me that sweeping them under a mat won't make them go away. Eventually, that rug will come up, and what's hidden will be exposed."

Katie raised an inquisitive brow. "Are you saying that I've been trying to ignore my worries?"

Rebecca nodded. "It certainly appears that way. You tried to scare me into leaving town to make sure I returned to my Amish roots. In my heart, I know that God would want me to do that on my own. Without a threat."

"I told you why I did it."

Rebecca shook her head. "Katie, it doesn't matter. I make my own choices. And I take responsibility for those decisions. That isn't to say we won't make mistakes. But in the process, we learn."

Katie paused. "That's an interesting way to look at it." She threw her hands over her face. "Oh, Rebecca. I've done something awful. I'm ashamed of myself. Can you ever forgive me?"

"Of course. But you need to apologize to Beth, Daniel, and William. Your actions worried them, too. Tell them how deeply sorry you are and why you did what you did."

"I will. I should try to be more like you, Rebecca. You're a role model."

Rebecca looked at her to continue.

"If you had been in my shoes, you would have thought of an honest way to talk to me about your concerns. You would never have done what I did."

Rebecca finally sat back in her seat, and a wave of relief swept through her. Even though Katie had been the cause of her pain, she had meant no harm. The threats had been a senseless mistake. Now, Rebecca could rest assured that she was safe.

Katie's voice broke her thoughts, and she startled.

"Rebecca, I can't undo the damage. But there must be some way to make this up to you. I really want us to continue to be friends. Is that possible?"

Chapter Twelve

Later that day, William regarded Beth with intense curiosity. Was she really going to teach him to drive? The question flitted in and out of William's mind as he sat in the driver's seat of her sleek BMW.

Everything about the car said luxury. The CD player. Stereo system. The open sunroof. The soft gray leather seat that had immediately molded comfortably to his body as if it had been custom designed for him.

With an eager smile, she handed him the keys. "Go ahead and start the ignition."

Unable to stop a grin, William took the key, inserted it, and gently turned it. The engine made a soft purring noise.

William sat up a little straighter. "I love this car."

He glanced at Beth, who was looking down at her seat belt while she fastened the buckle. After the click, William followed suit. In front of him loomed the black panel with all sorts of buttons. But the technology was no mystery.

He knew the dash by heart from the manual in

the glove compartment. He'd imagined driving this vehicle so many times, he already felt at ease behind the steering wheel.

Beth instructed him to put the gear in reverse, back up with caution, and to move the lever to the forward position. As he did so, he reached for the Ray-Bans his father had lent them. He slid them on, glanced in the mirror, and smiled. On the country road, William clutched the wheel. He couldn't believe he was driving.

"How does it feel?"

William nodded, keeping his eyes on the blacktop. "Great." His answer didn't do justice to her question. In fact, it was a huge understatement. As his gaze stayed on the narrow road that seemed to go on forever, he wondered if life could get any better.

From his peripheral vision, he caught Beth darting him a look of curiosity.

For the purpose of conversation, he said the only thing he could think of. "I'm surprised it's so easy to control."

"Would you like to try the cruise?"

"Sure." She explained how to set it. Of course, he knew. Still, he was fully aware that she was granting him a huge privilege in allowing him to drive her BMW, and simply thanked her for her instructions.

William darted a quick glance at the roof and squinted. The orange sun poured into the car like a fountain of warmth. The brightness made the jet-black dash take on a light gray appearance.

"My father taught me to drive on country roads."

"Really?"

"Mm-hmm. I learned on a stick shift." She laughed

a little. "There were a lot of starts and stops while I tried. But eventually, I caught on. He was the most patient person I've ever known."

"Why? Was it hard to drive?"

"It's far from an automatic. I kept letting up on the clutch too quickly, and the car would jerk and die. The trick is to let up slowly. Anyway, I finally got it."

William wanted to make Beth aware of his gratitude. He felt awkward because of the bad feelings he'd felt toward her. Besides, he hardly knew his stepmom. Not sure what to say, he decided to make it simple.

"Thanks for this, Beth."

He caught her wide grin. "My pleasure." She paused. "But if you'd like to say thank you, you can thank Rebecca."

He raised a brow. "Rebecca?"

"Mm-hmm. It was her idea, you know."

"No, I didn't."

"That girl looks out for you, William. You're one lucky man to have someone like that rooting for you. She's amazing."

"Don't I know it." He grinned. "And I'm fortunate I'm driving an automatic and not a stick like you learned on."

"Indeed."

He passed fields of corn and beans. For the first time since his arrival, he wished he were in Arthur. As he cruised ahead, he imagined waving to his Amish friends. He could envision the surprised looks on their faces if they could see him now.

As he thought of Aenti Sarah hanging clothes on the line, he breathed in the fresh country air that smelled of a mixture of woods and freshly mowed grass.

"Where should we go?"

She pointed. "Keep heading west. There's something I'd like to show you."

William didn't ask what it was. He'd find out soon enough.

Beth continued. "In about five miles, we'll come to an intersection. That's where we'll swing a right."

William nodded. Suddenly, his curiosity was piqued. What did Beth want to show him? The enthusiastic lift to her voice indicated it must be something interesting.

To his astonishment, he felt at ease with her. He yearned to open up, but what would he say? He didn't know her well. In fact, this was the first time they'd actually been alone. He noticed that she had become unusually quiet. Perhaps she was experiencing the same awkwardness.

It wasn't long before he approached the intersection. Following her instructions, he slowed the car. When he did so, she turned toward him a bit and motioned to the signal to the left of the steering wheel. "I know there's no one around, but why don't you flip that up for a right turn?"

She added, "Just for practice."

He did as told. As soon as they changed directions, the blinking sound went off, and the lever kicked back into place. Beth moved forward to the edge of her seat. "You can slow down now. We're almost there."

He could see her squint as she appeared to scrutinize the thick woods looming in front of them.

William caught his breath. The terrain was more beautiful than anything he had ever seen.

The woods behind the Conrad home was gorgeous, but this view was particularly amazing because of the uneven landscape and the way the different species of trees and brush seemed to grow over each other.

He marveled at the large array of tall oaks that hovered prestigiously, as if utilizing their wide, full branches as shields to protect the ground from the sun.

Beth's voice broke into his thoughts. "Here's where you pull in." She motioned to the side.

William turned onto a narrow gravel lane. The thick layer of rocks crunched under the tires. Very slowly and with great care, he followed the path that wound its way through the thick, massive forest. The shade created by the foliage blocked the sunlight. He removed his sunglasses and returned them to the holder on the driver's door. He blinked to adjust his vision.

He was about to reach for the button to turn on the lights when the trees miraculously disappeared, and a huge lake presented itself. Its deep blue color reminded him of a soft, thick blanket that Aenti Sarah had knit for a neighbor.

The bright sun reappeared. At the edge of the pond, William had no choice but to put the car into park. Totally smitten with the view, he drew in a long, deep breath and stared at the enormous round body of water surrounded by woods.

When Beth put a gentle hand on his arm, he drew back. Her touch came as a surprise. He'd become so enamored with the beautiful vista, he'd forgotten she was next to him.

"Sorry. I didn't mean to startle you."

He smiled a little. "It's okay."

"Are you up for a walk?"

"Sure."

William unfastened his seat belt and stepped out of the car. Amid the quiet serenity, the only sounds were the doors slamming.

Why were they here? Was the place owned by a friend? He hadn't seen signs indicating that it was a public area. Beth motioned to a dirt path that appeared to wind its way around the vast area of lake. He followed her.

"This is beautiful." William listened to the birds singing. A red fox darted in front of him, and he stopped a moment. He kicked a large green hedge apple out of his path. The view in front of him oozed peacefulness and tranquility.

He glimpsed the dark blue hues of the water. The color was as tranquil and mysterious as photos he'd seen of the Indian Ocean. Purple and golden wildflowers decorated the shore.

Beth's gentle voice seemed to float through the air. "I knew you'd like it here. This is Daniel's favorite piece of land." She paused to glance at William. "In fact, he's talked for years about bringing you here." She pulled in a little breath. "He always wanted to take you fishing."

William couldn't hide the surprise in his voice. "He owns this?"

Beth nodded.

William looked at her to continue.

"He was always consumed with work. It's sad to say

that he's never set foot on here since we bought it."
She shrugged. "You know how that goes."

William nodded. He was all too aware. Daniel
not only was too busy to fish, but he'd been too pre-
occupied with his business over the years to visit
his own son. But William had seen his dad's work
orders. With a customer list of that size, William
would bet that his father had never taken a vacation.

Beth resumed the walk, and William followed her
on the narrow path.

"William, when Daniel picked out this property,
all he could talk about was how you would love it
here. He had big dreams, you know. He even planned
to get a boat."

William frowned in doubt. "Beth, you're painting
a nice picture of Dad, but I can't believe he really
wanted to take me fishing."

"Why would you think that?"

"Because we've never done anything together."

She shook her head. "It's too bad. Some people
think they have all the time in the world to do the
things they want to do. I suppose Daniel's one of
those people."

After a lengthy pause, Beth took a deep, unsteady
breath. "William, you may not believe this either, but
you're the apple of Daniel's eye."

Her voice took on a nervous, breathless tone.
"Time passed us by. I suppose that expression about
never putting off the things you want to do holds a
lot of truth. I'm fully aware that talking is different
than doing, but I hope you'll believe me when I tell
you that I truly wish the three of us could redo the
years you and your father spent apart."

William's chest rose and fell rapidly. In a shaky voice, he responded, "Me too."

"We both should have spent more time with you, William. I'm ashamed that we didn't."

William pursed his lips as he considered Beth's admission. He didn't know her well, but suddenly felt the need to spill his guts.

"Why didn't you? You had a car."

Beth slowed. The path had widened just enough for them to walk side by side. William's shoulder brushed hers.

She stopped to look into his eyes. What he saw was defeat. Despair. Regret.

In fact, the expression on her face was so remorseful, it lessened his irritation. To his surprise, his anger diminished. It was replaced by a sense of loss and grief.

"Work. And Daniel's strong need to do as he believed your mother would have wanted."

"That doesn't explain why you didn't keep me during the summer. Dad could have surely found a couple of weeks to spend with me. You know, like a stepparent's time with his kid."

Beth squeezed her eyes closed and nodded in agreement. When she opened her lids, drops of moisture clung to her eyes like morning dew on a leaf. "We should have done better, William. I'm not making excuses, but from the day he left you in Arthur, Daniel struggled with what to do. But regardless of his decision to leave and not take you, we should have made you our priority. We failed."

When William didn't respond, Beth went on. "Daniel wanted you. At the same time, he was convinced you were happy with Aenti Sarah."

"I was." William's voice cracked with emotion. "But I missed him. I've told him how I felt when he left."

She lowered her gaze to the ground. "You probably experienced the same agony he did after he left. No sleep. Nightmares. It was a pretty rough time. I offered to adopt you, William"—she hesitated— "but it didn't matter. In the end, Daniel yearned to do what would have pleased your mother."

William's gut ached. Pain traveled from his stomach up to his chest as he thought of the lost time with his dad.

"Daniel isn't a good communicator, William, but there's no doubt that he loves you. He wishes he could make up for lost time." She threw her hands in the air. "He can't."

"No."

"But"—she let out a deep sigh—"maybe the two of you can start over. At least, you're both alive. God does offer second chances, and this is surely one of them. That doesn't mean everything will be perfect, but it can be good. Daniel obviously loves you enough to ask you to take over his business."

She motioned to the lake. "He also cares enough about you to do this."

William raised a curious brow. "What?"

"This property is a gift to you and Rebecca from Daniel and me. We would love it if you built here. Of course, we'll help. Can you imagine a better place to raise your children?" She took a deep, satisfied breath. "Our grandchildren."

William's breath caught in his throat. "Dad wants me to have this?"

Beth nodded. "Of course, it can't compensate for

growing up without him, but in his own way, your dad's trying to show you he loves you."

As William digested what she'd told him, he considered what Rebecca's reaction would be. His temples pounded with uncertainty. Turmoil brewed inside of him. He wanted to work with his dad and become his friend. He also yearned to marry Rebecca. There wasn't a way to do both.

Beth's voice was low and serious. "I'd like to be close to you, too, William. I realize that this is a lot to think about. It's something you and Rebecca will have to decide together."

"I don't know what to say."

"Right now, you don't need to do anything. Daniel and I are just happy to have the opportunity to get close to you. That is, if you'll give us a second chance." After a lengthy pause, she spoke in what was barely more than a whisper.

"Will you?"

Later that afternoon, all Rebecca could think about was Katie. What she'd done was bad. But the intentions behind her actions were good.

In the shop office, she told William what she'd learned. He frowned. As she went on, the concerned creases on his forehead became more pronounced. Rebecca noted the firm set of his jaw as she related the bizarre story of Katie's threats and the reason behind them.

William kept silent while he listened. She knew she talked a mile a minute, and the more she told him, the faster her words came out.

He motioned to the door. "Let's go outside."

Slow steps took them down the hill behind the shop. The path behind the Conrad home had become their place for serious talks.

Rebecca continued telling him about Katie. When she finished, she stopped and caught her breath. William turned to her. She crossed her arms over her chest and glanced up at him, searching his perplexed face for answers.

They locked gazes. She barely heard the sound of hammering coming from the shop. Her mind was in a whirl.

A combination of surprise and bewilderment filled his eyes as he stared back at her.

Rebecca's heart pumped hard as the breeze caressed her face. Under normal circumstances, the soothing coolness against her skin would have prompted her to relax. Not today.

Her mind was in a state of chaos. As her thoughts flitted from fact to fact, she found it difficult to stay focused. Recalling pieces of her conversation with Katie, she wasn't sure if she wanted to cry or scream about the injustice she'd suffered.

She gazed into the sky as the sun made its way west. Usually, the warmth calmed Rebecca. But right now, her entire body shook.

William shook his head in disbelief. "I can't believe what you've told me, Rebecca. Katie must be nuts." He shoved his hands into his pockets. "All these days and nights, I've worried about how to protect you. I've tossed and turned in bed wondering what I'd do if something happened to you. We've even changed our plans, in order to keep you safe. All the while, we thought poor Natalie was jealous of you. And who was really behind all of this? Some innocent-looking Amish girl?"

He harrumphed.

At a loss for words, Rebecca remained still.

As William tapped his foot, he straightened his shoulders. "Who would've guessed that Katie was the source of those awful messages? Boy, did she have us fooled."

"I know."

William bit his lip. The pink in his cheeks turned to a shade of red. Rebecca tried to get a grip on her emotions as she watched him curl his hands into fists. William's knuckles turned white.

The pulse in his neck picked up speed. Suddenly, he waved a hand toward the house. "I'm not letting her get away with this."

"What are you going to do?"

She stepped quickly behind him as he pulled her forward.

"We're going to pay Katie a visit. Right now. I'm going to warn her to never set foot on this property again. If she comes anywhere near you, she'll pay."

Rebecca stopped and tugged at his arm. She tried to catch her breath. "No, William. That's not the solution." She swallowed. "What good would that do? The damage is already done. There's no need to counter Katie with a warning."

He threw her a confused look.

"We've got to look at the positive side. Thank goodness, I wasn't harmed. Really, I was never at risk of being hurt. I'm safe. And we're lucky to know the source of the threats."

"Rebecca, you're downplaying this. What Katie did was unimaginable."

"Yes. But in the scheme of things, it could have been much worse."

William rolled his eyes. "I'm fully aware of that. But we can't let her get away with this." He looked down at Rebecca. "You surely don't want to drop this."

Rebecca thought a moment. The home was in view. She looked forward to sharing her story with Beth. William's step-mamma would be shocked at Katie's actions.

They proceeded to walk in silence. Rebecca wondered how the woods could seem so tranquil when her world was so chaotic.

Urgency edged William's voice. "Rebecca, we've got to do something. What she did wasn't just on the crazy side. It was mean. And whether or not she actually posed a threat, her actions affected all of our lives."

Dried leaves crunched under their shoes. The smell of pine from the large trees filled Rebecca's nostrils. She breathed in the refreshing scent. But not even the woods could slow the fast, uncomfortable beat of her heart.

William blew out a low whistle. "You can decide for yourself, but I'm not letting this woman get away with scaring the daylights out of us. She could have caused Dad another heart attack. Furthermore, it kills me to think of how this scheme of hers was planned with the motive to get you away from here so you wouldn't be tempted to leave the Amish faith."

Rebecca moaned in distress. "It's hard to believe. It was poor judgment on her part, at best. But William, at least she realizes she did wrong. That's a start. I don't think she comprehended how her actions would cause us to suffer. She apologized. And she's sincere. I know that."

William kicked a dead branch out of the way. He bent to pick up an acorn and threw it. "I don't give a hoot. I need more than an apology."

Rebecca shrugged. "I'm not sure what else she can do. She can't go back in time and undo her threats."

William's voice was edged with anger. "That still doesn't make it right."

"No. But what does? Is there a perfect solution? I know what happened is crazy, but really, the only way to deal with it is to put this behind me."

"And you plan to do that?"

Rebecca nodded. "I have to."

William raised an irritated brow. "How?"

"By forgiving her."

When they stopped and turned to each other, William's gaze locked with Rebecca's. His eyes sparkled with a combination of anger and concern. He was upset, and she loved the way he tried to protect her.

When he spoke, his voice was barely more than a whisper. "What kind of man would I be if I just dropped this?"

Rebecca considered the question. "William, this has nothing to do with you. It's all about Katie and her lack of faith in me. Now it's over. I know you'd move the earth for me, but in this case, you can't."

Impulsively, she lowered her voice. "And as far as you being a man?" She smiled a little. "You're definitely a man. And I love when you defend me. Knowing you're behind me is all I could ask for. What on earth would I do without you?"

"I'm still in shock that Katie would do such a thing."

"And I'm ashamed to admit that I thought Natalie was the guilty person."

The statement brought a sudden glow to William's cheeks. His lips curved up into a wide grin. "Poor Natalie. Katie makes Henry Kreggs's daughter look like a saint."

His comment prompted Rebecca to giggle. William joined her in laughter.

"It's not easy to forgive, is it?"

Enjoying their closeness, Rebecca whispered, "No. But it's the only way to get past what happened. And I certainly can't expect you to forgive Daniel and Beth if I don't do the same with Katie."

William's eyes glistened with moisture. As she looked into his deep, turbulent eyes, she trembled. At that moment, she knew in her heart that William Conrad was the only man she could ever love. He was her soul mate. She couldn't exist without him.

"Rebecca, I don't deserve you."

She stepped closer. His warm breath fanned her lips. The sensation made Rebecca's heart skip a beat. She'd never felt such a bond with anyone in her entire life. "Why do you say that?"

"There are a number of reasons. Your thoughts are so much purer than mine, Rebecca. Your heart is genuine and forgiving. This unstable woman has threatened your life and scared the living daylights out of both of us. Anyone else would be pounding at her door right now. But you? Your solution is to forgive her. You amaze me."

When he whispered in her ear, a shiver of delight zoomed up her arms. "I still want to be your protector. I intend to keep you safe the rest of my life. I really want to confront her, Rebecca. I need to get my anger off of my chest. Are you sure . . ."

Rebecca gave a firm, decisive nod. "Let it go, William. Let's just be thankful that we know the source of the warnings and that there's nothing to worry about. Talking about this has really helped to ease my mind. To be honest, I'm relieved it's over. And I'm happy I no longer have to worry about someone harming me. It's a huge weight lifted from my shoulders."

"Mine, too." He paused. "Look, I'll refrain from going to her home, if that's what you want . . . but if I see her again?"

Rebecca raised an inquisitive brow.

"I won't hesitate one minute to let her know how she betrayed us all. That what she did caused us tremendous worry and that her actions were cruel, at best."

"Fair enough." Rebecca sighed. "In my heart, I truly believe she thought she was doing what was right for me."

"It doesn't matter. That wasn't her decision to make."

"I know. I think she realizes that, too."

A mélange of clouds swept across the sky and blocked the sun. For a moment, the light dimmed. The eerie appearance above matched the strange sensation that swept through Rebecca's body as she considered what Katie had put her through.

A cool breeze rustled the leaves on the oak trees before the setting sun finally appeared again.

"Thanks for being here for me, William. I feel better now that we've talked."

Reluctantly, Rebecca made her way to the house. There was something so comforting about the outdoors. Fresh air helped her think clearly. Being close to nature gave her an added feeling of security.

She squared her chin and hooked her arm in William's. She darted him a glance.

"We've both been put to the test, haven't we?"

"What do you mean?"

"Exactly what I just said. We face huge challenges. I have to deal with Katie's betrayal. And you've got to forgive your father and Beth. Those aren't easy things to do."

"When I was little, I heard the word 'forgiveness' a lot in church. At the time, I really didn't give it much thought. Because it's used so often, a person doesn't realize what a gigantic word it is." He shook his head. "Forgiving isn't easy."

"No."

"Helping in my dad's shop isn't difficult because it's a physical task. In fact, I can do anything I set out to do with my hands. Lifting a heavy bale of hay isn't even that hard. Things that don't involve the mind can be done without much effort. But forgiveness is a different issue. Because it has to come from the heart."

He stopped a moment. "But I think I'm getting there."

He flexed his fingers while he related his recent conversations with his dad and Beth.

"Oh, William." Inside, her heart warmed. She closed her eyes a moment and said a silent prayer of thanks. Her third goal was coming true. She could leave Indiana guilt-free. Even though there was no need to go home now, Rebecca knew it was time. She'd done her best. And her parents needed her.

"William, you don't know how happy that makes me."

"Honestly, I want to forgive my dad for leaving me, Rebecca. I'm really trying hard to understand the turmoil he went through."

"We've talked before about life not being perfect."

"To be honest, I'm ready to let go of the huge weight I've carried on my shoulders. For years, I've been miserable inside, trying to figure out why he deserted me. After we came here, my feelings grew stronger. But things are slowly starting to work out."

He related parts of his conversation with Beth. He went on to tell her about the car ride and how it felt to be behind the wheel. At the end, he related what Beth had said about his folks wanting William and Rebecca to build on the land by the lake.

"Even though I don't agree with what Dad did, she helped me understand what was going through his mind. At least, it puts me more at ease."

"William, sometimes we don't get answers. We just have to realize that things are the way they are and move on. Forgiveness will happen. Because you've asked God to help you do it. Never doubt yourself. And don't doubt Him."

She let out a small sigh. "There's no rule that says you have to do it overnight. Just like we didn't get the Kreggses' order out right away. But eventually, you must forgive because you can't have a happy future harboring resentment."

When he glanced at her in understanding, she raised a thoughtful brow. "Just think of forgiving as removing roadblocks so your horse can get you to where you're going."

"What?"

Rebecca let out a pleased laugh at her analogy. "Your horse can't get you home if the road is covered with barricades. And when you think about it, the same goes with living a happy life. Mental roadblocks, like grudges, will stop you from moving forward unless you push them out of the way by forgiving." She giggled. "Old Sam would be proud of me, wouldn't he?"

William nodded. "I think you're inheriting his wisdom. And that's not a bad thing."

He stopped. When their gazes locked, he grinned. "You have an interesting way of looking at things, soon-to-be Mrs. Conrad."

She took a deep, excited breath as she thought about becoming William's wife. She yearned to go back to Arthur. To marry William. To have a family.

But a barricade was in their way. One that could stop Rebecca's dream from materializing. If William decided to run Daniel's business, he would be here permanently. Away from Rebecca's family. And Rebecca hadn't yet determined if she could leave her family to be with him.

Now, to make matters worse, Daniel was offering a plot of land where William and Rebecca could build a home. She didn't blame Daniel. But it seemed as though every time she turned around, there was another challenge to overcome.

What she didn't tell William was that she, too, carried a heavy weight on her shoulders. It involved their future. But she kept quiet. At this point, she should be satisfied that her third goal would come true.

She'd promised William never to keep anything from him. But to achieve her goal for the bishop—to help bring William and his father closer—she didn't want to interfere by muddying the waters.

William's dreams were important to her. More so than her own. She wouldn't be selfish. She'd wait for his decision and then go forward.

In spite of the uncertainty, she hoped that God would take care of them and bless them with a life together. Relaxing, she smiled a little. "Let's make each other a promise, William."

"Anything for you."

"I'll concentrate on putting Katie's threats behind me. And you continue to ask God to help you forgive Daniel and Beth. It may take time, but if God works with us, we'll do it. And if we can put those two things behind us?"

"We'll have it made," he commented.

She looked at him for an answer. "So, what do you say?"

He nodded. "Deal."

In the living room that evening, William stared at the cover of the fly-fishing magazine. Everyone had gone to bed. But his pulse was still too fast to sleep.

His folks had been relieved to know Rebecca was safe. So was he. At the same time, what he'd learned troubled him. He flipped the channels on the remote until he got ESPN. He laid the remote on the table next to the couch and crossed his legs.

As he stared at the tennis game on the large screen, his thoughts flitted from one thing to another. Katie. Beth. His father. The business. The land his dad and Beth wanted him and Rebecca to build on. Rebecca's desire to return to Arthur. His longing to becoming English.

It seemed too much to deal with. At that moment, he missed life with Aenti Sarah and Uncle John. But he couldn't ignore his problems. He recalled what Rebecca had said about our success in life being determined by how we deal with our issues.

After a while, his temples started to pound. He squeezed his eyes closed and pictured a beautiful home on the plot of land Beth had shown him. He imagined taking his little ones fishing while Rebecca made floral arrangements in her kitchen.

The visions prompted a grin. His smile grew wider as he imagined his father and Beth taking his kids for piggyback rides.

He opened his eyes. As a commercial for cereal flashed across the set in front of him, reality struck him. He'd love things to be settled. And they would be. Wouldn't they?

He opened the fishing magazine and flipped through the pages. While he stared at a huge grouper being reeled in, he imagined fishing with his dad. An ache filled William's chest until he closed the magazine and rested his head against the leather cushion.

A noise prompted him to look up.

"I thought you'd gone to bed."

His father joined him on the couch. As he glanced at the magazine in William's hand, he raised a curious brow. "I guess my love of fishing's no secret."

William had an idea. But he was afraid to voice it. Then he recalled Rebecca's philosophy about life. If Rebecca were in his shoes, William knew what she'd do. She'd tell the man next to him what was on his mind.

William raised his chin and turned. "Dad, that's one nice lake you've got. How 'bout we go fishing?"

Chapter Thirteen

A galaxy of stars sparkled outside of Rebecca's bedroom window. With the lights off, she gazed at the beautifully decorated sky and considered some of her conversation with William. Old Sam had once told her that serious issues weren't resolved overnight. Rebecca wondered just how long hers would take.

She thought of William and squeezed her eyes closed a moment. When she opened them, she realized just how much she really loved him. How badly she wanted him to turn down Daniel's offer.

But the decision had to come from William. Otherwise, he would have regrets the rest of his life. And how could they have a happy marriage with that on his shoulders?

Rebecca's gut ached as she thought of Katie and what she'd done. But something even more disturbing weighed on Rebecca's mind.

If William accepted Daniel's offer, she'd have to decide whether or not to live with him in Indiana. There had been plenty of time to consider the invitation, but putting it off wasn't the answer. Her decision wouldn't be any easier tomorrow. Or next week.

Now was the moment to make up her mind. When she and William had talked this evening, the subject hadn't come up. Perhaps William assumed that she would be with him whatever he decided.

Rebecca flipped on the light before reaching inside of her hope chest to pull out her diary. On the floor, she leaned back against her bed and recorded the date on the top right corner of the page.

Soon William will decide whether or not to join Daniel in his business. If he says yes, I'll have to make the biggest decision of my life. Whether or not to live in Indiana.

Rebecca squeezed her lids closed a moment. When she opened them, tears burned her eyes. *I'm still unsure of what I'll say. However, I am certain of two things.*

She sniffed back a tear and sat up a little straighter. She bent her knees and rested her notepad on her thighs. *I want William to join Daniel. At the same time, I yearn to live forever in my beloved little town where I will grow old with my family.*

She paused and pressed her lips together in thought. *Maybe William will decide to forfeit Daniel's offer.* She shook her head sadly. *When he tells me he accepts, what will I say? Is it possible to give him what he wants without sacrificing everything that's important to me?*

The questions she'd written were potent. So strong, she put down her paper and pressed her hands together in prayer. With every ounce of hope, she spoke. "What should I do, Lord?"

In silence, she asked Him over and over to help her make the right decision. Finally, she sighed with relief. God would tell her what to do. She had no doubt about that. But when?

She continued with her diary. *I'm guilty of impatience. And right now, I wish my faith were stronger.*

She stood and returned the journal to her hope chest. As she closed the lid, she traced a finger over one of the flowers Old Sam had carved into the wood. At the thought of him, she smiled a little. She wished she had his wisdom. His experience.

Letting out a yawn, she returned to her bed, where she opened her prayer book and flipped through scriptures. She attempted to apply the Biblical verses to her life. She said a silent prayer for Katie and asked God to help William forgive Daniel and Beth.

As Rebecca got comfortable, Katie flitted in and out of her thoughts. Rebecca kicked the covers down to the end of the bed, wiggled her toes, and thanked God that she was safe.

But what would she tell William should he accept Daniel's offer?

She imagined the happy expression on William's face if she told him she'd make her home with him in Indiana. At the same time, she pictured her mother and father's sad, teary eyes when she explained to them she was leaving for good.

The thought of hurting her parents prompted an ache in Rebecca's gut. The pain became so intense, Rebecca rolled onto her stomach and closed her eyes. As she tried for a solution that would please everyone she loved, a tear slipped down her cheek. More followed.

Before she knew it, she was crying her heart out. What seemed an eternity later, she caught her breath. She sat up and grabbed a tissue, sniffled, and composed herself.

As her gaze landed on the delicate-looking cover of her mother's handmade book, she realized that the only place to find her answer was in those verses.

Turning onto her back, she picked up the book and focused on the scriptures. The answer she needed was here. She knew it. She just had to find it. The fresh scent from the green-blue eucalyptus leaves on the bed stand helped her relax. The cool night breeze floated in from the window screen.

An hour later, Rebecca read the last sentence, closed the book, and glanced up at the wooden blades of the ceiling fan. The slow whirl made a faint whistle.

As she enjoyed the airy ambiance, Rebecca thought how ironic it was that she'd finished Mamma's book just as her stay in Indiana was coming to an end.

Now that she was out of danger, she didn't really need to leave. But her instincts told her that it was time to go home and regroup. And it would be to her benefit. Having the security of her family would help her think more clearly.

Perhaps a different environment was what she needed to find her answer. It was important to clear her mind so she could make the biggest decision she'd ever made.

At the thought of her homecoming, she sat up. She couldn't wait to see her family. To catch up on the news.

It was up to her to put to rest any rumors about her becoming English. It was indeed her sole responsibility to reassure her parents. And she would. Soon.

As she thought of being without William, a lump formed in her throat. She sat very still and recalled a verse from the book of John. It had been printed in her mother's neat hand on the very last page of the book. In a low, thoughtful voice, she repeated it.

"'I am the bread of life. He who comes to me will never go hungry, and he who believes in me will never go thirsty.'"

A sense of calm flowed through her body. She finally had the answer she'd so desperately sought. It was in that very scripture and her mamma's neat printing.

Whatever Rebecca decided, she would be okay. So would William and her family. Because God would take care of them. He would help her make the right choice. Her Savior knew what William sacrificed if he stayed in Arthur. At the same time, her Father in heaven was fully aware of what she forfeited if she moved to Indiana.

Why on earth had she worried so much over something that was really up to God? The question prompted her to let out a small laugh. She pulled the book to her and held it close to her chest.

She ran her hand over the cover. As she touched the soft fabric and the colorful stitches, she imagined Mamma making it. Whatever happened, God had blessed Rebecca with the best parents in the world.

They had instilled in her everything they believed in. All that was important and all that they wanted

Rebecca to know. Most importantly, they'd made sure she knew God was in charge of her life. With those strong values, how could she go wrong? Rebecca moaned satisfaction as she realized what a lucky girl she was.

A smile tugged at her lips. Why had she fretted so about making the much-thought-over decision when it really wasn't hers to make? She'd been carrying the burden on her shoulders when all she'd had to do was give it to God.

She recalled the verse about the footprints in the sand. From now on, there would be only one set of footprints. God's. He would carry her the rest of the way.

Suddenly, the heavy load of stress she'd lived with evaporated. She was more at peace with herself than she'd ever been.

Filled with renewed contentment, she lay on her pillow and pulled the covers up to her waist. The breeze coming in through the window was soft and caressing. Crickets chirped. The gentle night sounds were music to her ears.

She let out a deep breath while her hand lingered on the cover. Mamma's book had become Rebecca's security blanket. Her Christian guide on how to face challenges in a new, uncertain world.

At that moment, she knew what to tell William should he decide to accept Daniel's offer. She pushed out a decisive breath and turned onto her side. The covers felt soft against her toes. The breeze coming in from the window would lull her to sleep.

And sleep, she would. Tonight she went to bed

with no worries, even though tomorrow would be a big day.

The next morning, Rebecca sat across from William at the breakfast table. Beth reached for the salt and pepper shakers, and Rebecca watched Beth's gold bracelet slide down her wrist as William talked with excitement about the fishing trip he and Daniel were planning. Rebecca smiled.

Beth salted her scrambled eggs. Daniel was asleep in his room. "I'm glad we don't have to worry about you anymore, Rebecca. What a load off of my mind."

Beth shook her head. "I still can't believe Katie was behind those nasty threats. I feel responsible for what happened."

William swallowed a bite of ham. He frowned. "Why would you even begin to think you're to blame for what Katie did?"

Beth glanced up and gave a helpless shrug. "If you'll remember, I introduced Rebecca to her. Call it poor judgment or whatever you want. My intentions were good. I thought I was helping Rebecca find a friend."

"You've known Katie for some time, haven't you?" He downed the rest of his orange juice.

Beth nodded. "I obviously didn't know her as well as I thought I did. I've bought eggs from her for years. Over time, we've had our fill of chats. She always seemed like such a sweet, responsible girl. I never had any indication that she would threaten anyone. My goodness, who would have guessed she would cause us so much worry?"

Rebecca's gaze drifted from William to Beth. "You certainly can't take the blame. It was just one of those things we never expected." She smiled. "But it's over. And we can relax. Thank God."

"Thank God," Beth echoed.

Rebecca stood to refill the pitcher of juice. Silence ensued while they ate scrambled eggs. The only sound was the clinking of silverware against china plates.

Then Beth said, "Rebecca, now that we know you're safe, there's really no reason to leave. You're not in danger. Won't you stay longer?" She paused. "I confess that my reasons are purely selfish. I'm going to miss you."

Rebecca smiled. "Thank you, Beth."

"I'm appreciative for what you've done. What you and William have accomplished together is nothing less than a miracle. But most of all, I'll be grateful forever for the emotional support you've given me during this most difficult time." She lowered her voice. "You are an angel."

Rebecca's heart warmed. She loved to be appreciated. With a slight nod, she said, "Being here has been a wonderful opportunity. And I'll miss you, too."

Rebecca buttered her croissant. "But it's time to go. My parents need me. I'm afraid they're going through their own crisis."

Beth looked at her to continue.

"They're suffering from the wrath of the grapevine." She winked.

Beth giggled. "You mean, the town has labeled you English?"

Rebecca nodded. "Oh yes. Gossip spreads like

wildfire. I'd love to come back and see you and Daniel. But my next visit will be after I reassure everyone at home that I'm still going to join the church."

The doorbell sounded.

Beth looked up. "Hmm. I wonder who that is."

William chimed in. "Could be the grocery service."

Beth shook her head. "Not today."

As Beth got up from her chair, Rebecca stood and put a gentle hand on Beth's shoulder. "Sit down and finish your breakfast. I'll get it. It's probably a neighbor checking on Daniel."

Rebecca stepped quickly. What a relief to answer the door, knowing her life wasn't at stake.

As usual, she looked through the peephole. Taking a deep breath, she slowly pulled the handle and stood face-to-face with Katie. The girl held a large white box in front of her. Conflicting emotions tugged at Rebecca as she struggled for something to say. At a loss for words, she glanced behind her, where Beth and William stood and regarded each other in silence. The sun shone in through the skylight.

Rebecca faced Katie and forced a half smile. "Gut morning, Katie."

Katie's eyes were filled with uncertainty. "Morning, Rebecca. May I come in?"

Rebecca motioned toward the kitchen. "Of course."

"Thank you." She glanced toward the living room couch. "I'll set this package down, if it's all right."

Rebecca nodded.

As Rebecca and Katie walked into the kitchen, William got up out of his chair and came toward them. Without a word, he signaled for Rebecca to step back as he squared his shoulders and stood directly in front of Katie.

Rebecca stood behind William as he looked down at Katie. He spoke in a firm voice. "You're not welcome here. You have no right to set foot on this property."

He motioned toward the entrance. "What you did was incomprehensible. How can you live with yourself? I want you to leave right now."

To Rebecca's surprise, Katie squared her shoulders defensively. "Please. I didn't come to make trouble."

Beth joined them. Beside William, she put her hands to her hips. "Katie, you've caused us so much worry. William's right. You should go."

Katie didn't budge. She swallowed. "I know. But my conscience won't allow me to leave this house before I tell all of you how deeply sorry I am for what I did. I'm here to apologize." Katie nearly choked on her words.

William stepped forward again. This time, he walked past Katie to the entrance, where he opened the door and motioned outside. The only sound was the low tone of the air conditioner. Katie's eyes glistened with moisture while she looked helplessly at William, then Beth.

Rebecca nodded to William. "Let her have her say. It's okay."

William frowned and tapped his foot.

Katie darted Rebecca a look full of regret and sadness. "I owe you another apology, Rebecca. I'm so ashamed of my actions. What I did was terribly wrong." She cleared her throat. "You were a good friend to me, and I betrayed your trust." She squeezed her eyes closed, then opened them and shook her head sadly.

"I wish I could undo what happened. You're the most forgiving person I know. If you'll give me another chance, I promise I'll be the best friend you've ever had. I never meant to hurt you. Honest."

William's voice shook as he spoke. "Katie, do you have any idea what kind of stress you've put us through?" He waved a hand toward Daniel's room. "My father suffered two heart attacks. To make matters worse, we've had to worry about Rebecca's safety."

Katie nodded. "I don't know what came over me. I was a terrible person and am sure God will punish me. I'll understand if you don't ever want to see me again. But before I leave, please accept this gift, Rebecca. I want you to have it."

Katie walked to the couch, lifted the oversized box, and handed it to Rebecca. "Obviously, this can't make up for what happened, but accept it as an apology. I wanted to give you the nicest thing I own, to let you know how genuinely sorry I am."

With a teary good-bye, Katie waved and made her way to the door. William nodded in satisfaction.

As soon as Katie had one foot outside, Rebecca stopped her. "Katie?"

"Yes?"

With a relaxed smile, Rebecca motioned to the box. "You came all this way to give me this gift. Aren't you going to watch me open it?"

Katie let out a sigh of relief. Standing still, she glanced at William and Beth for approval. Finally, Beth waved a hand. "Go ahead. I'm curious now."

Rebecca darted a skeptical look at William. As their eyes locked, a concerned crease made its way across his forehead. His jaw was set. Not sure what to do, Rebecca's heart beat nervously.

But she was certain of one thing. In her heart, she had forgiven Katie. That admission filled her spirit with immense happiness.

But Katie hadn't convinced everyone in the room of her remorse. Rebecca eyed William with suspicion. Unusually quiet, he looked on in disapproval. Rebecca wanted him to be comfortable with her decision to let Katie stay. If he wasn't . . .

Finally, he rolled his eyes. "All right. Who am I to think I can win against three women?"

Rebecca whispered, "Thank you," and he responded with a quick nod. Rebecca focused her efforts on the package and placed it on the floor. The gift was too large to hold for long. "What on earth could be inside?"

As Katie grinned, Rebecca muttered. "It's big. But it's so light."

Bending, she removed the lid and laid it on the nearest armchair. Thin white tissue paper protected the contents. With great care, Rebecca removed the present. She put a hand on her chest and gasped in surprise.

"Oh, Katie." With Beth's help, Rebecca gently unfolded the beautiful quilt and laid it over the back of the couch for display.

"That's got to be the most gorgeous work I've ever seen," Beth said, running her hand over one of the corner handkerchiefs.

In awe, Rebecca studied the unique work that

represented Katie's family. "This is the project you did with your grandmothers' handkerchiefs?"

Katie nodded proudly.

Rebecca eyed the delicate piece. As she did so, joyful tears stung her eyes as she thought of the work Katie had invested and the heritage behind it.

Rebecca gently touched one of the handkerchiefs and looked up. "They're far from ordinary." She glanced back down. "In fact, they're exquisite."

"They are."

Suddenly, Rebecca remembered the auction and put a hand over her mouth in astonishment. She recalled Katie's comment that it would be extremely difficult to part with the quilt because of the unique connection to her ancestors. Indeed, Katie's gift to Rebecca was much more than something appealing to the eye. It was a family heirloom.

Taking the material by a corner, Rebecca turned to Katie. "Thank you for this, Katie. But I can't accept something so special. You made this to raise money for the new school. That's what it should be used for."

Katie shook her head. "It's yours, Rebecca. I want you to have it. Years from now, you'll look at it and remember our buggy rides. Consider it a gift from a friend."

Their gazes locked. Rebecca wasn't comfortable accepting something so special.

Katie winked. "Enjoy it. You can pass it on to your own daughter."

Letting out a deep sigh, Rebecca squeezed Katie's hands. "Thank you. I will put it on top of my hope chest. When I look at it, I will remember our buggy rides."

In an emotional embrace, the two girls hugged. Rebecca silently thanked God for giving her another chance with Katie. With the threats behind them, maybe their friendship could grow. Rebecca didn't know what God had planned for her. She only knew that He had answered her prayer. She forgave Katie with all of her heart and soul. Now, if William could forgive Daniel . . .

Outside that evening, on the soft, thick blanket, the cool breeze caressed Rebecca's face. The bonfire crackled. Rebecca watched as William added brush and poked the logs with a stick. Bright orange flames sprang up and then settled. The burning heat forced Rebecca to stand and pull the blanket a distance from the fire.

William helped her to straighten the corners. As he took a seat next to her, she bent her knees and put her arms around them. At ease, she considered her stay in Indiana. Tomorrow, she would leave. But she would go home a stronger person. In silence, they sat together and looked up at the stars that sparkled like bright glitter.

"What a day," William said softly.

Rebecca nodded in agreement. Between Katie's unexpected arrival and other interruptions, she hadn't even had the chance to tell William of her decision.

His voice was soft. "I'm going to miss you, Rebecca." Before she could respond, he added, "A lot."

She turned to him. "I'll miss you, too, William."

She let out a nervous laugh. "I can't believe it's our last night together."

He frowned. "Just for a while."

Rebecca didn't comment. Her eyes burned with moisture at the thought of leaving him. She should relate what she'd decided last night. But not right now. She didn't want anything to spoil this precious moment.

The flecks in William's eyes held that mesmerizing metallic look that made her pulse speed up. His jaw was set. The light from the fire made the color of his hair appear a couple of shades lighter. For now, all she wanted was to savor this special time alone with him.

Tonight was for being with the man she loved. For roasting hot dogs. Enjoying the light that the full moon cast over the yard. And reflecting on what God had in store for her.

William leaned toward her so their cheeks brushed. The light sensation made her close her eyes until the blissful feeling passed.

"Rebecca, will you stay?" A hint of sadness edged his voice. "Beth's right. There's no need to leave now that we know you're safe."

"No, William. It's time to go." She tried for a positive approach. "But I'll leave with a good feeling inside of me. I've been here longer than we originally anticipated. And as much as I'd love to be with you, I can't forget the responsibility awaiting me."

When he didn't respond, her chest tightened. "Just think of all we accomplished, William. Daniel's business is back on track. Even more importantly, the two of you have established a bond."

She gave a happy shrug of her shoulders. "What more could you ask for?"

When he started to speak, she held up a hand to stop him. "Your relationship with your father might not be exactly what you want, but it's a start. It's definitely better than it was."

William nodded. A smile tugged at his lips. "Don't forget that beautiful garden you planted for him."

"Jah."

They sat shoulder to shoulder. Questions flitted through Rebecca's mind, but the lack of answers no longer bothered her. She was finally at peace.

Letting out a lazy sigh, she lay back and propped her upper body with her elbows. Looking up at the sky prompted her to dream. If God could create this awesome, endless universe, surely He would guide her life and fulfill her with happiness.

She turned to William and studied him. The light from the fire accented the small groove under his lips.

His voice was low and serious. "I wish I could read your thoughts."

"I'm thinking of how a person's face reflects who he is."

He whispered, "And what do you see when you look at me?"

The fire popped, but Rebecca didn't flinch. She was so intent on the expression in William's eyes, her gaze never left his. As she stared into those mysterious depths, a happy chill rushed up her spine.

She leaned closer to get a better glimpse. "When I look at you, I see incredible inner strength. Honesty.

And most of all? Determination that can't be broken, even under the most tempting circumstances."

"I wish you were right, but I'm afraid I'm far from the strong man I'd love to be."

"No you're not, William. Your fear is on the surface. Underneath that layer of skin lies a steely, unbreakable character. I know it's there. You just can't see it."

He was so close, his warm breath caressed her lashes. He raised an amused brow. "Would you like to know what I see when I look at you?"

She lifted her chin. "Tell me."

"A compassionate and understanding face. Beautiful eyes that can light up my darkest day. You need security. But more than anything, Rebecca, you need me."

Rebecca had difficulty breathing. His gaze never left hers.

"You know what?" she said.

"What?"

"I have almost everything I could ever want. The most important thing to me is my future with you. I want us to both be happy, William."

"What are you getting at?"

"It's time to have that discussion on whether or not you join Daniel. You have my blessing." She lowered her voice. "I'll move to Indiana, if that's what you want."

For long moments, the earth seemed to stand still. In silence, he looked at her.

After a slight hesitation, Rebecca gave a firm nod.

She heard his quick intake of breath before he spoke in a low tone. "Oh, Rebecca. You don't know what it means to hear that." He looked down before meeting her gaze. "The offer has been weighing me down. I can't believe what you just said. Thank you."

She noted the excitement in his eyes. The happiness in his voice. She'd had her say. "I guess the next step is yours to make."

Confusion reflected across his face.

"Will you say yes to that partnership with Daniel? Or will you move back to Arthur, Illinois?"

Chapter Fourteen

Later that night, Rebecca pulled her diary from her beautiful hope chest. Relaxing on the floor with her back against the bed, she looked around the room. She would miss this place, Beth and Daniel, even Katie.

She glanced down at the lined paper resting on her thighs and jotted the date in the upper right-hand corner. Pursing her lips thoughtfully, she began to write.

I feel closer than ever to William. Ironically, the conflict between us has made me stronger and has also forced me to think about what I truly want out of life. When I told William I would support him working with Daniel, I had hoped he would choose instead to raise our family in Arthur. He didn't.

Rebecca stopped to think

If William decides to stay in Indiana, my life will change forever. Tonight, while I gazed into his eyes, I realized an even bigger question has yet to be answered. If William remains here, will he stay Amish?

Tensing, Rebecca sat up straighter to consider the

potent question. She studied the hope chest and wondered what Old Sam would do in her situation.

She knew how much he'd loved his wife. She could read it in his eyes. Hear it in his voice over and over when he'd spoken of her. But had that love been strong enough to have pulled him from the Amish faith?

Rebecca glanced down at her diary to write and stopped. As she pondered the possibility of William becoming English, she couldn't continue her journal. She would live with him in Indiana, if that's what he wanted. But if he were to become English?

Early the following morning, William carried Rebecca's small suitcase down the stairs. At the front entrance, he set it next to the large box containing Katie's quilt and the smaller one with Rebecca's hope chest. He smiled a little. "The driver's coming soon. I can't believe you're really going home."

"You knew . . ."

He nodded, shifting his gaze to the hardwood floor and back to her face. "But now that it's actually happening, it's harder to accept."

"I know."

Rebecca hesitated. "William, there's something I'd like to talk about with you." She motioned. "Want to go outside?"

"Sure."

He opened the door and followed her. Above, clouds circled the sky while the sun shone bravely in its halo of blue. Hand in hand, they meandered to the garden and stood side by side. Rebecca smiled in satisfaction at the pastel colors, the neat rows, and the arrays of different flowers.

As she breathed in the pleasant fragrance that reminded her of Beth's sweet perfume, she marveled at each beautiful yet unique plant. Even though she preferred some over others, they all came together to produce this amazing picture.

It must be the same with God's children. Every Christian and faith contributed to His work. He sought everyone's talents and efforts to make a better world.

Salty tears burned her eyes as she thought of leaving William and his parents. She blinked at the sting. She loved Beth and Daniel, even Katie.

"Hey, are you okay?"

She sniffled and composed herself. "I'm all right. It's just my emotions at work. Saying good-bye is proving more difficult than I had imagined."

She added, "I feel good about my stay here, William. I made a difference." She straightened her shoulders. "I set out to accomplish three goals for the bishop. That's not to say it was easy. But I gave it my best shot. And now?" She let out a satisfied sigh. "I'm leaving without regrets."

His mouth twitched. "I'm sure Katie's apology played a role in this."

"Of course. It sure made forgiving easier. I admit that I'm relieved she was sorry for what she did. The quilt was a huge sign of remorse on her part."

"I'm with you on that one. It must have taken months to make it. I've never seen anything like it."

"Me neither."

"Since Katie showed up at the house yesterday,

I've thought a lot about forgiveness. At first, I was ready to boot her out."

Rebecca eyed him skeptically. "But you did the right thing. I'm glad you let her speak her mind. If you'd made her leave, I wouldn't have closure." She shrugged. "Don't get me wrong. I'm in no way condoning what she did, but everyone who is truly remorseful deserves a second chance, don't you think?"

"Maybe. I credit her for apologizing. What she did took courage, Rebecca."

"Yes."

"Remember the pact that we made?"

Rebecca raised a brow.

"You know. The deal that you would put Katie's threats behind you if I forgave Dad?"

"Of course."

He hesitated. "I'm praying every day for God to give us a second chance. I'm even starting to think it's possible for us to be close."

"That's all you can do. Don't expect things to be perfect, William."

"I won't."

"We already know Daniel's strength isn't in his communication skills. He's told you as much."

William nodded.

"But just think; your whole life is ahead of you. You can make it whatever you want. Take the bull by the horns."

William threw her a startled look, and she giggled. "I heard Daniel use that expression."

He rolled his eyes.

"Why don't you have another heart-to-heart with your father? Talking with him will get easier. In fact, each time you tell him what's on your mind, you'll do better. And vice versa."

William shrugged. "Unfortunately, the communication problem works both ways. It's not easy opening up to him."

Rebecca pressed a firm hand on his shoulder. "Then change that. Don't be like him, William. Be bigger. Speak your mind. We don't get much time on this earth. Life is too short to keep things inside. I believe Daniel could communicate better . . . all he needs is a little push."

"And if he can't?"

"Be positive."

"Right now, I've got a bigger problem."

"What?"

"I don't know what I'll do without you. I miss you already." His voice quivered.

Adrenaline pulsed through her veins as reality sank in. "I'll miss you, too. But you'll be fine, William. You're capable of running the shop."

He frowned. "But I need you." He shrugged in a frustrated gesture. His voice went hoarse. "Like I need the air I breathe."

As she observed the man she loved, she noted the tiny lines of concern etched around his eyes. His jaw was set. The look in his eyes mesmerized her until a nervous laugh escaped his throat.

"I guess that now is as good a time as any to test my communication skills."

She waited for him to go on.

The faint trace of a smile lightened his face. "You're the first thing I think about when I wake up and last on my mind before I go to sleep at night." He swallowed. "We'll be apart, but not for long.

Dad's going to be okay. I really believe that. And as soon as I can leave with a good conscience, we'll be married. After that, I'll never leave your side."

"That's what I want to talk to you about. William, I've prayed about Daniel's offer to make you his partner. Of course, I'm rooting for the two of you to be close. At the same time, I've had conflicting emotions. You know what they are."

He dipped his head.

She glanced at the front porch and motioned. "Let's sit down."

William's eyes reflected a combination of uncertainty and curiosity as Rebecca led him to the swing, where they rocked back and forth. Bright green blades of grass dusted the edge of the patio while a lawn mower hummed in the background. Rebecca smiled a little at the squeaky swing chain and their shadow on the concrete.

As she took in his woodsy scent, Rebecca gave him a reassuring glance. For blissful moments, she enjoyed being next to him. While she studied his handsome profile, she realized how lucky she was. Her heart belonged to him and no one else.

With a newfound confidence, she focused on what she wanted to say. There wasn't much time. When the swing slowed, she turned to William. "William, giving you my blessing was a huge decision. I wasn't sure what to do. Of course, I supported your partnership with your father, because that's what you wanted."

Her pent-up thoughts suddenly flowed freely. It felt good to put them out in the open. "At the same time, I wasn't sure I could live the rest of my life without my family. I couldn't have both, so obviously, something had to give."

To her surprise, William interrupted. "I've been going through the same thing. Of course, we'll make our own family wherever we are."

When she started to continue, he held up a hand to stop her. "But moving to Indiana has been on my mind. When Beth offered us the land, deciding what's best became even tougher. At the same time, it seemed like it was all coming together. In fact, God must have been listening to my prayers. But I've tried to consider everything. Not just the business relationship with Dad."

"Your aunt and uncle?"

He nodded. "I never was crazy about leaving Aenti Sarah and Uncle John. After all they've done for me, how could I even consider moving away? What would I do without them, Rebecca?"

She responded with a sympathetic smile.

"I love them." He gave a slight shrug. "I'm ashamed to admit I took for granted all they've done for me."

Rebecca nodded in understanding. "That realization alone makes this experience worthwhile. But back to the offer . . ." She patted her palms against her thighs. "I've had both of my parents my entire life. On the other hand, you've been without Daniel most of yours."

"Sad, but true." His voice broke on the last word.

"I've been blessed with a mom and dad who watched over me and nurtured me with every ounce of love and affection they could offer."

For a moment, she looked off into the distance. "But they did more than that. They taught me well.

Mamma raised me to think of others. To make good decisions."

With an appraising gaze, he ran his hand over her shoulder. "And I'm the one who benefits."

She raised a mischievous brow. "I'm not getting a bad deal, either. I think the world of my parents. At the same time, I love you with all of my heart."

"I've watched you help my folks, and for that, I'll always be grateful. Not only have you worked, but you've been a blessing to everyone. Especially me. You're the source of my strength."

Rebecca's voice softened. "Thank you for that."

"It's true."

"William, like I said, not only do I give you my blessing to become your father's partner, but if that's what you choose, I'll be right at your side. Whenever you need me . . . even if it's in Indiana."

She waited for a response. Something! Instead, nothing.

Finally, she glanced at his arms. "You're shaking."

A rosy pink filled his cheeks. "I'm nervous."

He squeezed his eyes closed. When he opened them, he sighed in relief. "Did I tell you that you're also the most generous person I've ever met?"

She smiled. "I'm not worried about the future because God will take care of us . . . wherever we are. What's most important is that we're together."

His eyes glistened. "Now it's time to let you know where I stand."

She frowned. As she contemplated his statement, a nervous tingle darted up her shoulders and made her shiver.

"Of course, I love you. I also love my father. And I believe my prayers are working. I've forgiven him and Beth." William leaned back against the boards and chuckled. "I guess you could call that a miracle."

"That's wonderful."

A huge grin lit his face. "I've made an important decision and want you to be the first to know."

Her heart picked up speed at his unusually confident tone.

He paused to gaze down at his shoes. When he looked up, his eyes sparkled with excitement. "Rebecca, I've missed Dad for years. But he left me of his own free will."

William's eyes danced with delight as she gazed at him in silence.

"I'm passing on Dad's offer."

Her jaw dropped in shock. Had she heard him correctly?

She turned to him for the answer.

As if reading her mind, he gave a slow, certain nod. A wide grin accompanied it.

A warm rush of emotion filled her heart. She drew her arms across her chest and lowered her head. As she bit her lip, joyful tears filled her eyes. It was difficult to believe that William would turn down Daniel's offer.

As she digested what he'd just told her, she raised her head and met his gaze with a newfound happiness. Taking his fingers in hers, she swallowed. "William, I can't believe what has happened. You've given up what you wanted most. For me."

He gently squeezed her hands. "For both of us, Rebecca. The past couple of weeks have been tough. I've searched my heart for answers." He let go of her and at the same time, they pushed the swing with their feet.

"After struggling with liking the conveniences of the English way of life and driving a car, I acknowledged that a partnership would be nice. In fact, just knowing Dad loves me enough to make such an offer is more than I ever dreamed possible. But in the end?" He paused. "That's not what I want most out of life. The whole time we've been here I've had everything I could want right in front of my eyes."

He lowered his voice several notches. "You."

She swallowed.

"I've learned that love doesn't come without a price. But you're worth more than anything money could buy."

They hugged. As Rebecca closed her eyes, the reassuring feel of his arms around her was all she needed to be happy forever. She couldn't believe her dream had come true. But it hadn't happened by chance. Her prayers had been answered. God had made sure that she and William would raise their family in Arthur, Illinois. What more could she want?

A voice startled them. They broke their embrace as Daniel stood in front of them. The swing slowed. There was a certain glow about him. Even a rosy color in his cheeks.

"Dad . . ."

A smile tugged at Daniel's lips. Without a doubt, it was the best he'd looked since her arrival. God certainly had been busy answering prayers.

"Son, it's a very good day. And I plan to take advantage of it." Daniel stretched his arms and let out a deep, satisfied sigh. "I've got a list a mile long to start on. But"—he paused—"before I begin, I need to talk to both of you. Together."

* * *

In the living room, William and Rebecca sat opposite Daniel and looked around. This was the last time she'd be in the Conrad home. At least, for a while.

Her conversation with William played over and over in her mind. Each time she thought of what he'd told her, she wanted to jump up and down.

Now, Daniel was about to say something. She couldn't imagine what it was. Did he know William had decided to turn down his offer? Trying to calm herself, she pulled in a deep, steady breath, swallowed, and considered how she had changed since coming here. She was excited, but also sad.

Soon, she would be home. And William would join her shortly. She imagined her family running to greet her. She looked forward to talking to Mamma. And Old Sam. Only this time, it wouldn't be by phone or letter. She'd see them in person. And there was so much to say, she wasn't sure where to start.

She stretched her legs and glanced out of the window to the road. That blacktop would lead her back to Arthur, Illinois.

The three goals: Amazingly, she had achieved more than she'd thought possible.

She would carry out her dream of owning a floral shop. Old Sam would surely let her use his old barn to get started. When she and William got their own place, she could work out of her home.

She broke the silence. "I want to remember this room exactly like it looks right now."

She glanced up at the beautiful white fan hanging

from the high ceiling. The breeze created by its slow circles caressed Rebecca's face.

A large gold-framed painting of a huge flower garden decorated the cream-colored wall. She took in the ornate gold doorknob. The large oval oil painting of Beth and Daniel.

Daniel stepped into the room and lifted his coffee cup in the air. "Anything to drink for you two?"

"No, thanks."

Beth joined Daniel on the love seat.

Daniel leaned forward and rested his hands between his legs. His gaze drifted from Rebecca to William. "There's so much to say, it's hard to know where to start."

Rebecca and William silently waited for Daniel to continue. William's foot tapped to a nervous beat. Rebecca sat up straighter. Her hands gripped the edge of the seat cushion.

"First of all, I want you kids to know that I'm fully aware of what you sacrificed to come here. And believe me, I'm the last person who deserves your help."

Rebecca leaned forward. "It was my pleasure."

"Mine too, Dad."

Daniel nodded and focused his attention on William. Beside him, Beth sat very still. "Son, I realize more than ever how much I'd love you to be my partner. Maybe it's selfish on my part."

"What do you mean?"

"I feel as if I'm compensating for the pain I've caused you. Trust me, I'd make sure you never wanted for anything."

Rebecca bit her lip. *Oh no. He thinks William's going to accept his offer.* Her grip on the cushion tightened.

Daniel put his cup on the lamp stand and stood. Looking down at the floor, he paced to the television and back, stopping in front of William. "Son, I've learned a very important lesson by watching you and Rebecca."

Rebecca tensed. Why was he taking so long to convey his message? She clasped her hands in her lap and waited for him to continue.

"After seeing how unselfish you are and how very generous your love for each other is, I've decided to show my love the best way I know how."

As Rebecca's heart rate picked up, Daniel sat down next to Beth and pressed his palms against his thighs. "I'm selling my business."

Rebecca's jaw dropped while she digested his statement. She sat very still.

William inhaled a deep breath, exhaled, and leaned forward. "You're what?"

Daniel nodded with a wide grin. "You heard me. That way, you and Rebecca can raise your family in Illinois."

Rebecca tried to figure out what selling his business had to do with her and William raising their family.

"Beth and I have regrouped. We love both of you." He winked at Rebecca. "We couldn't ask for a better daughter."

Beth directed her attention to William. "And you're the best son we could ever have."

Daniel nodded. "That's why we want to move near you to help raise our grandchildren." He hesitated. "I'll have to learn to deal with the shunning. But it will be worth it to be close. Will you let us do that?"

Rebecca and William glanced at each other. At the same time, they stood and hugged each other. Rebecca's breath caught in her throat. When William released his hold on her, his eyes glistened with moisture.

They turned to Daniel and Beth.

The Conrads stood and faced them. "I wasn't there for you, son. But it's never too late to start. Isn't what they say? Maybe God will grant me a second chance with my grandkids."

"Dad . . ."

Rebecca cleared her throat. "Oh, Daniel. I don't know what to say. I can't believe you're making such a sacrifice for us."

William gave his father a long hug. As Rebecca watched them, she said a prayer of thanks to God.

When William broke the long embrace, Daniel raised a hand. His voice hinted at mischief. "There's only one favor I'd like to ask."

They waited for an answer. *There's more?*

"I'd like to use some of the profits from the shop's sale to help you build a house."

Rebecca closed her eyes in happiness. She was afraid to open them for fear of having heard him incorrectly. When she did, she saw tears in Beth's eyes.

Beth hugged William. Then Rebecca. At last, the four of them embraced.

Rebecca's heart danced with a newfound joy. The blissful feeling of unity was overwhelming. Who would have dreamed that God would answer so many prayers at once?

When they broke away, William took Rebecca's

hand. His eyes held an excited, hopeful gleam. The look on his face was of pure satisfaction.

Rebecca knew that this was a new beginning for all of them. And life would only get better. She'd never lost faith.

The price of love had been paid with love. God had blessed her with everything important. And she would spend the rest of her life thanking Him.

Up next in the Hope Chest of Dreams series . . .

Annie's Recipe

*Three young Amish women,
each gifted with a hand-carved hope chest,
find that one by one, with patience and faith,
their most blessed dreams for the future can come true . . .*

Annie Mast and Levi Miller were best friends until
his father was shunned by the church. Now, ten
years later, Levi has returned to Arthur, Illinois,
for a brief visit, and he and Annie discover
their bond is as strong as ever.
Spending as much time together as possible,
Annie finds herself dreaming of a future with Levi.
And Levi is soon dreaming of building a home on
a beautiful local hillside—to live in with Annie.
Yet their longings are unlikely to become reality . . .

Levi is part of the English world,
and while Annie cannot see herself there,
she knows she must reveal her heart's truth to him.
And Levi, strongly reminded of his Amish roots,
knows he must heal the bitterness of the past.
And together, with love on their side,
they just may find their way
to an answered prayer . . .

Also available . . .

The Amish Christmas Kitchen

by Kelly Long, Jennifer Beckstrand,
and Lisa Jones Baker

Something's always baking in an Amish oven,
and at Christmastime,
all the ingredients for joy are at hand.
Wrap yourself in the warmth of the Amish home—
and the Plain peace of hearts joined by love.
Each story includes a recipe from the author!

Emma drew a star at the top of Amos's English homework page and wrapped an affectionate arm around him. "Excellent work! You got every answer right!"

The corners of Amos's lips drew up into a huge grin that showed a row of straight teeth. The child had a kind face. And an even warmer heart. Every time Emma looked at him, the small boy's innocence tugged at her emotions.

As the first December snowfall touched the bare, frozen ground of Arthur, Illinois, the flame in the fireplace at the two-story Troyer home popped. Amos and Emma jumped at the same time. Laughter followed.

Automatically, Emma didn't waste time pulling the front of his black hand-knit sweater together. She tried to avoid mentioning Amos's unusual heart defect, but it was more important than ever to make sure he stayed warm. At the young age of six, Amos hadn't known any other way of life.

But good news had broken a year ago when he

had visited a doctor at the Mayo Clinic who could fix it. Because they were Amish, they had no insurance, but thanks to the news reaching the media, there was huge support for an upcoming auction in their community to raise money for the unique procedure to take place in Rochester, Minnesota.

The smell of lemon-scented furniture polish loomed in the air. It was no secret that Amos's mother, Esther, kept the cleanest house in town when she was well. But unfortunately, she was forced to spend bouts of time in bed when the Epstein-Barr virus set her back. But even then, her sisters made sure the Troyer house stayed well kept!

As Emma regarded Amos, he turned to face her. The unexpected seriousness in his deep brown eyes took her by surprise.

When he tugged at her arm, his small white hand remained on her wrist. "Emmie, does this mean I get a cookie with icing?"

Emma broke out in laughter. For some reason, that was the last question she'd expected. He was referring to the star she'd drawn. Honored that her only student considered her Christmas cookies the best he'd ever tasted, Emma stood and proceeded to the thin red plastic platter she'd brought to his house that morning. Amos knew he had earned a cookie. And she loved making him happy. "Which one do you want?"

He quickly and eagerly joined her, pointing to the edible with peppermint icing. She plucked the chosen treat between two fingers, grabbed a napkin with her free hand, and laid both on the table.

While chewing the buttery dessert, he glanced

back at her and grinned. "I like this better than the one you drew."

Emma sat next to him. "I'll bet you do."

He lifted a skeptical brow. "In my opinion, this is my favorite."

She gave an appreciative nod. "That's good to hear." Amos was fully aware that Emma changed her recipe a tad each time for Amos to decide which batch was the tastiest. When she altered the mixture, sometimes adding more butter, or vanilla, or flour, she documented her adjustments so when Amos decided which cookie won, she would use that formula for the auction, to take place in less than two weeks.

As she put his schoolbooks in a neat pile, his soft voice made her look up. "Emmie, when I have the operation, I won't have to wear this anymore, will I?" He looked down at his heavy knit sweater, and the corners of his lips dropped.

Contemplating an answer, she shoved her chair closer to the table. The quick motion made a light squeaking sound on the tiled floor.

While he chewed the morsel, Emma pressed her lips together thoughtfully. Somehow she knew that being positive would play a very important role in the outcome of the operation.

"You won't have to wear it in the summer. But in the winter?" She lifted a brow. "It's pretty cold. You'll probably want it on."

Her answer seemed to satisfy him. After gobbling down the snack, he wrote out the answers she'd asked him to do on the paper in front of him. She watched his feet, which almost touched the floor, swing back and forth while he concentrated.

A bright beam of sunlight swept through the

kitchen window and landed on his beautiful thick mass of hair, lightening it to a softer shade of reddish blond.

Finally, the six-year-old dropped his pencil on the table and handed the paper to Emma while displaying a proud look on his face. "That was easy, Emmie. What next?"

The adultlike way he spoke at times prompted a smile. If only every child liked homework as much as Amos did. She tried not to overreact to the high academic level he'd achieved at his age; she never wanted it to go to his head.

She quickly put another project in front of him. "Here. Read it to yourself, then see how many answers you can get." She followed the order with a wink.

Without wasting a second, he started the new project as if he was playing with a toy. Emma already knew that Amos would get every answer correct. She wasn't sure whether his reading ability was related to his inability to play outside with other children, but whatever the case, his level in English skills was heads above kids his age.

After he glanced at the page, he surprised her by dropping his pen next to the paper and looking straight ahead. Emma lifted a curious brow. Her instincts told her that some of his interest in completing his schoolwork was to please his tutor. He loved spending time with her. And vice versa.

He turned and crossed one leg under the other while getting comfortable on his chair. The serious look in his eyes hinted that he wanted to talk about something.

She hesitated. "Amos, is something wrong?"

He glanced down at the table and frowned. She tried for a positive thought to make him smile again. "Just think, Amos, it's only a matter of time before the surgery takes place. And you'll be as good as new!"

When he looked up, his expression was uncertain. He lowered the pitch of his voice until it was barely more than a whisper. "What if there aren't enough cookies?"

"You mean donations?"

He offered a slow, sad nod.

She reached across the table and used her pointer finger to lift his chin a notch. Their gazes locked. "Amos, I have every bit of faith that God will help us get enough money."

She used her most confident voice. The last thing she wanted was for him to lose hope. "I have a list of cookie donations that would reach all the way to the North Pole!"

He laughed.

She went on to explain. "The cookies will help, that's for sure. But as I've told you, most of the revenue will come from more expensive items. Tables, chairs, and furniture that men in our community are working very hard to make."

When he didn't say anything, she proceeded in her most reassuring tone. "Other donations will help, too. From what I've heard, one of the farmers in our community will even auction off some of his land to go to your fund."

Amos pulled in a deep breath and rolled his eyes in disbelief.

"That goes to show just how special you are."

His pupils got larger.

"Because so many people across the state are aware of this surgery . . . and of you . . . folks have committed out of the goodness of their hearts."

He frowned and scratched his nose. "You mean they're giving money without getting anything back?"

She smiled at the way he worded the question. His thoughts were so straightforward. Honest. There was never a guess where he was coming from.

The mooing noises from the cattle lightened the silence.

"You know that people all over are rooting for you to get your surgery. Even the doctor who will perform the procedure is forfeiting what he would make."

An emotional breath escaped her. She blinked when salty tears stung her eyes. She leaned closer to Amos and whispered, "Do you know just how special that makes you?"

To her surprise, he didn't grin. The expression in his large, hopeful eyes was unusually serious. "Do you know what I'm gonna do first thing after I get my heart fixed, Emmie?"

She looked at him for an answer.

"Play tag with Jake and Daniel. And nobody's gonna catch me!"

The admissions tugged at Emma's heartstrings until her chest ached. Automatically, she rested her hands below her neck and closed her eyes a moment. His wants were so simple. She knew of healthy kids with much stronger desires, but this little guy only wanted to run and play outside.

To Emma, raising sufficient funds for the operation would be one of God's greatest gifts. When Amos had asked her about it, she had stood firm that the funds would come in. But she was saying double prayers for it to actually happen.

How could any child be more precious than Amos? Emma was sure it wasn't possible, as she took in the small boy's endearing features and swallowed an emotional knot. Amos's thick mass of unruly hair fell lazily over his forehead and caressed the tops of his brows.

The child's deep brown eyes reminded her of autumn. Of pumpkin pie–colored leaves falling from tall trees. Tiny freckles on the bridge of his nose matched his pupils. And a narrow set of shoulders was the reason his suspenders continuously slipped down his arms.

Amos's wide smile was full of hope. Filled with an innocence that made Emma want to do everything she could to see him run around and have fun with kids his age.

And soon, he would get the long-awaited surgery that would allow him to have a normal life. The upcoming auction would be the ultimate blessing.

She'd been asking God for this miracle. Her faith was strong. And she knew her Lord and Savior wouldn't let her down.

The end of the school week was here. After Emma hugged Amos good-bye, she watched him tote his books to his room. That was the normal routine. Because the youngster was incredibly studious and also because she knew him so well, she didn't have to guess what he would do the rest of the evening.

As happy steps took him to his room on the ground floor, Emma took in the stairway that glistened with furniture polish. Before slipping inside of his door, he looked back at her and grinned. She offered a quick wave.

She had no doubt that he wouldn't waste time before checking out the story she'd just given him. She always took great care when selecting his material. This particular library book was about a child who had undergone surgery to correct his foot from turning inward. When she'd told Amos the theme, he'd immediately flipped open the cover.

As the fire crackled, Emma ran her hands up and down her sleeved arms. The unusually cold winds competed boldly with the gas heat, as well as the warmth from the fireplace.

As she considered the twenty-minute walk home, she pressed her lips together in a dread-filled sigh. She made her way to the dining room table to slip her teaching materials into the oversized bag her mamma had given her.

As soon as the books were tucked neatly inside the vinyl holder with extra-strong handles, Emma slipped her arms through her heavy wool coat and proceeded toward the door. As she passed the gas heater, she stopped and smiled a little, trying to savor the moment; she knew what to expect when she opened the front door.

As soon as her fingers touched the brass knob on the inside of the door, a stern voice stopped her. Automatically, she turned to face Amos's older brother, Jonathan, who regarded her with skepticism.

She forced a polite smile. "Jonathan."

His face still held a slight tan from the summer. In his coat, he looked unusually large. It was common knowledge in their community that he was easily one of the strongest men around.

"You surprised me. I thought you were out feeding the cattle."

"I finished." He hesitated, and a set of dark brows drew together into a frown. "You got a moment?"

Before she could answer, she took in the dissatisfied look on his face that told her something was awry. But she wasn't surprised. It seemed as though nothing could please Amos's older brother these days.

She offered a slight shrug. "Sure. What's up?"

He motioned to the back door. "Let's talk while I drive you home." For a moment, Emma drew in a grateful breath. At the same time, she wondered if it was proper to accept a ride from a single Amish man. She quickly decided that it was. The weather was dangerously cold, and this was common courtesy on Jonathan's part.

As if reading her mind, he smiled a little. "I don't want you to freeze to death, Emma."

"Okay."

He motioned and followed her out. The unusually high wind shear stopped her breath. She pressed her lips together to prevent the air from going down her throat. The fierce coldness stung her eyes, and she automatically lowered her lids a moment to adjust. When she opened them, she drew in a deep breath and shivered.

"You okay?"

The concerned tone of his voice prompted a comforting sensation. She parted her lips in reaction. The question showed thoughtfulness, a side of Jonathan that was endearing. She pulled in a deep breath.

"Denki." She smiled a little. "What's on your mind?"

As she stepped inside of the carriage, Emma tried to stop her teeth from chattering. She knew without question that Jonathan obviously wanted to discuss something away from Amos. But the coldness quickly turned to a much-appreciated warmth as Jonathan turned on his gas heater.

Some Amish didn't use anything to make their cabins of their carriages more comfortable; she was happy he did. And the cabin in the buggy wasn't tight, so the fumes posed no danger. She relaxed a little and flexed her fingers in reaction to the change in temperature.

He cleared his throat. "It's the auction."

Emma darted him a quick glance to continue ahead.

"When you and the others voted for this fundraiser, I never actually thought it would materialize." He turned to her and lowered his pitch to a more serious tone.

"Emma, I appreciate all you've done for Amos. Everything you do for him. Since Dad passed away, the kid hasn't been the same. It doesn't much help things that Mom is down with the virus at times. And when we found out last year about the heart defect . . ."

He shook his head. "It's been a bad time. But since you started tutoring him . . ." He paused. "It's hard to explain. But he smiles. Laughs. And you've helped him discover his love of reading."

Emma almost choked with shock. Getting a compliment from Jonathan was rare. And what he'd said forced her heart to a happy beat. What on earth, then, was wrong?

"I'm so glad to play a role in Amos's life. And let me tell you, he's given me much more than I've offered him."

When the wind picked up speed, the buggy rocked a bit from side to side. As she eyed the dull gray sky looming in the distance, Emma yearned for the season to change. But she knew that winter was just beginning.

They were nearly home when she glanced at Jonathan and noticed his somber expression. He looked at her, and their gazes locked. "I suppose it's no secret that I think you focus way too much on English and not enough on math. Don't numbers deserve more attention? When he's running his own business, he'll need to know figures."

She gave a firm shake of her head.

"When Amos is older and has a farm, he'll use math skills on a daily basis. Amos will compute profits and manage the budget." Jonathan threw his head back and chuckled. "Sorry we don't see eye to eye, but I hardly think English is gonna help him with that."

She gave a stronger shake of her head. "I disagree. In the long run, his English knowledge will actually be much more important than math." Before Jonathan could cut in, Emma substantiated her statement. "Just think of how important the scriptures are. He'll read them every night. And most communication requires literacy. Amos loves books. And that's how you build vocabulary."

"That's not my main complaint, though." He cleared his throat. His voice took on a firmer, more direct tone. "Please don't take this the wrong way,

Emma. But the auction's been causing me to lose sleep."

She pressed her lips together in deep deliberation.

"I've been giving this a lot of thought, and to be honest, I'm still not comfortable accepting donations for the surgery. From the get-go, you've played an important role in getting this thing going. Now I want you to stop it."

His unfair order made her bite her tongue. His demand prompted her to forget the brief compliment he'd paid her. She didn't try to hide how upset she was. Trying to think of an appropriate response, she lifted a defensive hand.

"Jonathan, are you crazy?" Without thinking, she raised her chin a notch. As she looked at him for an answer, she glimpsed his deep green eyes. The shade reminded Emma of a beautiful stone she'd seen on an English girl's finger.

Wavy jet-black hair stuck out from the bottom of his hat. His jaw was square, and a dark set of thick brows hovered beneath his forehead.

To her astonishment, the expression on his face was that of amusement. She was happy she hadn't further irritated him; that was the last thing she wanted to do.

He lifted a defensive hand to stop her. "I'm well aware of the benefits. It's just that . . ." He stared straight ahead and cupped his chin with his hand. When he turned toward her, the expression in his eyes was of sadness.

Her heart pumped to an unsettling beat.

"I'm not happy taking money from people I don't know—or even those I do." He lifted a defensive hand. "I was raised to be humble and taught that pride isn't a good thing. But I'm flawed, Emma. Something inside of me likes to be able to support my family without accepting charity. It's all about self-respect."

He offered a helpless shrug. "I'd rather earn the money myself."

"Jonathan, swallow your pride. This should be about Amos."

The emotion in her voice was so fierce, she nearly choked on her words. "As soon as this procedure's over, think of how his life will change. I know you'll see things differently."

She threw her hands up in the air. In a swift motion, she stuck her hand out to count with her fingers as she ticked off reasons. "He'll be able to do things other kids his age do. Play outside. Not wear a sweater all summer long. Or take medicine four times a day."

She continued her argument with emotion. "Do you know what your little brother wants more than anything?"

He eyed her.

"To play tag with his friends."

A hard knot in her throat made it difficult to talk. Her pulse nearly jumped out of her wrist in protest as she went on.

"Do you have any idea of the work we've put in for this auction? I've practically pulled teeth to get it. And finally, *finally*, Jonathan, momentum is on our side. People are talking about it with excitement. In fact, as soon as the press got wind of it, attention poured in from everywhere in Illinois. Don't you understand that the entire state is rooting for little Amos to get well?"

She paused to shrug. "We *will* raise enough money for little Amos's operation. But now you're telling me to stop it? *Why?*" She lifted her chin a notch, squared her shoulders, and planted her palms against her waist.

A long, tense silence ensued. She took in Jonathan's features and pressed her lips together thoughtfully.

"I'm telling you, Emma, I won't take their money. It just doesn't feel right."

She closed her eyes and silently counted to ten. "I admire your self-respect, Jonathan. And at least, you admit it's in the way. But sometimes you've got to look at the bigger picture."

"I feel like I've failed. I mean, I'm the father figure in the boy's life. What's wrong with me that I can't take care of him like I should?"

He lowered his voice. "And how could he possibly look up to me when he sees I can't handle something like this without everyone else having to pitch in?"

Emma wasn't sure what to say. Because she realized what she was up against. How could she ever convince a man who was used to doing everything by himself, that this was a situation where he needed help?

Books by Bestselling Author
Fern Michaels

___The Jury	0-8217-7878-1	$6.99US/$9.99CAN
___Sweet Revenge	0-8217-7879-X	$6.99US/$9.99CAN
___Lethal Justice	0-8217-7880-3	$6.99US/$9.99CAN
___Free Fall	0-8217-7881-1	$6.99US/$9.99CAN
___Fool Me Once	0-8217-8071-9	$7.99US/$10.99CAN
___Vegas Rich	0-8217-8112-X	$7.99US/$10.99CAN
___Hide and Seek	1-4201-0184-6	$6.99US/$9.99CAN
___Hokus Pokus	1-4201-0185-4	$6.99US/$9.99CAN
___Fast Track	1-4201-0186-2	$6.99US/$9.99CAN
___Collateral Damage	1-4201-0187-0	$6.99US/$9.99CAN
___Final Justice	1-4201-0188-9	$6.99US/$9.99CAN
___Up Close and Personal	0-8217-7956-7	$7.99US/$9.99CAN
___Under the Radar	1-4201-0683-X	$6.99US/$9.99CAN
___Razor Sharp	1-4201-0684-8	$7.99US/$10.99CAN
___Yesterday	1-4201-1494-8	$5.99US/$6.99CAN
___Vanishing Act	1-4201-0685-6	$7.99US/$10.99CAN
___Sara's Song	1-4201-1493-X	$5.99US/$6.99CAN
___Deadly Deals	1-4201-0686-4	$7.99US/$10.99CAN
___Game Over	1-4201-0687-2	$7.99US/$10.99CAN
___Sins of Omission	1-4201-1153-1	$7.99US/$10.99CAN
___Sins of the Flesh	1-4201-1154-X	$7.99US/$10.99CAN
___Cross Roads	1-4201-1192-2	$7.99US/$10.99CAN

Available Wherever Books Are Sold!
Check out our website at **www.kensingtonbooks.com**